D0369843

UNDERCOVER

Gerard Brennan

First published by Blasted Heath, 2014
copyright © 2014, Gerard Brennan

Cover design by JT Lindroos and Kyle MacRae
Photo by Giuseppe Milo

ISBN: 978-1500295127
Version 2-1-3

CHAPTER I

If you're standing between me and the goal, you're not my friend.

Rory Cullen, *Cullen: The Autobiography*

Cormac Kelly nibbled on the inside of his ski mask. He'd been given the only one without a mouth-hole and it was driving him nuts. The damp fibres irritated his lips. He'd already swallowed four or five little balls of chewed wool but couldn't stop himself from biting off another tiny piece. They stuck to the walls of his dry throat. He'd be hawking up hairballs all night.

It didn't matter what line of work you were in, the new guy always got the crap. A ski mask with no mouth-hole, a dinged-up old Ruger Security Six revolver in serious need of a clean, and the shittiest job – babysitting.

The kidnapped man slumped in the middle of a bare mattress pushed up against a damp wall. The boy sat slightly apart from his father. His knees were drawn up to his chest and his arms wrapped around his shins. His head tipped back to rest against the wall. He hadn't uttered a peep since Big Frank had scared him with a few dummy digs for the camera. Once or twice the boy had glanced at his father with disappointment etched deep in his face, as if he wondered how his guardian, his hero, his protector, had let them get into this mess.

And it didn't look as if Daddy was going to spring into action mode any time soon. Although the boy wouldn't understand it, this was the best thing his father could do for him. Heroics got people killed.

Big Frank blundered into the room. He moved without grace and his footsteps clapped like thunder. The boy tensed at the sight of the juggernaut who'd bullied him for the camera. Built like a silverback on steroids, Big Frank would scare the life out of most men. Put him in a ski mask and he became the stuff of nightmares. His lips stretched wide as he treated Cormac to a craggy-toothed smile through the mouth-hole of his ski mask.

"The boys are waiting for the bitch at the cottage."

The father's frame tensed. He breathed deep but didn't complain. The boy shot a death stare at Big Frank. Looked like he was ready to jump up and lamp the giant. Fiery wee bastard.

Cormac kept an eye on the boy as he responded to Big Frank.

"Great."

"Aye, she'll be scared shitless. That wee video turned out a beezer."

"Okay."

"Amazing what you can do these days, isn't it? I mind a time when you'd have to send fingers through the post to get what you wanted. Everything's digital now."

"Aye."

"It's like living in the future."

Cormac could see that Big Frank's brainless chatter poked at the boy like a rusty spike. His little fists clenched up into white-knuckled knots of fury. He was bound to do something stupid if Cormac let the oaf ramble on.

"Would you put the kettle on, mate?" Cormac said. "I've been gasping for hours."

Big Frank took a step back. "Get away to fuck. You think this is a day at the office?"

"Don't know, big man. Aren't you the one gabbing away like we're on our tea break?"

Big Frank's teeth disappeared behind a tight-lipped slit. He turned in a clumsy half-circle and headed for the door.

Cormac couldn't resist a parting shot. "And tell that other fat shite-bag to come in here and do a turn. He's not even offered me so much as a toilet break."

"You can piss yourself, you wanker."

Big Frank clattered out of the room and slammed the door behind him. The father and son flinched, though Cormac thought he could see the trace of a smirk on the boy's face. He was tempted to engage the young fellah in some idle banter but knew it to be a bad idea. So he went back to chewing on his damp bala-clava. It passed the time.

Lydia Gallagher stepped onto the cast-iron doormat of the cottage and rummaged through her handbag for the key. Her rain-soaked hair clung to her face. She wished for an umbrella, gave up the hunt for the key and hammered on the door with the side of her fist.

Footsteps thudded on the other side of the win-dowless slab of oak and she brightened in anticipa-tion of John's welcome. It had been a long day and she craved a decent glass of Pinot. She turned to wave her taxi away. Its tail lights disappeared behind the hedging on the side of the main road.

The door creaked open. Lydia gazed deep into the twin barrels of a sawn-off. The shotgun's hollow stare watched without passion. She took one step backwards. Gravel scrunched under her heel.

Run.

But she couldn't.

Lydia looked over the sawn-off at the gunman. Eyes as dispassionate as the shotgun muzzle nestled in the peepholes of a black ski mask. She raised her hands.

The gunman reached out and grabbed Lydia's lapels with his free hand. He kept the shotgun trained on her face and walked backwards into the hallway. Lydia followed without resistance. She listened out for her family. Nothing. The light in the kitchen was out. A telltale sign that Mattie, her son, hadn't mooched in the cupboards for a pre-dinner snack. Whatever was going on had started a few hours ago.

"Where are they?"

The gunman said nothing. He yanked her into the living room.

The television played on mute. Two more masked men sat on the sofa and gazed into the pale blue light of a documentary about sharks. They didn't look up at her, but Lydia noticed one of them lift a handgun from the arm of the sofa and thumb a little switch on the side. Acknowledgement enough.

She tried again. "My son. My husband. Where are they?"

The silence crept into her bones. She could have screamed, but it seemed wrong. Like belting out a football chant in a chapel.

The first man shoved her into the armchair closest to the TV – furthest from the door. He stood in front of her. Lowered his sawn-off.

"What the fuck do you want?" Lydia was hyper-aware of her London accent in the eerie calm. She could feel the panic take hold of her heart. Claw at her lungs. Tie knots in her bowels.

The man with the sawn-off leaned forward and back-handed her across the face. Instinctively she kicked out at him. Her leg arced upwards as she aimed her shin at his groin. He parried her kick with his knee and slammed the palm of his hand into her forehead. The dull thwack juddered her vision and shoved her head against the back of the seat. She blinked away black dots. The pain faded quickly but left a hangover of weakness and humiliation.

The men on the sofa shifted forward and perched on the edge of their seat. With elbows on knees, they watched. Lydia tried not to think about what they might be expecting to happen. She squirmed. Needed to pee.

"Take off your shoes."

The gunman's Belfast growl matched his mask.

Lydia raised her hands to ward off another attack. "What is this? I don't… Are you an IRA man?"

He swept her hands to the side and slapped her again. It stung like he'd shoved her face in nettles. One of the sofa jockeys sniggered.

"Shut your mouth and do as you're told, wee girl."

Lydia kicked off her heels. The tingle of fresh circulation in her toes didn't bring the usual relief. All she felt was fear and confusion. She didn't understand why he wanted her shoes. Maybe he was worried that she'd try and hit him with one of them. She prayed that he wouldn't ask her to remove anything else.

The gunman punted her shoes into the corner of the room.

"Give me your handbag." In his thick Belfast accent it sounded like he wanted her *hawndbeg*.

Lydia handed it over. He studied the brand logo on the buckle.

"Is this a real Lewis Vuitton?"

Lydia paused a second before she nodded.

He curled his lip in distaste and tossed the bag into the corner with her shoes. The contents clattered.

"Now your coat."

"How far is this going to go?"

"Don't flatter yourself, love."

Lydia struggled out of her knee-length coat. She was afraid to stand in case she earned another slap so she shifted from side to side as she dragged it out from under her bum. Just another indignity.

The gunman threw the woollen coat into the corner and moved to the other armchair. A black canvas holdall sat on the cushion. He unzipped it and poked around inside.

Lydia's skin tightened into gooseflesh. The house was cold. It smelt wrong. The scent of strange men.

The gunman pulled a smartphone from the holdall and handed it to one of the sniggering sofa jockeys. "Get the thing working."

He tapped the screen a few times and passed it back to the gunman. He brought it to Lydia and dropped it in her lap.

"Watch."

Lydia picked up the phone and squinted at the little display.

A masked man stood over Mattie – her thirteen-year-old son – with his fists curled. Mattie scuttled backwards on all fours, his mouth pulled back in a ghost train grimace.

Lydia sprang out of the armchair and launched herself at the gunman. She clawed at his eyes and caught a handful of ski mask. The gunman danced backwards and batted her hands away. He was light on his feet and skilled. Lydia shrieked and stepped up her attack. Swung arms and legs at the dancing bastard. He side-stepped. Buried the butt of his sawn-off into her solar plexus. Air whooshed from her lungs. She wheezed and crumpled face-first into the carpet. Hitched her breath, sputtered and pulled her knees under her chest.

The ten seconds of footage from the video clip played on a loop in her mind.

She cried.

A rough hand seized a fistful of hair from the back of her head and hauled her to her feet. She tried to strike out behind her with the heel of her shoeless foot. Earned a kick in the backside for her troubles. Hot breath blasted in her ear.

"Settle yourself."

The fight drained from her and she sagged. The gunman practically held her up by the hair. He led her back to the armchair and dropped her into it.

The gunman adjusted his ski mask and sighed. "Your son hasn't been hurt. Yet. Neither has your husband. But we *will* hurt them if we don't get what we want. Hurt them a lot and then kill them. Let that sit with you for a second or two. See how it makes you feel."

Lydia gripped the arms of her chair. She opened her mouth to speak.

The gunman raised a gloved finger to the lower part of his ski mask. Lydia clamped her mouth shut.

"Now, Missus Gallagher. You listen to me and do exactly as I say."

She swiped fresh tears from her eyes with the sleeve of her suit jacket. "Okay."

Cormac had almost gnawed himself a ragged mouth-hole when Paddy waddled into the room. Paddy weighed about as much as Big Frank did, but he was made up of doughy fat that drooped from his bones like custard in a condom. His arms were always in motion as if they couldn't find a casual spot on his soft body to rest against. Paddy was the lame duck of the crew. A blood connection with the boss was the only thing that booked him a place on these jobs. And yet, he still ranked higher than Cormac.

Paddy brandished the hi-tech phone that they'd filmed the boy and Big Frank on. "I've the woman on the blower. She's to talk to the kid."

Cormac flapped his hand at the boy. Paddy walked past the father to hand over the mobile. The boy took a deep breath before speaking.

"Hello...? Yeah, it's Mattie, Mum." He screwed up his face. "I'm fine." Then he glanced at his father, his young face hardened. "Yeah, he's okay too."

Paddy snatched the phone away from Mattie's ear and pressed it to his own. "Right, that's all you get for now, missus." He disconnected the call.

Cormac nipped across the room to cut the departing Paddy off at the door.

"Lend us the mobile for a bit, will you?"

Paddy gave Cormac one of his watery-eyed looks. His nose twitched visibly under his ski mask. "What for?"

"I'm bored shitless here. Wouldn't mind a wee tinker on it to pass the time."

"You going to call one of them dodgy numbers, big lad? Heavy breathing and all that?"

"Fuck off. I'll just piss about on the apps or something."

"What are apps?"

Cormac shook his head. "Can I have it or not?"

Paddy shrugged and handed over the touch-screen phone. "Whatever. Just don't get too distracted, all right? You're meant to be working."

"No sweat, boss."

Paddy puffed his chest and his considerable man-boobs strained the front of his black cotton shirt. Suitably inflated by an ounce of respect, he gave Cormac a curt nod and waddled out.

Cormac turned his back to the family, gave the phone a quick once over, then flipped open a tiny flap on the side of the casing. He took a miniscule memory card from the watch pocket of his jeans and slipped it into the slot. A few taps of the screen later and he had the video of Big Frank threatening Mattie on the card. He ejected his little piece of evidence and tucked it back into his watch pocket.

A present for his handler.

CHAPTER 2

It can be weird when you read about yourself in one of the tabloids. Mostly flattering, though. Even when they're printing bullshit about you, it means they still care. It'd be crap if you weren't important enough to take the piss out of.

Rory Cullen, *Cullen: The Autobiography*

Lydia checked her phone reception. Strong as could be. She made sure the ringer was at full volume and tucked it back into her handbag.

Hawndbeg.

She squirmed in her seat. Recalled the threats from the previous night; the sound of Mattie's voice as he played brave for her; how the slaps to her face had stung and throbbed. It'd taken more makeup than she would normally wear to cover the red patches on her cheeks. She tried to convince herself that nobody would notice but it felt like she'd been done up by an Oompa-Loompa beautician. Somebody would figure out what she was up to.

"Lydia?"

Lydia snapped back to the current situation. She was in the back of a hired Mercedes with her star client, Rory Cullen. Manchester City's latest signing; a record-breaking deal for the new-money club. He'd cost more than their last Brazilian , but Rory was actually worth the millions. The release of Rory's controversial autobiography had taken them on a tour of Northern Ireland, his home country. She detested him for it.

Rory had wanted to play up to the "New George Best" hype. They'd flown in from John Lennon Airport in Liverpool to George Best Belfast City Airport. That had been Rory's idea too. Every photographer and reporter in Ulster was crammed into the terminal, snapping pictures and roaring questions. And it was most likely from that point that the fuckers Lydia had spent the previous night with had started to tail her and her family.

"How many times are you going to check that phone today?" Rory asked.

Lydia stopped her hand before it slipped back into her handbag. She gave Rory a weak smile.

Rory squinted at her. "Are you okay?" His tanned, unlined brow rippled ever so slightly. "You look a bit... I don't know. Off?"

"Probably jetlag."

"We only flew for forty-five minutes."

She twiddled with the buckle on her handbag. *Lewis Vuitton.*

"I'd a late night."

Rory smirked. "Oh, aye?" He tapped the side of his aquiline nose. "Say no more... you good thing."

"Oh, give over, Rory."

Rory's smirk stretched into his signature toothy grin. He'd a mouthful of Belfast teeth. Somewhere between Robert Carlyle and Tom Cruise before the Hollywood megastar got his work done. For all of his careful metrosexual preening, tailored suits and fifty-quid haircuts, the teeth were a welcome reminder of Rory's working-class background. As was the dog-eared tabloid resting on his lap, page turned, as always, to an article about himself.

"I'd a late one myself," Rory said. "Called a couple of old mates and hit the Merchant Hotel for cocktails and society girls."

"Sounds... expensive."

"Ach, these were fellahs I grew up with. It was nice to treat them."

Lydia knew the night had been more about rubbing his friends' faces in his success than anything else. Altruism was not one of his strong points.

Rory shifted away from Lydia and looked out the window at the passing scenery. A blur of red bricks and paramilitary murals. Welcome to Belfast. There'd been a distinct lack of that sort of thing on the Discover Northern Ireland website.

Lydia slipped her mobile out of her bag and checked it again. Good network coverage – not always the case on the outskirts of Belfast. Still no fucking call from the bastards.

Rory maintained his silence until the gates of his old primary school were in sight. Then he needed her reassurance.

"They're going to hate my guts in here."

"Rory. You're a superstar. These kids will be falling over themselves for a quick chat and an autograph."

"You don't know what it's like on the Lower Falls. People don't like to see you do too well, you know?"

People don't like to see you do too well. She'd heard the phrase before. Her husband, John, was particularly fond of it. John's mother and father were from Belfast; the same neck of the woods as Rory. And even though John's Northern Irish accent had softened to a weird London Irish hybrid, he still had a rattlebag of phrases and sayings that he unconsciously drew on from time to time. Mattie loved to mimic his dad's sayings, though his impressions had got more sarcastic in recent years.

Lydia imagined Mattie's smartass sideways grin. She would do whatever was needed to see it again.

The driver navigated the little street, narrowed further by lines of parked cars on either side, and stopped at the school gate.

An impressive gabble of blasphemy rolled off Rory's tongue.

Lydia cleared her throat and pitched her voice just a little too high. "Yes, I can see what you mean, Rory. I imagine you'll be torn apart here."

It looked like every kid in the school and all related to them had turned up for Rory's visit. Kids, teenagers and adults stood crammed together in the primary school playground. The majority held banners and picket signs with Rory's name on it but a fair number of the adults had turned up in Manchester United jerseys to welcome City's latest addition. This would be the Northern Irish sense of humour she'd heard so much about. She didn't really get it.

Lydia instructed the driver to move off and find somewhere safe to park for an hour. Then she practically shoved Rory out onto the footpath. A roar lit up among the crowd and he flinched. Confident as he was, Lydia worried for a second that it was all going to be too much for her boy wonder. But he turned to her and flashed that imperfect set of teeth.

"Look at these pricks. Go and tell them I'm not setting foot in that school until they get rid of those United tops."

"Are you serious?"

Rory winked at her, popped the collar of his suit jacket for the bad boy effect, and shrugged.

"What do you think?"

Cormac snapped out of a dazed half-sleep. Paddy stood by the bedroom door. He cleared his throat.

"All right, Sleeping Beauty?"

Cormac tugged at his ski mask. "Just checking my eyelids for holes."

Paddy nodded towards the man and boy on the mattress. "No trouble, then?"

"None. I think the kid needs a toilet break, though."

"I'll get him a bucket, maybe."

Cormac wanted to smack him in his stupid grinning mouth.

Paddy leant against the door frame. "Jesus, don't be so serious, big man. We'll sort them out in a bit. You've to go downstairs first. The boss is back."

Cormac stood up and stretched. His spine popped and crackled. Bliss. He tucked the Ruger into his waistband and scooted past Paddy.

"Keep my seat warm, eh?"

Cormac closed the door and whipped off his ski mask. He rubbed some life into his cheeks and ran a clawed hand through his hair. A quick trip to the bathroom was the top of his agenda. Ambrose O'Neill would have to wait two minutes for him; bad tempered wee shite or not.

The whole gang, bar Paddy, were clustered around a poker table in the kitchen. A game of cards was the last thing on O'Neill's agenda, though. He sat with the air of Christ in Da Vinci's *Last Supper*. But with his slicked-back hair, widow's peak and thick mono-brow he looked more like the messiah's counterpart. His three unlikely apostles sat in reverential silence, Big Frank at his right hand and the brothers grim, Mick and Pete Scullion, on the left. The brothers' cherubic cheeks and soft brown eyes lent them a look of innocence. Cormac knew their form, though. They'd gut you as soon as look at you.

"Cormac Kelly." O'Neill indicated a chair directly opposite him. "Take a seat, young fellah."

Cormac sat, mindful of his body language. He'd long since learned the importance of primal posturing to men like his current "boss". Men who detested weakness and craved admiration. Alpha morons.

"Cheers, Mr O'Neill."

O'Neill sniffed and scanned the faces of his cronies. "You hear that, boys? A bit of respect. There's hope for these young ones yet."

A couple of grunts and nods acknowledged the boss's approval.

O'Neill laid his broad hands on the table and edged forward on his chair. "How's the family, Cormac?"

"Mine or the one upstairs?"

Big Frank groaned. "Just answer the question, smart-arse."

O'Neill shushed the cranky giant and waited for Cormac to respond.

"They're grand. Very quiet and it looks like they're going to behave. The da knows not to try anything stupid." He thought about mentioning Mattie's edginess but decided against it. He didn't want the young fellah to get slapped around.

"That's good," O'Neill said. "Let's hope they stay that way. They're going to be here for the long haul."

Cormac scratched his head. "How long?"

"You'll know when you need to."

"Am I on babysitting duty for the whole job?"

"Yes."

"Then I need to know how long, Mr O'Neill."

"No, you don't. We've all got our areas and that's yours. You stay available until the job is done and then you get paid. Next time you might get to know a little more. For now you're on the bottom rung. Be a good boy and you won't get knocked off it."

Eat shit and smile, in other words.

"Okay, Mr O'Neill. But we need to sort them out with food and water if they're staying any longer."

"We've thought of that, Cormac. This isn't amateur hour."

"Fair enough." He rubbed his stomach. "I'm a bit hungry myself, by the way."

O'Neill licked his thumb and smoothed the spot where his eyebrows met. "Put on the kettle, then. We could all use a refuel. There's bread in the cupboard and ham in the fridge."

Big Frank pushed his chair back and raised his arse off the seat. "And for dessert, you can suck my dick."

Mick loosed a camp whoop and Pete made kissy faces at Cormac. Such wit. Cormac looked to O'Neill to gauge an appropriate reaction. The boss gave him nothing. Pure poker face. Cormac bit back a quip about Big Frank's sexuality and kept his cool. They wanted to put the new kid in his place. He could play along for now. His time would come soon enough.

Cormac set the crew up with a tall stack of sandwiches. He laid the heavy plate on the table and almost lost his arm in the feeding frenzy. At least he'd had the foresight to hold a few rounds back for himself. The first bite barely touched the sides. He'd just sunk his teeth into the second mouthful when the screaming began.

Cormac spat out the sandwich and bolted for the stairs. He took the steps three at a time. The commotion in the bedroom kicked up a gear. Cormac drew his gun and shoved open the door.

Paddy towered above Mattie. The young fellah was curled up on his side, red-faced and wheezing. The fat bastard launched a kick into the boy's ribcage. John, the father, was on his knees. His nose had been bust and blood streamed through his fingers. He tried to get to his feet but pain and panic slowed his actions. Useless. Paddy drew his leg back to deliver another kick. Cormac hammered the butt of his revolver into the back of Paddy's skull. The fat man wobbled on his feet. Cormac snagged him by the back of his collar and jerked him away from the kid. Paddy landed flat out on his back and Cormac raised his foot to stomp on his face.

"Don't even think about it, big lad."

O'Neill, ski mask in place, snatched a handful of Cormac's hair and dragged him out onto the landing. Cormac grabbed at O'Neill's wrist with his free hand and broke the shorter man's grip. O'Neill tried to sweep the legs out from under Cormac with a low round-house kick. Cormac folded the boss's arm and trapped it against his heaving chest. He raised the Ruger and pointed it at O'Neill's face.

The metallic swish of a well-oiled automatic slide sounded in Cormac's ear.

"Let go of your gun," Big Frank said.

O'Neill, teeth bared in anger, pain and frustration, raised one side of his mono-brow. Cormac's millisecond assessment: cornered rat in front of him, in his ear an automatic pistol with one round chambered, huffy gorilla at his shoulder with a trigger finger set to twitch – check. Too close to checkmate to risk another move.

Cormac lowered his weapon and uncurled his grip. The revolver hit the carpeted floor with a thunk. Big Frank swept up the abandoned Ruger and returned to the background. O'Neill snatched his arm from Cormac's grasp and rotated each joint in turn; wrist, elbow, shoulder. His dented pride raged in his eyes.

O'Neill pushed Cormac aside and went into the bedroom. Cormac watched through the open door as the boss hunkered down beside his cousin and checked his neck for a pulse. He grunted and slapped Paddy about the jowls.

Cormac couldn't see the kid from his vantage point but the sound of Mattie coughing reassured him. The father sobbed.

"Is the boy all right?" O'Neill asked.

He didn't get an answer.

O'Neill didn't ask again. He clicked his fingers and the Scullions barged past Cormac to get into the room.

"Carry this fucking lump into the next room," O'Neill said. "Frank, you watch these ones for a bit."

"No sweat, boss."

O'Neill pointed a thick finger at Cormac. "You. Get downstairs and wait for me in the kitchen."

Cormac knew he'd fucked up big-time. It'd be a scramble to maintain some semblance of cover in a face-to-face with O'Neill. He had to put Mattie and John out of his mind and focus on self-preservation. Without him, the boy and his father were as good as dead.

Tighten up. There's worse to come.

###

Lydia wiped watery puke from her lips with a scrunched-up sheet of coarse toilet paper and dropped it in the bowl. She pulled the chain and negotiated her way out of the miniature cubicle. Her lower back strained as she stooped low to rinse her mouth out in the little sink. She straightened and checked her face in the mirror. Her lippy was slightly smeared. Nothing a quick touch-up wouldn't fix, but she didn't reach into her handbag for the makeup right away.

Rory's little book signing in the assembly hall had bought her some quiet time. She'd slipped out while he held the audience's attention with stories about scratched knees in the playground, jumpers for goal-posts and teachers who'd encouraged him to develop his natural abilities. As an oasis of calm, the school WC left a lot to be desired. The infant-sized cubicles and sinks made for slightly ludicrous surroundings. Ordinarily she might have made the appropriate clucking noises at the cutesy proportions, but with the taste of vomit still fresh in her mouth and a ball of tension rolling about in her stomach, the diminutive porcelain facilities mocked her. Jangled the emotional wounds the men in ski masks had left her with.

She deep-breathed her way through another wave of nausea. There was nothing in there but bile and it would burn its way up her oesophagus if she didn't regain some control. Falling to pieces wasn't going to get her family out of trouble.

A rumble of applause from the assembly hall got her moving again. She fixed her lips and ran a brush through her chestnut layered bob. There wasn't much she could do about her breath until she got her hands on some gum. She'd just have to avoid face-to-face conversation until then.

The assembly hall began to empty out as Lydia left the little bathroom. She negotiated her way back towards the hall against the flow of noisy munchkins. Rory, a yellow indoor football tucked under one arm, looked a little lost among the remaining teachers and local politicians who competed for his attention. His face brightened when he caught sight of Lydia. He raised his eyebrows and she zeroed in for a subtle rescue.

"I *hate* to drag you away, Rory," Lydia said. "Unfortunately, we've a timetable to stick to."

Rory passed the ball to the local priest, shook hands with the men in suits, promised to stop in again and managed a sincere-ish look of regret as Lydia led him out of the school. The driver was parked across the school gates, all the better for a quick escape. They waded through the growing cluster of children and hopped into the back seat of the Merc.

"Have fun?" Lydia asked.

"What a load of shite."

Lydia thumbed through the organiser on her phone. "We've an hour and a half before you visit the secondary school."

Rory groaned. "Thank fuck I didn't go to university, eh?"

"Hmmm. You have a little time to recharge your batteries. Do you want to grab a bite somewhere?"

"If we can find a quiet place. I can't be arsed putting on the PR face."

"Here," the driver said. "What about the Manchester United supporters' bar? It's not far from here."

Rory sighed. "Ha-fucking-ha."

He told the driver to take them to Andersonstown and find a quiet café. The driver nodded at him in the rear-view mirror then went back to cursing at black taxis and pink buses under his breath.

"Is your son enjoying the wee trip?" Rory asked.

Lydia fixed her eyes on the driver's headrest. The thought of Mattie's "enjoyment" drove a jagged icicle through her heart. "You know what kids are like. He's bored to tears without Sky TV and Xbox Live."

"I kind of miss my Xbox too. Is thingy... um, John. Is John not dragging him to all the usual spots? The Causeway and all that."

"We're trying to save that sort of stuff for when I can go. When your schedule clears... in a day or two." She checked her phone. "Are you doing anything tonight?"

Rory didn't register the subject change. "Clubbing, probably, if I can find somewhere with a bit of life. I'd forgotten what a backward shithole Belfast was. It doesn't even have any strip clubs, like."

Yeah, that's the worst thing about this country, you spoiled bastard.

The car juddered to a halt on a bus lane. The driver shut off the engine and Lydia realised they were parked. She glanced out at what looked like a construction site. Beyond the mess of red and white plastic barriers and temporary steel fencing was a squat building that claimed to be a leisure centre. The driver pointed to a row of houses converted to shop units a few yard up the street.

"Not the best place in Andytown," he said, "but they do a decent cuppa, you know, like?"

Lydia couldn't figure out if he required some sort of response. She avoided eye contact in the rear-view mirror.

"They do an all-day breakfast with a pot of tea for £3.95."

Rory patted his stomach and gave the driver the thumbs up.

"That looks like the business to me. Haven't been to a good old-fashioned greasy spoon in years."

Lydia's stomach lurched at the thought of an Ulster Fry, but she reckoned she could manage a cup of tea. "Yes, great. Let's go."

"Driver, come on in with us," Rory said. "I'm sure you could use a bite yourself."

The driver didn't need to be coaxed. He was the first one out of the car.

They sat at a small square table in the far corner of the café, Rory and Lydia beside each other and the driver opposite them. The table was one of half a dozen lined in rows of three along splotchy magnolia walls. Worn lino barely covered the floor. Three of the tables were yet to be cleared of the leftovers from the last wave of customers. The elderly lady behind the counter seemed to be in no rush to remedy this. The driver reached over to the next table and lifted a coffee-stained copy of The Sun. He started reading it from the back page.

"I don't suppose you're a City fan?" Rory asked.

He barely looked up. "United."

"Right."

"Always have been. No offence, like."

"Hey, I wasn't always a City lad myself."

The driver perked up a little. "Aye?"

"I followed Liverpool when I was a kid."

"Oh." He went back to his paper.

Rory turned to Lydia and crossed his eyes, his signature expression of exasperation.

"What are youse having?" The elderly lady's voice clawed its way out through a sixty-a-day ravaged throat. She hadn't moved from her spot behind the counter. Probably would have been too much for her lungs to handle.

"Three fries," Rory said.

Lydia cut in. "Make that two. I just want some tea."

"Ach, come on," Rory said. "When in Andytown..."

"I ate a big breakfast earlier."

"But we might be—"

"Just tea, please."

Lydia turned away from Rory and fiddled with her phone. She imagined him giving his cross-eyed look to the driver. *Let him put it down to PMT.* Her phone vibrated in her hand and squawked the chorus to Lady Gaga's *Bad Romance*.

Lydia stared at the display. Private number. It was them.

"Jesus, Lydia," Rory said. "Lady Gaga? Do us all a favour and answer it, will you?"

She jolted upright and was out the door before her toppled chair hit the linoleum.

CHAPTER 3

It's hard not to feel sorry for some of the international players. A few of these guys really do miss the family they left behind. It can be tough. They must get at least a little comfort from drying their tears with fifty pound notes, though.

Rory Cullen, *Cullen: The Autobiography*

Cormac waited: controlled, quiet, calm. He was back at the round table in the kitchen, seated at O'Neill's instruction. The boss paced a short stretch of tiled floor on the opposite side of the table. His natural boxer's strut did not go unnoticed. Cormac predicted that fists would fly before the end of their chat.

"I'm still trying to understand why you would pistol-whip my cousin." O'Neill said. "Do you want to help me out at all?"

Cormac took a deep breath and sneered. He leaned forward to occupy more of O'Neill's field of vision. "I thought your cousin was going to kill the child."

"Ach, wise up. He just got smacked about a wee bit."

"The kid was on the floor and that fat shite was hoofing kicks into his chest. If Mattie's not got broken ribs I'll—"

"Mattie, is it? Did you make friends with our wee hostage last night?"

"I barely said two words to him."

"That right?"

Cormac sat back in his chair and folded his arms. He nodded.

O'Neill planted his hands on the table and bent at the waist. He eyeballed Cormac. "Because you seem to be getting on better with the hostages than you are with the rest of the crew. You smart-mouthed Frank last night, tried to kill Paddy—"

"It'd take more than a bang—"

"Don't interrupt me."

Cormac reeled in the urge to argue his case. O'Neill wasn't ready to hear from him yet, even if this was a questioning. Cormac realised he'd be better off shutting the fuck up until the boss man finished ranting. Cops or robbers, it didn't matter. When your superior got in a mood, it was usually best to say as little as you could until it let up a little.

"You think you're a cut above the rest of us. Don't you? Just because you've a couple of dissident connections you reckon you should be running the show here. I've put you at the bottom for a reason, son." His decibel levels hit a sudden spike. "So why don't you lose the fucking attitude and learn your place here? Or do you want me to knock that smirk of yours off your smug fucking face!"

O'Neill swiped a string of spittle from his chin with the sleeve of his sweater. His mono-brow had formed an obtuse v-shape during his ball-chewing. He thumbed the little patch of coarse hair that joined his two eyebrows as if they needed manual adjustment to level out again. It seemed to do the trick too. He rolled his head like he was working the strain of a full-on bout of sparring from his bunched shoulders.

Cormac took this post-fight display as a sign to speak. "Okay. So, I'm sorry, Mr O'Neill. I'll apologise to Paddy as well, if he'll accept it."

"What makes you think you're going to get the opportunity to apologise to Paddy? Do you not think I should send you packing?"

"With all due respect, Mr O'Neill, we both know you're not in a position to do that."

"Am I not?"

Cormac knew he was juggling chainsaws, but he had to make sure that he saw the job through. The whole investigation would fall to pieces if he got kicked off O'Neill's crew.

"Those connections you mentioned, Mr O'Neill... my Real IRA friends... I'd have to call in a favour or two with them."

O'Neill looked Cormac in the eye for a couple of heartbeats. Then he lunged as fast as a cobra strike. Cormac kicked himself away from the table and toppled his chair as he rolled off the back of it. He tried to push himself upright. O'Neill scrambled over the table and landed a push-kick on his sternum. Flipped him onto his back. O'Neill drew his gun. He aimed at Cormac's face.

"You stupid bastard," O'Neill said. "Threatening *me*?"

Cormac puffed hard. He thought he might be able to kick the gun out of O'Neill's hand from his position on the floor. Anger had made the boss a little sloppy. But he held still.

O'Neill stepped back a few paces. "Get up."

Cormac got to his feet, slow and steady, never taking his eyes off O'Neill.

"Maybe I can't get rid of you," O'Neill said. "But

I can't let you off with such a lack of respect either."

O'Neill double-stepped on his diagonal and flanked Cormac. His arm arced in a cross between a hook and a hammer blow. Cormac caught the butt of O'Neill's automatic pistol on the back of his head. The lights went right out.

###

"You were meant to phone hours ago."

"Wind your neck in, woman. We phone when we phone. Be grateful for it."

Through her blend of rage, panic and utter confusion, Lydia registered that the voice on the other line was different from the last. She wondered if this was the one who'd been videoed with Mattie and entertained a brief revenge fantasy that was heavy on castration.

"Just let me talk to my family."

"Mummy?" It was Mattie but something wasn't right. His voice was higher-pitched and he hadn't called her "Mummy" in years.

"Oh, sweetheart, are you okay?"

Mattie snuffled and squeaked. He was having trouble catching his breath.

"Did they hurt you?"

"Fat guy... got me."

"Oh Mattie, sweetheart. Are you okay?"

"Kicked—"

Mattie's voice was cut off by a rustling at his end. Lydia figured somebody had snatched the phone by the mouthpiece.

The gruff mystery voice returned. "That's your lot."

"Wait. What happened to my son?"

"The boy's fine."

"Let me talk to him again. Put him on the phone now!"

"You don't call the shots, woman."

"Did you hurt him?"

"*I* didn't, no."

"You bastards!"

The line went dead. Lydia had aimlessly walked in circles outside the café as she spoke to Mattie and his captor. She found herself at the Merc they'd arrived in. Without thinking, she drove a high-heeled kick into the passenger side fender. The impact rattled upwards from her toes to her hip. She twirled on her left foot as the right flared in agony. Then she leant backwards against the car and laid a hand across her mouth. Her guts burbled a threat and she fought hard to contain it.

And then Rory was in front of her. "What the fuck's wrong, Lydia?"

She held up one finger and shook her head as if she'd a mouthful of steak to chew through before she could speak. Rory hopped from foot to foot. Waited for her to respond.

"I got some bad news," Lydia said. "Nothing for you to worry about. Just a deal gone wrong for another client."

Rory looked pointedly at the small dent in the Merc's bodywork. "Must have been a hell of a deal."

"You have no idea."

He looked her up and down. Lingered on her eyes, which Lydia knew had to be puffed up and set to burst. Then he slipped his hands into his pockets and casually kicked at a loose stone on the badly surfaced footpath.

"Who was it?" he asked. "Trabucco? I heard a rumour that AC Milan was courting the glory-hunting bastard."

"I can't tell you."

"Ach, come on. This is me you're talking to. Do you think I'd leak it to the tabloids or something?"

Lydia pushed her bum off the side of the car and edged a little closer to Rory. She wanted to fall into him. Feel the comfort of his strong arms around her. Let him whisper in her ear that everything would be all right. Instead she tilted her head and did her best to feign coyness.

"This is football, Rory. You know the score."

Cormac cracked one eyelid. The light in the room, dull as it was, stabbed at his eyes like a demon's pitchfork. A slow throb warmed the back of his skull. He probed the area with tentative fingertips. They came back coated in sticky flakes of blood. He held his breath and examined the area more thoroughly. Pain ripped outwards from the wound. His whole scalp tightened and a muscle in his neck twanged. But he persevered until he could assess the damage. He guessed the cut in his scalp was about an inch long and not as deep as he'd first feared. It had probably bled like a bastard at the time, but it had been stemmed by a coagulated mess in the time he'd been unconscious. He guessed it'd been a few hours since O'Neill's attack.

With a deep bracing breath he popped open his other eyelid. Didn't get half the pain he expected.

The room wobbled a little as he righted himself into a sitting position and it took him half a minute to place himself. He registered the kid first, sat cross-legged on the mattress. A pair of big cartoonish eyes locked in on Cormac's. He looked more curious than afraid.

"He's awake."

Mattie had directed this update at his father. John was a blurred image, slightly behind Mattie. The kid's arms were crossed, hands cradling his floating ribs. It looked like an attempt to hug himself.

Cormac focussed on the father. He stood at the right of the mattress with his back to the rest of the room. His forehead rested against the wall. Shoulders slumped in defeat.

Big Frank's legs cut across Cormac's field of vision. The steroid-popping ogre stood as tall and broad as a mighty redwood. One swift stomp from his size fourteen Timberlands would end Cormac. Big Frank offered his hand. On acceptance, Cormac was hauled to his feet like a toddler. He held on until a severe spell of dizziness passed. The big palm was coarsened by a neat line of calluses, most likely from a fully loaded weight bar. Cormac broke out of the iron grip when he was confident he would remain upright. His fingers pulsed as the circulation kicked in again.

"You all right?" Big Frank asked.

Cormac nodded and instantly regretted it. "I've been better, like. Could use a couple of paracetamol."

Big Frank's expression was hidden behind his ski mask but his stare was as serious as a heart attack. Eyes set like granite. He clapped a meaty hand on Cormac's shoulder and leaned in a little to mumble in his ear.

Cormac just about made out the words through a fresh wave of disorientation.

"For what it's worth, I think you were right when you knocked Paddy out to fuck. The fat cunt has no self-control. God knows what could have happened.

But O'Neill's pissed and he's my boss, so if he decides you're to be punished for beating down his cousin, I'll go with it. I'll try to make it as easy on you as I can, though. Just try not to resist when the time comes. It'll be easier."

"You going for Mother Teresa's old title?"

Big Frank's lips twitched in an almost-smile. Then he went to the door.

"He's back in the land of the living." Frank's words rumbled like a bowling ball on its way down the stairs.

Chairs scraped against tiles in the room below. Cormac guessed the whole crew was going to hold some sort of court to decide what to do with him. It was probably a bad sign that they hadn't replaced his ski mask. They were no longer worried if the family could identify him.

O'Neill led the pack as they crowded into the bedroom. Cormac filled his lungs with a huge, calming breath. Whatever way it worked out, he intended to go down swinging.

The Scullions' soft brown eyes had narrowed into jackal-like slits. The pair of them practically panted. Paddy barged past the bloodthirsty brothers to stand by his cousin. Righteous anger puffed his chest. He placed his hands on his wobbly hips and jutted his treble chin. A roll of fat slipped out from under his ski mask.

"Let's get the air cleared, Cormac," O'Neill said.

Fucking bastard had used his name in front of the hostages. The sound of it had the same effect as the *shuck-shuck* of a pumped shotgun. They were hanging him out to dry. The assignment was fucked. And so was he.

O'Neill rolled his bulldog shoulders. "You

shouldn't have hit our man here."

"If I hadn't, we might have been dealing with a dead hostage right now." From the corner of his eye, Cormac saw Mattie stiffen. "I think the fool got off light with a bump on the head."

"Funny, he thinks the same about you."

Cormac's hand hovered above his own head injury. "How about we call it eye for an eye and let it be, eh?"

Paddy shook his head. "I didn't get the pleasure from it."

"So what? You going to crack me one now too? Fuck's sake, my skull won't hold up to it."

"We thought about that," O'Neill said. "So he's going to break a couple of fingers instead."

Cormac raised his hands. Before he could form any sort of guard the Scullions were on him. They seized a wrist each and pulled him into a Jesus Christ pose. Mattie started to keen. His father wrapped his arm around the kid's neck. Mattie buried his face in his father's chest.

"Does my son need to see this?"

O'Neill looked to Mattie and John and sucked air through his teeth. "Get John out of here." He pointed at Big Frank. "Take him into the other room."

"What about my son?"

"He started this shit storm. Maybe it'll put some manners on him."

"Are you fucking—?"

Big Frank stomped over to John. He grabbed the smaller man by the arm and cranked it up his back. He squeaked like a kicked shih tzu. Mattie scrambled to his knees and tried to grapple with the brute hurting his father. Big Frank shoved the kid away.

"Dad! Don't go, Dad!"

The boy's piercing command set the father off on a more frenzied struggle. Then he was on his tiptoes and howling.

"Enough, enough. You're going to fucking break it."

"No. Dad!"

Frank eased off on the pressure just enough for John to settle.

"I'm okay, son." He hissed through clenched teeth. "I'll come back as soon as I can. Be good."

Big Frank wrapped an arm around John's throat. He dragged the defeated man out of the room.

Mattie backed into a corner and squirmed.

Cormac struggled against the Scullions but they held fast. His shoulders burned with exertion as he spat and cursed and jerked. The brothers mocked him with their own high-pitched F-words.

"Would somebody panel this fucking wriggler?" Mick asked.

O'Neill nipped forward and caught Cormac with a textbook uppercut. Cormac's head snapped back and his crown bounced off the wall behind him. The room disappeared in a brilliant white flash. His wound reopened and warm blood coursed down the back of his neck. The floor dropped away from his feet. He started to sink; slow and lazy like a falling feather. The Scullions gave his arms a tug o' war heave. And the floor was back. His knees trembled slightly but his feet stayed under him.

A little voice at the back of his mind suggested he say a quick decade of the rosary.

He chased away the fear and tried to focus. Clarity came back with a vengeance. O'Neill had his crazy eyes on. He drew his Glock and pointed it at Cormac's face.

The boss's fat trigger finger went white-knuckled with pressure.

O'Neill stepped forward and pushed the muzzle into Cormac's face. Ground it into the flesh below his cheekbone. Cormac could smell gun oil. It stuck to the back of his throat like smokers' mucus. He breathed the scent deeper. Drew it into his lungs. Imagined it hardening in his core.

And then O'Neill put his gun away.

"We'll not kill you yet," he said. "Don't want you stinking up the place. Might be here a while."

Cormac jutted his chin at the boss. "What are you going to do when word gets back to my friends? You know they'll not be happy about this."

O'Neill's mighty mono-brow bowed in the middle. "We'll think of something, son. Don't worry. Plenty of ways a lad can get himself killed on a job like this. Maybe I'll tell them John Gallagher did you in during an escape attempt. Just off the top of my head, like."

Cormac snuffed air through his nose. Composed himself. He subtly tested the Scullions' grip on his arms, just a small shift in pressure here and there to see if they'd dropped their guard even just a little. Solid as shackles. O'Neill motioned Paddy forward.

"Go on, fat man," Cormac said. "Have your pound of flesh."

Paddy waddled forward. He stood with his nose inches away from Cormac's. His breath reeked of raw onion.

"This could have all been avoided, you know," Paddy said. "If you'd just had the sense to stop for a second and ask me what happened... why I had to sort the wee shite out... Ach, why bother? You're a stupid bastard. I'm not even going to justify myself to you."

Cormac tensed, expecting Paddy to grab a handful of fingers and get to work. But the fat man turned away from him and beckoned the kid off the mattress.

Mattie stood slowly, his face wrought with trepidation. Then he darted forward. He dummied to Paddy's left. The fat man fell for it and Mattie dashed to the right. He almost made it to the door but in a moment of action that took everybody by surprise, himself included, Paddy kicked out backwards like a surly mule. The kick caught the door and swung it shut. Mattie got sideswiped in the arc and was shunted to the side. He bounced off the stud wall and stumbled backwards. Mick caught up with the moment and left Cormac's side to grab Mattie by the scruff. The kid flailed his arms in all directions, caught Mick by surprise and ran at the door again. But he'd lost his chance. Paddy grabbed him by the waist and dumped him on the mattress. Mattie refused to stay down. He sprang up and threw a low punch. Paddy went back, arse first, and avoided a brutal thump in the balls. Mattie took advantage of a lowered target and caught Paddy's jaw with an efficient right hook. He primed his fist for another swing but Mick had shaken off Mattie's wild attack. He stepped in and kicked the kid's legs out from under him. Mattie crashed to the floor and stayed down.

Paddy coughed and gulped air, the sudden exertion too much for him. Mick Scullion stood between the fat man and the boy. Dared him to have another go so he'd have an excuse to batter him. Mattie knew he'd been beat but he returned Mick's stare and dared him right back.

Cormac started to weigh up the situation. There might have been a chance to gain some sort of advantage over the other three while Mattie had pinballed around the room but that frantic moment was lost. He'd been too wrapped up in watching Mattie's sudden charge. But the balance had shifted. Cormac, one arm now free, primed himself for the right moment.

"You wee fucker." Paddy's breathless voice whined. "Did you not learn your lesson the first time?"

Mattie paled. He knew what had to be coming next. Cormac couldn't help but admire him. No tears, no begging. Just cool silence and that tough little look of defiance.

Paddy pushed Mick out of his way. "Keep that prick busy." He pointed at Cormac. "You know what he's like."

Pete let go of Cormac's arm and stood shoulder to shoulder with his brother. They shifted into loose boxing stances and invited Cormac to have a go with matching perverse smiles. Paddy advanced on the boy, his guard held low to shield his groin. Mattie scrambled to his feet and backed away from the fat man. He held up his small hands, palms out, to ward him off.

Cormac could no longer wait for the perfect opening. He charged the Scullions and tried to clock Mick with a straight left. Mick bobbed and the blow glanced off the top of his head. Cormac moved to his left and stuck close to Mick. Pete tried to weigh in but couldn't get past his brother. Cormac threw a jab. Mick swatted it away and countered with a right cross. Landed it on Cormac's cheekbone. He followed up with a left hook. Cormac, barely fazed by the first strike, ducked and came up with an uppercut. Connected clean to the chin and Mick staggered backwards. Pete pushed his stunned brother to the side and leapt at Cormac. The enraged Scullion absorbed a couple of tight left hooks and wrapped his opponent up in a clinch. Cormac struggled against Pete's berserker rage but couldn't get a handle on him. Mick rallied and returned to the fray. He rounded the wrestling pair and got to work. Cormac took a couple of blows to the kidneys. He allowed his knees to buckle and Pete let him drop to the floor. The brothers kicked and stomped but Cormac rolled out of their path.

Cormac drew his knees up to his chest and tumbled backwards onto his feet. Adrenaline took the edge off his pain and honed his vision. He embraced it. Cormac beckoned the brothers with his open-handed guard. Taunted them. They edged towards him, lead feet testing each floorboard as if they expected mines.

The brothers' reluctance allowed Cormac a few seconds to focus beyond them. He saw Paddy slap Mattie's already bloody face. Then the bastard took the young boy's left wrist and wrapped his fat hands around his little fingers. Cormac snarled and clenched his fists. He collided with the Scullions but couldn't get through them quick enough to prevent the snap of bone. Mattie shrieked.

Cormac took it up a gear. He lashed out and landed strikes. Felt their resistance sag. He pushed them to the limit. One of his obstacles went down. Cormac trampled over him and fought harder. Another fell to the wayside. And he was on the fat, useless bully that had damaged the kid. Paddy's face squished under Cormac's left-handed grip. He swung down hard with his right elbow.

There was screaming. Some sort of explosion. More screaming. Cormac was dragged backwards. He railed against the unseen force and it almost withered.

Then nothing.

CHAPTER 4

No, I've never been in the IRA. Growing up on the Falls Road isn't the only qualification required for the job. Can we put that question to bed now?

Rory Cullen, *Cullen: The Autobiography*

Lydia stood in the living room in front of a blank television screen. She held an unfamiliar remote control in her hand. Her thumb hovered over the red standby button.

She'd parted ways with Rory after his book signing at the secondary school. The format had been much the same as the primary school visit, but Rory's short attention span had sapped his enthusiasm. He'd rhymed off his speech about the "Explosive!" autobiography to the pupils with a weary lack of enthusiasm and rushed his way through the meet and greets that followed. They were in and out in double time, and Lydia was left with extra hours to pass on her own.

Lydia let the remote fall to the floor. It bounced off the carpet and the batteries popped out. She considered the sofa but her nerves jangled too much to allow her to sit.

In the kitchen, she opened the fridge door and peered inside. Her stomach rumbled at the prospect of food but she just couldn't be bothered with fixing herself something. Didn't even have the drive to butter a slice of bread. She considered a half-empty bottle of chardonnay but nixed the notion pretty quickly. What if they phoned and she didn't have her wits about her? She'd never forgive herself.

The old cottage brimmed with weird noises that Mattie's natural clamour would have covered. Lydia knew that the sounds she heard were nothing more mysterious than a clanking pipe or a shifting floor-board, but every little creak tingled down her spine. She'd never felt so lonely.

Lydia paced the house, up and down the narrow hall, in and out of the rooms. She straightened pictures on the wall, adjusted and readjusted the hang of the curtains in each room and stripped down all the beds so she could make them all over again. It passed an hour.

When Lydia finished her series of utterly pointless tasks she felt like she could actually sit for a bit. She flopped down onto the sofa and placed her phone on the armrest. The same spot where one of the masked men had rested his pistol the night before. She lifted the phone and placed it on the opposite arm. Then she sat back and waited.

Lydia snapped back to life from a muzzy drowse at the sound of her Lady Gaga ringtone. Her collar was cold and damp with sweat and her mouth tasted of morning breath. Her voice cracked a little as she answered the phone.

"I want to speak to Mattie."

"Whoa there, missus. You'll talk to the boy soon enough."

"What do you want from me? Where's my family?"

"Two of my men will be there soon. Be a good girl

and let them in, will you? You don't want them kicking the door down."

Lydia sprang off the couch. "Why are they coming here?"

He killed the connection.

She thought about the chef's knife in the kitchen drawer. A true-blue Norman Bates effort. Considered hiding it up her sleeve.

Get a grip. You'll probably end up slashing your own wrist with it.

She knew it was stupid. What would she do with a knife anyway? Kill the two visitors and then try to find her family? Kill one and torture the other for information? They had her family and the blade would do nothing to change that fact.

A ruckus erupted out in the hall. A boom at the door followed by a splintering crack and a crash. Lydia screamed and fumbled her phone but managed to hold onto it. She slipped it into the pocket of her trousers and swallowed hard. The bastards had kicked the door in without as much as a warning knock. She heard their boots on the hallway's laminate floor and tried to brace herself for more terror. When they entered the living room she realised that there was no preparing for certain things.

The sight of them in their dark clothes and ski masks combined the memories of the previous night's fear with a brand new sense of dread. Lydia wished she'd fetched the knife after all. Her sudden vulnerability wiped her mind of all thoughts but survival.

Judging by their height and build Lydia placed them as the sofa jockeys. She got a better look at their eyes in the early evening light. Both men had distinctly dark brown irises that might have been attractive if they weren't framed by ski mask eye-holes set above maniacal grins.

The one on the left spoke first. "How'd you get on today?"

She offered a blank look in return.

He elaborated. "With Cullen, you stupid bitch. Did you get anywhere with Cullen?"

"How could I? We—"

"That's for you to figure out. Our job is to remind you that we have your family and we won't let them go until you've given us what we want."

"But you can't expect—"

The man on the right slapped Lydia's face. "Shut the fuck up."

Lydia stumbled backwards. The masked men closed the gap she created right away. Lydia was painfully aware that they were maintaining a striking distance. She raised a hand to her hot cheek.

Lefty waggled his finger at Lydia. "The longer it takes you to get us what we want, the longer we keep your family."

Righty's mouth contorted into a killer clown smile. "Have you nothing to say for yourself, gorgeous?"

"She's probably afraid you'll smack her again," Lefty said.

"Sure that was only a wee love tap."

"Got a wee thing for her, have you?"

Righty tugged at the crotch of his jeans. "Nothing wee about it, kid."

Lydia felt grimy as the two thugs looked her up and down, tongues practically lolling from their smirking mouths. She drew her knees together and crossed her arms in front of her breasts.

Lefty nudged his partner like they were in some

twisted version of the Monty Python "say no more" sketch. "You can see where her son gets his looks from, can't you? Could have a thing for him and all."

And with that they'd crossed the line. Lydia curled her fingers into claws and went for their eyes. She cut off their demonic cackles with an alley cat attack. Lefty jerked backwards and dodged her swipe. Righty wasn't fast enough. Lydia grunted with satisfaction as her fingers slipped into his eyeholes and tore flesh. Righty screeched and backpedalled. He pulled off one of his gloves, cupped his hand and pressed it against his left eye. Blood ran through his fingers.

"She fucking blinded me!"

Lefty tutted and turned on Lydia. "That was stupid."

He put all his weight behind a solid body shot. Lydia wheezed and went to her knees. She fought for air but couldn't draw anything into her winded lungs.

The uninjured thug left her gasping on the floor, turned to his partner and examined his eye.

"The eye's still there. It's just scratched."

"Hurts like a bastard."

Lefty clapped Righty's shoulder and for a second Lydia thought they might hug. But then Lefty curled his fist to grasp a handful of Righty's sweater. He dragged him over to Lydia.

"I think you should put some manners on this bitch."

Righty stared her out with his one good eye. Lydia renewed her effort to get her lungs working properly. Her mind screamed at her to get up and run but she hadn't even the juice to stand. Righty placed the sole of his boot between her breasts and pushed her backwards. She toppled over and continued to wheeze.

"Get up."

Lydia rolled on to her front and pushed herself up onto her hands and knees. One of the men behind her whistled.

"Not a bad view, eh?" Lefty said. "Looks like she spends a lot of time at the gym sculpting that arse."

"It'd be a lot nicer if I could see out of both my eyes."

Lydia used the couch for support and fought gravity to get to her feet. She turned to face the men. Righty closed in on her. He took his hand from his injured eye and reached out towards her face with it. Lydia could smell his blood. He brushed back a strand of her hair with his bloodstained fingers and sighed softly. Then he leant in as if to kiss her cheek. Hot breath dampened her ear.

"If you're still here by tomorrow night I'm coming back to fuck your brains out." He traced the line of her jaw with his bloody fingertips. "You've work to do in London, bitch. Get that lovely arse in gear."

###

Cormac woke up with cotton-mouth, a thumping headache and pins and needles prickling the length of his right arm. He tried to shake some life into the sleeping limb and blanched. It felt like his brain had been shook loose and it rattled in his skull with every movement. The pain blew the cobwebs from his mind. He realised he hadn't come out of a deep slumber. He'd been knocked out and had regained consciousness. It was a wonder he'd come to at all.

He pushed himself upright and sat with his back to the bedroom wall. Scanned the room with blurred vision. Mattie was on the mattress, pale and in obvious discomfort. His dad hadn't returned and the little guy looked even smaller in his isolation. He looked to Cormac and nodded a slight acknowledgment. Cormac tried to smile but his face wasn't having any of it. The skin on his cheeks tingled with each fresh thud from his heart and his lips were thick with swelling.

"You look fucked," Mattie said.

Cormac surveyed Mattie's face. A purple bruise blossomed around his left eye and there was dried blood under his nostrils and in the corners of his mouth. His left hand rested in his lap, badly swollen yet still slender and birdlike.

"What age are you, kid?" Cormac asked. "Twelve?"

Mattie bristled. "I'm thirteen."

Cormac had figured the boy was closer to eleven but had upped the number to compliment him. Still, it was good to see that Mattie had enough fight left in him to be insulted by Cormac's *faux pas*.

"You're a bit young to be using the F-word."

"I'm a bit young to get my fingers broke by that shower of cunts as well. Didn't make much difference, though, did it?"

The boy had a point. And the fact that he referred to the rest of the crew as "that shower" implied that he didn't count Cormac among their number. Small comfort though it was, Cormac entertained hopes that he could form some sort of alliance with Mattie.

"Cormac, isn't it?"

"Aye."

"Thanks for standing up for me."

Cormac laid his head back against the wall. "For all the good it did either of us."

"Still..."

Something clicked in Cormac's mind. He sat up straight and looked from left to right. "Did they leave us here on our own?"

Mattie nodded. "I heard some of them go out a good while ago. They left the bastard with the big muscles to watch us but he's been downstairs for a while now."

Cormac's eyes went to the door.

"It's locked," Mattie said.

The door was a whitewood panel effort and would have been no bother to get through, locked or not. But Big Frank would be up the stairs at the sound of the first kick and Cormac was in no shape to deal with him.

"How long was I out?" Cormac asked.

Mattie shrugged then winced as it reminded him of one of his injuries. "I don't have a watch."

Cormac looked to the window. An orange streetlight glow crept under the curtains. Hours had passed but it could have been anywhere between ten o'clock at night and three in the morning.

"No sign of your da?"

"I heard him shouting a while ago but I don't think anybody was hurting him or anything. I didn't want to shout back in case we got in more trouble."

Cormac cocked his head to listen for life beyond the bedroom. Deathly silence. He figured it'd be safe to move about without attracting immediate attention. Safe but not easy. The full extent of his injuries began to make itself known with every slight movement he made. His lungs couldn't hold a deep breath without complaint from his ribcage. The muscles in his legs were cramped up and his lower back ached. He longed to empty his bladder but suspected his piss would be tinged crimson with blood. Nausea tightened his stomach. He battled against his gag reflex and stood.

"You look like my granny trying to get off a beanbag."

Cormac grunted. "Funny little fu-fellah, aren't you?"

"Fu-fellah?"

"Shut up."

"You can curse in front of me. I won't tell, like."

Cormac moved to the window and whipped back the curtain. A couple of hooks pinged loose but it held on to the rail. The PVC window had a little lock on the catch. Cormac tried to turn the handle but it held firm. He pushed the bottom corner of the frame and it gave way slightly under the pressure. One good shove would probably pop it.

"What's the point in that?" Mattie said. "We're upstairs."

"You're a very negative person. I'm just weighing up the options. Have you a better idea in mind, like?"

"We could take the legs off that chair and brain the next bastard that comes in here."

"Chair legs against guns...? Yeah, I can see how that trumps the window."

"They're going to kill us anyway. May as well go down swinging."

"Nobody's going to get killed."

"Wise up. Maybe there's a chance that I'll get out of this, but you're definitely fucked."

Cormac didn't know whether to hug or strangle him.

CHAPTER 5

They'll name an airport after me some day.

Rory Cullen, *Cullen: The Autobiography*

The hired Merc swept into the M3 fast lane. A long distance lorry flashed its lights in protest as it was forced to shift down a gear. Just a couple of yards later, the driver slotted the Merc back into the inside lane, this time upsetting a Fon-A-Cab driver who laid on his horn for a good five seconds. The sideward momentum from the lane-hopping rocked Lydia and Rory in the back seat. Lydia welcomed the distraction but Rory looked a little green around the gills as he clenched the door handle for support and assurance. She thought about asking the driver to slow down but didn't want to risk missing the flight back to London.

"I still don't understand what the big panic is." Rory's voice croaked from the punishment of the previous night's debauchery.

"You can't keep these people waiting, Rory. When a slot comes up in their schedule, you have to jump at it. Your book's in everybody's mind this week. Next week they'll have wrung it out."

"But I have commitments here."

"Nothing that can't be postponed. You've done the important ones, anyway. It's forgetting where you came from that's the cardinal sin. After the school visits the corporate events don't really matter."

"They were paying gigs, though."

"Oh, please, Rory. Peanuts compared to what this crowd can bring in for you."

"But you've always handled my sponsorship deals. Won't you be out of pocket if this thing goes through?"

"I still get a cut of what they make for you, and believe me; it'll be a lot more than I could ever pull in. No, unless you want to end up doing ads for crisps, this is the agency you want on your side. They've the contacts to land you your own clothing line."

Rory opened his window, hawked and spat a gob that got whipped away in the slipstream. "Fashion shows, though? Wouldn't that be a bit gay?"

Typical footballer bullshit. Lydia never met a client she didn't want to strangle at some point in their dealings.

"You'll not be expected to sit by the catwalk. It's just your name, Rory. Come on, is it fair that it's always the United boys that get these gigs? Think of the pride you'll bring to the City of Manchester when you top the biggest transfer deal in Premiership history with the biggest sponsorship deal. The fans will think the sun shines out your arse."

"They don't care about that shite. It's how many goals I score that'll matter."

"Football's not that simple anymore. Everything matters. And the more popular you get, on and off the pitch, the bigger the bargaining chip you arm me with next time your contract is up for renewal."

"I've only just signed this one."

"And you pay me to think of the next one."

Rory fiddled with the rear passenger air vent in the car's door pillar. To Lydia's relief, he'd asked enough questions and his interest was spent. He fished a can of Red Bull out of his hand luggage and cracked it open. His face crimped as he took his first sip.

"Ah, Jesus. This tastes like there's vodka in it."

"Must have been a heavy night."

"Ugh. I don't want to talk about it yet."

They made it to George Best Belfast City Airport in record time. The driver jumped out and snagged a luggage trolley. He trundled it back to them, his face blank and joyless as he went through the motions of a well polished routine. Rory stood at the side of the car with a wheelie case and a rucksack. Lydia had a light overnight bag slung over her shoulder. The driver offered them the trolley.

"I think we've got it covered," Lydia said. "Thanks anyway."

The driver grunted and left the trolley at the kerbside. Rory intercepted him on his way to the car.

"Hold up, mate." He rummaged in his hip pocket and pulled out a twenty pound note. "Here you go."

"Cheers."

"No worries, but put that trolley back where you got it, will you? I hate to see them lying about."

The driver made a face, looked at the crisp note in his hand and then shrugged. "Certainly, sir."

Rory snapped up his shirt cuff and checked the time on his chunky blinged-out timepiece. Mid-morning light glinted off platinum and ice. "We've twenty minutes to get checked in. Fancy a bit of breakfast?"

"After we get through security. It'll be more relaxing."

He crossed his eyes and smirked. "You're such a geek."

"No. I'm organised."

The early morning commute rush was over and the hangar-sized terminal building exuded an eerie calm. A handful of tardy business types rustled newspapers and periodically glanced at the flight schedule monitors dotted about the waiting areas. Lydia was overly aware of the echoed clip-clop from her heels as they marched to the check-in desk. The orange-faced Ryanair rep beckoned them forward from the red line on the floor they'd obediently stopped behind despite there being no queue. The rep rattled through her list of security questions in a robotic voice and was satisfied with Rory's equally robotic answers. Then she weighed and sent Rory's case down the conveyor belt.

As the case disappeared behind a rubber flap curtain Rory came to a realisation. He pointed at Lydia's hand luggage.

"Is that all you're bringing with you?"

"Em, yeah? You realise that I haven't got John and Mattie with me either, don't you?" Her insides knotted at the thought of her family but she kept herself in check. Maintained a mask of calm.

Rory's face reddened. He coughed into his fist. "Aye, right enough. Sorry, I've only just woke up to be honest." He drained the dregs of his Red Bull can and shuddered with displeasure. "So what's the story? They taking a later flight?"

"No, I'm going to come back in a few days and finish up the week with them. No point cutting their holiday short when it's only a quick flight back over. It wouldn't have been fair on Mattie."

"Thought you said he was bored."

Lydia picked at an imaginary thread on the sleeve of her coat. Her eyes stung with the threat of tears. "Well, yeah, but you know kids. They'd get bored on a rollercoaster then moan when the ride ends."

Rory shrugged. He hadn't a clue about kids and didn't pretend otherwise.

Airport veterans both, Lydia and Rory breezed through the security process. They had all their toiletries in clear plastic bags, wore slip-on shoes and didn't bother with belts. When they got to the departure lounge, Rory led them straight to the coffee shop. Lydia's mouth watered at the smell of fresh scones, bagels and fried bacon but when Rory offered to buy her breakfast she passed.

"That's the second time you've knocked me back in two days. One more KB and you might just hurt my feelings."

She forced a smile. "It's not you, it's me."

"You'll waste away."

"Chance would be a fine thing."

"Ach, wise up, you eejit. I could pick you up and stick you in my pocket."

A devilish look crossed his face and he stepped towards her with his arms outstretched. "Come here and I'll show you."

Lydia reeled backwards. "Stop it. Don't touch me." She crossed her arms in front of her breasts and shuddered.

Rory's face dropped as if she'd just slapped him. "Fuck's sake, Lydia. I was only joking." He slipped his hands into his hip pockets and bunched his shoulders. His expression went from angry to bewildered.

Her skin crawled at the memory of the previous night's humiliation. She could still feel the bastard's sticky fingerprints on her face. Organising the flight to London and trailing Rory out of his bed had allowed her to push her disgust to the back of her mind, but one little joke was all it took to bring the horror back with a vengeance. She couldn't act like this around Rory, though. For the sake of John and Mattie, she tried to shake it off. She forced a laugh that had as much humour about it as a death rattle.

"Ignore me. You just caught me off guard. Didn't mean anything by it. I'm dead tired and, you know, it's that time of the month and all…"

Rory's face scrunched up for a second then ironed back out to expressionless cool. He nodded meaningfully and then turned to study the chalkboard menu behind the coffee shop counter. She knew it was a cheap trick to play the "time of the month" card but it had done the business.

Without turning to face her Rory asked, "Will you have a coffee, even?"

"How about a bottle of water?"

"No sweat."

She dropped her overnight bag at his feet. "Will you watch this while I nip to the ladies?"

He waved her away, a little too eagerly. She hadn't the time to worry about it. On the way to the toilets she dug her phone out of her pocket and called the office. Gloria, her PA, picked up.

"Benson and Gallagher. Can I help you?"

"I hope so."

"Oh, hi, boss. How's bonny Ireland?"

Bonny? Jesus. "It's lovely, Gloria. I'm tripping over leprechauns every ten minutes. Look. I need you to get me a meeting with Jeremy at PHQ. Pretend that you're tipping him off for sending you that bottle of bubbly at Christmas."

Gloria immediately lost the office girl ditz and went into shark mode. "Will do. What's the tip?"

"Rory Cullen wants to outsource his sponsorship business to a heavy-hitting marketing agency. And he's got my blessing."

"Why the hell would you do that, boss? You've been massaging L'Oreal for weeks to get him that shampoo ad."

Like she needed the reminder. "I don't have time to go into it."

"You know best. Shall I set up a meeting, then?"

"Yeah, get him a spot at three o'clock today."

Gloria choked a little. "I'm not sure I can make that work."

"You can if you tell him we're meeting with McGoldrick at four."

"And are you?"

"That's up to you. Phone McGoldrick after you set things up with Jeremy. Tell him we're in talks with PHQ but we're willing to throw him a bone."

"But if they phone each other to check for bullshit they'll know we're playing them."

"For Rory Cullen they won't risk the call."

"If you say so..." Gloria cleared her throat. "I better get... Oh, wait. You and Rory are in Ireland. How's this going to work?"

"We're at the airport now. Just a few hours away."

"God, whatever you're planning must be massive."

"You've no idea."

Lydia cut the call and dropped her phone back into her bag. Her spine tingled as she sensed somebody behind her. She turned on her heel expecting to find Rory. A small lady in a blue smock gave her a nervous smile. Her hands were wrapped around the shaft of a mop. The head was dunked into a huge bucket on wheels filled to the brim with grey water.

"Can I get past you, love?"

Lydia realised she was stood in front of the door to the ladies.

"Yes, sorry. Work away."

On her way back to the coffee shop Lydia considered the day ahead. It was destined to go tits up but as long as she thought of a decent cover story to sell to Rory when it did, she just might get through it and get to work on the kidnappers' list of demands.

She was within backstabbing distance of Rory when she realised she really did need to go to the toilet. And if she didn't go fast, she'd end up puking in the middle of the departure lounge.

Cormac chewed through the final thread holding the two halves of his bootlace together. He re-laced his boot, skipping the hooks at the top, and tied a short-looped knot. Then he repeated the process with his other boot.

"What are you doing?" Mattie asked.

Cormac looked up and winked at the kid. "I'm making a rope so we can climb out the window."

"Have you a hole in your skull?"

Cormac patted the blood-crusted hair at the back of his head. "Not for want of trying." He held a hand out to Mattie. "Come over here a wee second."

"Why?"

"Just come here and sit in the chair, please."

Mattie grunted as he raised himself off the mattress. The damage he'd taken off Paddy had stiffened and slowed him visibly. He moved like an eighty-year-old arthritic. A fresh blast of fury heated Cormac's skin, much of it directed at himself for failing to protect the boy.

Mattie took his seat and tilted his head as Cormac knelt in front of him.

"Let's see your hand, Mattie."

Mattie twisted slightly in his seat and drew his left hand away from Cormac. "What for?"

"I'm going to strap it up for you. It'll ease the pain a bit, I think."

"You *think*?"

"I know, I know." Cormac held the laces up. "I'm going to buddy them with your index finger and pinkie to keep them straight. It'll lessen the chances of jarring them by mistake."

"How do you know?"

"I used to hurl for Antrim. I've had my fair share of broken fingers."

"Hurl?" Mattie's face brightened. "You mean like puking?"

"No, you eejit. Hurling. The game with a stick and a ball. Fastest sport in the world?"

"Oh, is it that hockey-type thing?"

"Hockey! Where are you from, the moon? They're a world apart. I thought your da came from Belfast…"

"Yeah, he did, but he only ever told me about that weird football you guys play. You know the one that's a bit like *rugby*?"

"Ach, you're winding me up now, aren't you? Rugby. You may as well compare Gaelic to golf."

Mattie shook his head. "Whatever. You're still not qualified to fix my fingers with manky laces."

"They're clean enough." Cormac held them up to the low wattage light bulb. "At least I hope they are. I've had them in my mouth."

"Gross."

"Look, quit your stalling and give me your hand."

Mattie looked at Cormac sideways then blew air through his teeth and slowly extended his arm. The fingers were swollen to more than twice their original size. He'd suffered a very bad break. Surgery bad, Cormac reckoned. And the young fellah hadn't bitched about the pain once. Tough little bastard.

"Jesus," Cormac said. "Fat arse did a real number on you. What the hell did you do to set him off?"

"The first time?" Mattie's lips quivered a little but the traces of a smirk slipped through. "He kept staring at me when he was guarding us. I told him to stop it. Called him a fat, ugly paedophile. He squared up to me and I punched him in his... you know... his nuts. Then the psycho flipped his lid."

"Can't imagine why."

"It was nearly funny. Except for this, like." He nodded towards his ruined fingers.

"We really need to get you to a hospital, kid."

"Yeah? Why don't you ask one of the guys downstairs to give us a lift? They could drop you off at the morgue."

"God, you're a dark wee man, do you know that? I bet you watch a lot of horror movies."

Mattie pointed at his hand. "Who's stalling now?"

"Right, right. Tell me if this hurts."

Cormac took the middle digit between his thumb and index finger and squeezed. Mattie growled through clenched teeth and bounced a little on his seat. Tears rolled and he curled his right fist. He punched Cormac's upper arm.

"Jesus, kid. Sorry. No need to break my arm, but."

Mattie snuffled hard and croaked. "Ah, shit. There's no way you're touching them again."

"It's okay, I'll be gentle."

"How about I fuck you gently with a chainsaw?"

Cormac bit down on the inside of his lips to hold back a chuckle. He unbuckled his belt, slid it out of its loops and folded it in four.

"Ever see an old cowboy movie, Mattie? The way they bite down on bullets when somebody digs an arrow out of their leg? Well, I don't have any bullets, but here." He pushed the folded belt into Mattie's good hand. "See if it works for you."

For a second Cormac thought Mattie might wallop him with the belt but the moment passed.

"Get it over with, then."

Mattie chomped down on the leather and held out the injured hand. It trembled ever so slightly. Cormac gently wound the lace around the pinkie and ring fingers. Tendons stuck out on either side of Mattie's neck, tight as guitar strings, as he bit harder into the belt. Tears squeezed through his clenched shut eyes. Cormac worked fast. He let go of Mattie's wrist to tie the ends of the lace together and quickly bound the other two fingers. The result was an abomination of a Star Trek salute.

"Live long and prosper, kid."

"Kiss my arse."

Mattie tossed the belt to Cormac and spat on the carpet. He swiped the tears from his eyes with the heel of his uninjured hand and sniffed. Cormac ran a finger across the deep indents Mattie's teeth had left in the belt leather. The thought of whipping Paddy raw with it played on his mind.

"What now?" Mattie asked.

"We get out of here, tough guy."

Cormac beckoned Mattie out of the chair and

upended it. He gripped two of the legs in his hands and pulled at them. They held fast. He laid the chair down, the backrest and legs parallel to the floor.

"We might need to move fast," Cormac said. "Whatever happens, don't think. Just run when you get the chance."

"What about my dad?"

"We're going to bring him with us. Don't worry."

Cormac raised his boot and stomped down on one of the chair legs. It came loose with a loud crack. He went to work on the next one. It held on until the second stomp. He scooped up both legs and handed one to Mattie.

"Aim for their knees, kid. I'll go for the head."

A voice in Cormac's mind screamed for him to drop the chair leg. Both of them were liable to end up shot. But Cormac could see no alternative. If he sat back and waited he'd end up dead and Mattie would have nobody to look after him.

Cormac booted the bedroom door. The wood splintered a little around the lock. One more kick would bust it open but he held back. He didn't want to run out into the hallway. It'd be much easier to attack whoever had been left to guard them if he waited for them to come through the door.

Footsteps thudded on the stairs and the bedroom door handle rattled. The lock clunked and the door opened a fraction. A gun poked in through the gap. Cormac and Mattie stepped to the side, away from the muzzle. Then Cormac brought the chair leg down on it. The gun landed on the floor. To Cormac's relief it didn't fire. He kicked it towards the mattress. The door slammed shut and Cormac snatched at the handle. The lock clicked into place before he could pull it open. He stepped back to boot it down. A fist-sized chunk of the upper panel blasted in on him. An ear-thumping boom marked it as gunshot.

Cormac scrambled backwards and grabbed Mattie by the arm. He dragged him towards the mattress, keeping his own body between the source of gunfire and the boy. Another bullet thundered through the disintegrating wood. Cormac flipped the mattress and pushed Mattie behind it. Then he cocked the pistol, rolled into the middle of the room and fired three bullets through the door.

The floorboards under Cormac's feet shuddered. Somebody had keeled over in the landing.

"Ah, fuck."

It was Paddy's voice.

Cormac sent two more shots out into the landing. The fat man cursed again and, judging by the second wave of tremors under Cormac's feet, toppled. Had he taken out two of the fuckers? He cocked his head and tried to listen through the ringing in his ears.

Hurried footsteps on the stairs. Heading down, not up. A man, maybe John, screaming. Front door opening. Slamming shut. Some whimpering from the landing.

Hunkered down, Cormac approached the door with caution. He thought he could hear a breathless recital of the Hail Mary. At least one of the fallen was still alive. Most likely armed. He weighed up his options. Stay put and wait for the cavalry or risk a bullet in the face for a quick peek into the landing. Not exactly a no-brainer, but he figured the longer he waited the worse things would get. He straightened slowly to his full height, slightly to one side of the holes in the door. Then he risked a glance out onto the landing. Two bloody forms were sprawled out on the carpet. He made out Paddy right away but the other man lay face down, his upper body out of Cormac's line of vision. Paddy stared up at the ceiling, his ski mask rolled up like a monkey hat and his panic-stricken face exposed. Blood had run from a ragged wound in his chest to paint bright red runnels on his pasty fat neck.

There was a gun in Paddy's loosely curled fist but it was pointed away from the bedroom, forgotten. Cormac decided to move. He shouldered through the remains of the door and skipped over Paddy's chest. Cormac pinned the fat man's gun to the floor with his foot. Paddy moaned.

"Get off my hand." His voice gurgled.

"Shut up."

Cormac looked over his shoulder at the other body. He realised who it was.

"Oh, no..."

He turned back to Paddy, not ready to consider the implications at that moment.

"Where's O'Neill?"

"Fucking your ma." He coughed up blood and whined like a crippled puppy. The hiss that escaped from his chest wound with each shallow breath did not bode well for his future.

"Don't waste time, Paddy. We might be able to get you to a hospital before you drown in your own blood. But I need a few answers first."

"You won't let me live."

"Paddy, I'm a cop."

Paddy double blinked. "Shit."

"Yeah, I know. So do yourself a favour. Talk to me and I *will* phone that ambulance."

"He's followed the bitch and her footballer over

to England. Wants to keep an eye on her. The Scullions are with him. Me and Frank were left here to watch you lot."

"Where's Frank now?"

"Don't know. Cunt left me here to die."

Cormac rubbed the back of his neck. "Fuck."

Paddy pawed at Cormac's lower legs with his free hand. "Will you call the ambulance now? Please?"

"Sorry, Paddy." Cormac smiled down at him. "I've no phone on me, mate."

"Use mine, you stupid prick."

"Aye, I suppose I could. First things first, though."

Cormac raised his boot off Paddy's gun hand and slammed it back down. Paddy's bones cracked and crumbled. He let loose a squeal that erupted into a coughing fit. A blood mist sprayed from his mouth and rained down on his face. It thickened with each cough. And then his eyes glazed over. He'd a few shallow breaths left in him, but they faded too. Cormac blessed himself and stooped to take the gun from Paddy's mangled hand. Then he rifled through the fat man's pockets until he found his mobile phone. It had been smashed by a bullet. Useless. As he stood up he saw Mattie come to the bedroom door.

"Stay in there for a minute, kid. Please."

Mattie ignored him and stepped onto the landing. His gaze passed over Paddy's corpse and came to rest on the other body, sprawled out at the top of the stairs.

"Dad?"

CHAPTER 6

Irish, British, Northern Irish… who gives a shit? Last year I was a Londoner and this year I'll be a Mancunian. It's just geography.

Rory Cullen, *Cullen: The Autobiography*

Stansted Airport was a world apart from the almost serene Belfast airport Lydia had left behind little over an hour ago. She moved from left to right to avoid blinkered travellers willing to walk through rather than around her while Rory waited for his case at the baggage reclaim carousel. Somehow, above the hustle and bustle, she heard her ringtone sound.

Private number.

She took a deep breath before answering the call.

"Hi, gorgeous."

It was one of her visitors from the night before. Just hearing his voice made her crave a shower.

"I'm in London," she said.

"I know. That's a nice suit you're wearing. Black pinstripe… very businesslike."

Lydia wheeled around looking for her caller. "Where are you?"

"Close enough. Just keeping an eye on you. The one you didn't try to claw out of its socket, you know?"

Lydia scanned the seething masses moving in and out of her view. Tried to locate the caller but it seemed like every other person had a phone pressed to their ear.

"I'm doing what you want," she said. "Leave me alone."

"Aren't you going to ask me about your family?"

"Would you tell me anything if I did?"

"No, but it strikes me as a little cold that you wouldn't even ask."

"Fuck off."

"That's lovely, that is. I might call you later for another dirty phone call. Your toy boy's on his way back."

The line went dead. Sure enough, Rory was headed her way. His little wheelie case trundled behind him.

"That's me all set, Lydia. Will we head on out?"

Lydia nodded and turned to lead the way to the exit. Rory laid a hand on her upper arm to halt her. She shrugged it off without thinking. He rubbed his palm down the front of his shirt as if to wipe off whatever Lydia found so repulsive.

"Are you okay, Lydia?"

"I'm fine."

"You look like you're about to cry."

Lydia shrugged. What could she say?

"Was that John on the phone or something? Everything okay?"

"Don't worry about it." Her voice cracked. "I'll just nip to the ladies and sort myself out."

Rory called after her as she hurried off. She stopped for a second, held up her hand with her fingers splayed and mouthed, "Five minutes."

It the bathroom she stood at the sink furthest from the door and ran the taps. The hot water was scalding but she dampened her hands with it and patted her face. She looked in the mirror and cringed at the sight of her puffy eyes. And through force of habit, she lightly touched her finger to the corners of her mouth. Not exactly marionette lines yet, but she could see their ghostly potential.

She tousled her hair to give it a little life then unzipped her hand luggage and retrieved some makeup from its clear plastic bag. As she worked on a quick facial spit-shine the puffiness in her eyes began to retreat. In a few more minutes she managed to make herself halfway presentable. She studied herself in the mirror and was satisfied that she looked calm and collected again. The luxury of a breakdown would have to wait until she was on her own. In the meantime, for the sake of John and Mattie, she had to smile on the outside and choke down the bile that burned her insides.

When she left the ladies toilets she found Rory with a balding man and a young boy. A quick look was enough to tell they were father and son. They bore identical close-set eyes and pudgy red cheeks. The father's mouth twisted in distaste at something Rory said. She guessed the boy was about ten years old. He fiddled with the hem of his T-shirt, embarrassed by whatever his father was saying to Rory.

Rory spotted Lydia as she approached and moved away from them. The father waved him off with a two-fingered salute. "Chelsea don't need you anyway, you stupid Paddy bastard."

"You'll not be saying that come the end of the season, mate." Rory's voice boomed with theatrical cocksureness. "The title's ours this year."

"It'll never happen, dickhead."

The boy blushed and drew his shoulders up to his scarlet ears. His father grabbed a random man by the arm and pointed Rory out to him. The unimpressed traveller shrugged Mr Rosy-cheeks off and rushed on. The Chelsea fan cupped his mouth with his hands.

"Your book's a load of bollocks as well, Paddy."

"Thanks for buying it, though," Rory gave him a little wave, "ball-bag."

Rory swaggered alongside Lydia like James Bond's slicker older brother. The little battle of wits had shifted his attention away from Lydia's tears and she was happy to let him replay it for her. They moved through the terminal as he gabbled, occasionally stalling to look for exit signs.

They eventually found themselves in the cancer cloud that hovered around the smokers gathered at the terminal doors. Downwind a few paces, they stood for a minute to suss out the day ahead.

"Home sweet home," Rory said. "Well, sort of. Home away from sweet home, really." He crossed his eyes at his own drivel. "Anyway, do we have time to go freshen up before we meet these people?"

"First meeting's not until three. We've hours yet."

"Great stuff. I'll meet you at your office about half two, then."

Rory reached into a pocket at the front of his case and pulled out his car keys. Then he flipped open his wallet to search out his car park ticket. Lydia pretended to hunt about in her handbag and hand luggage for her own keys. After a plausible amount of time she cursed softly, but not too soft for Rory to hear.

"What's the matter, Lydia?"

"I've not got my keys with me."

"Your car keys?"

"Car keys, house keys… nothing. For God's sake. I must have left them at the cottage."

"You should phone John. Make sure you haven't

just lost them."

"Yeah, yeah. I'll text him in a bit. What the hell am I going to do right now, though?"

"Can I help?"

Lydia rapped her forehead lightly with her knuckles. "So stupid... I don't know, Rory. Do you think you could give me a lift to a hotel or something?"

"A hotel? Wise up. I've tonnes of room at my place. You can stay with me until you figure out how to get your keys."

"I couldn't put you out like that."

"Are you kidding? After all you've done for me over the years? I insist."

Lydia stood on her tiptoes and gave Rory a little peck on the cheek. "Thank you."

Rory smiled and a faint blush showed through his sunbed tan. It hurt Lydia deeply to know that he was so pleasantly surprised by her little scrap of forced affection. Her Judas kiss.

Cormac checked John for a pulse. He found it right away. Mattie stared, expectant. Cormac gave the kid a nod.

"He's still alive."

Cormac knew the safe house was bang in the middle of a vacant terrace and so it was unsurprising that the police hadn't flooded the scene. But they had to get moving before Big Frank came back with a small army.

"Did he get shot?"

Cormac nodded. He pushed up John's bloody shirt and found a wound to the left of his bellybutton.

Mattie took a step closer and hissed at the sight of it.

"Hold on," Cormac slipped his hands under John's back. He planned to roll him onto his side and check out the wound.

John howled.

Cormac covered John's mouth with the palm of his hand. "Take it easy, mate."

Mattie pulled on Cormac's arm. "Stop it, you'll hurt him!"

"He needs to calm down or he'll do damage to himself. Just stand back, Mattie. I'll take care of this."

Cormac removed his hand when he felt some of the tension leave John's face. His palm was slick with the other man's sweat. Cormac looked him in the eye.

"You're in shock, John. I'm going to roll you onto your side in case you throw up. I'm hoping to see an exit wound on your back. Do you understand?"

John didn't answer.

"I'm taking that as a yes. Brace yourself."

Cormac moved John with one steady push. John grunted and cursed. The exit wound was as big as Cormac's fist. He was glad to see it, ugly as it was.

"Okay, John. It's as good as it can be. I'd tell you you're lucky but..."

"Fuck yourself."

"There you go. Mattie, I might need your help, kid. Do you think you'll be able to stomach it?"

"What do you need me to do?"

"Put pressure on your father's wounds until I can cobble together some sort of dressing."

Mattie nodded. "I can do that."

Cormac went to Paddy's body and tore strips of material from his XXXL T-shirt. He folded them into a pair of thick pads and handed them to Mattie.

"One for the front and one for the back. Squeeze them together as hard as you can. I won't need you to do this for long, okay?"

The kid went right to it. He used the heel of his left hand for the entry wound to protect his broken fingers. There was pain in his expression but he didn't complain. Cormac returned to the mammoth task of tearing cloth from a dead fat man. Sweat sprang up on his forehead. It was like manhandling a small whale. The slow burn of a vigorous weightlifting session warmed his muscles.

"You nearly finished?" Mattie's voice was edged with strain.

"Two seconds, Mattie. Hold on."

Cormac kicked it up a gear and knotted together a bandage.

"My dad just puked."

"That's forgivable kid. He's been gut-shot. Hang tight."

They worked together to get the bandage around John's waist. Cormac did the heavy work – compared to lugging a dead Paddy about John seemed as light as a rag doll – and Mattie pulled the makeshift dressing tight and tied it up with admirable efficiency considering he had to work with one hand. He compensated for his broken fingers by pulling one end of the bandage with his teeth.

"Okay. Nice work, Mattie. You ready to get moving?"

"Why are you helping us? You're one of them, aren't you?"

Cormac held his hand out. "Detective Cormac Kelly. Pleased to meet you, Mattie."

Mattie looked as serious as a funeral director as they shook.

"Are we safe now, then?"

"Almost. We need to get your father out of here and get him some medical attention, but we're nearly home and dry."

So long as we stay a few steps ahead of Big Frank.

Lydia eyed the security cameras above Rory's front door. Her client unlocked three bolts and then, just inside the hallway, he tapped a seven-digit code to disable his alarm system. She felt something tug on her stomach. The kidnappers wanted her to breach *this* system? Rory directed her up the stairs to the guest room.

Lydia dropped her overnight bag at the foot of the bed. The floorboards creaked under a threadbare carpet as she crossed the room to the window. She drew back the heavy homemade curtains to reveal an old-fashioned net blind, yellowed with age. Parts of it stuck to the condensation-slick window pane. She pulled the blind away to look for weak spots. The window was double-glazed and the frame rigged with security sensors.

The guestroom was at the front of the house and it looked out on an idyllic leafy suburb complete with smiling kids on bicycles, and old codgers walking dogs. Teddington seemed like an odd place for a professional footballer in his twenties to put down his roots but Lydia could see the appeal. Merely a stone's throw from Kingston upon Thames and a short trip into central London, it was a peaceful spot that didn't seem like the arsehole of nowhere.

The guestroom would have benefited from an aesthetic update. From the built-in wardrobes to the bedside cabinets, none of the furniture matched. The walls boasted two wallpaper designs separated in the middle by a chipped dado rail. And little reminders from the previous occupants remained; peeling football stickers on the inside of the door, tears in the wallpaper where posters had been removed and a burnt patch on the carpet in front of the mirrored wardrobe door. This house had been lived in.

Rory's voice rang loud from the bottom of the stairs. "You want tea or coffee?"

"Tea, please."

"Milk?"

"That'd be lovely."

Lydia checked her mobile. No missed calls. Like she could have missed one. She scrolled through the text messages she'd received on the drive to Teddington from a withheld number.

Watchin u

No cops

Dont make us hurt ur boy ☒

She noticed that the battery was down to its last bar so she rooted out the charger from her bag and took it downstairs with her. Rory buzzed about the kitchen putting together a plate of sandwiches to go with the tea. Her stomach rumbled at the sight of the thick white bread, the slabs of cheese and fresh slices of ham. Simple, wholesome food. Lydia's mouth watered and she hoped she might actually be able to handle a couple of bites. She needed fuel.

"Can I plug my phone in somewhere, Rory?"

He plonked the plate of sandwiches on the tabletop and pointed towards the microwave on the countertop. "There's a free socket there."

There was a bunch of brown envelopes propped

against the side of the microwave. They had all been opened, the contents removed and stuffed back inside for future consideration. It looked like a mixture of bills and credit card statements to Lydia and her heart beat out a quick drum roll. But she didn't linger. She took a seat opposite Rory and loosed a little sigh of gratitude as he poured her a cup of tea.

"Everything okay for you upstairs?" Rory asked.

"Yes. Thanks." She tried to come up with a compliment. "The bed looks lovely and comfy."

Rory blew on his tea. "I know it's not exactly the Ritz, like..."

"It's fine. Really."

"I'd always meant to get the place redecorated, you know. Never got around to it. Maybe if I'd picked up a WAG she'd have sorted it out for me."

"Yes, I suppose so." *Shut up, shut up, shut up.*

"Well, I'll be looking for a new place in Manchester now. Don't want to have to travel every day for training." He pointed to the plate. "Help yourself."

Lydia hefted a sandwich. The weight of the cheese surprised her a little. She bit a small piece off the corner and chewed. It was better than an orgasm.

Rory choked down a hunk of his piece and chased it with a gulp of tea. He patted his chest and said, "What about Mattie, by the way? He's a Chelsea fan. Is he pissed off that you sold their best player to the enemy?"

Her stodgy snack stuck to the roof of her mouth. She washed it away with a mouthful of suddenly over-milked and tepid tea. It took all her might to hold back a grimace.

"Well, he's probably not your biggest fan these days."

Rory shrugged and went back to attacking his food while Lydia broke up what was left of her bread and fillings to make it look like she'd eaten more than she really had. When Rory was finished he eyed her leftovers, pinched a particularly inviting chunk of cheese off her plate and popped it in his mouth.

"You're not eating enough," he said between chews.

"No appetite. Think I might have a stomach bug or something."

Rory wrinkled his nose. "Well don't give it to me."

"Relax. If it was contagious my whole family would have it and they're... fine."

"I was going to suggest we head out for dinner after we've been to those meetings, but if you've a dodgy tummy it might not be such a good idea."

"That's a nice thought, Rory, but you're right. Why don't we pick up a bottle of bubbly, though? Have a few celebratory glasses here tonight? I'm sure I could handle that."

"Now there's a plan. A wee champers or two would go down a treat."

Lydia winked at him. "An early night wouldn't do us any harm either."

Rory cleared his throat and regarded Lydia, his eyebrows drawn downwards as he tried to figure out if she'd just flirted with him. Lydia did nothing to clear up the confusion. It hadn't occurred to her until then, but she knew that if it came down to it she'd do anything to get her family back from the kidnappers. Anything.

CHAPTER 7

Sponsorship is great, like. Very lucrative. I just don't understand what football has to do with crisps, though. Surely as role models we should be promoting apples and bananas or something like that.

Rory Cullen, *Cullen: The Autobiography*

Paddy's car handled like a half-charged mobility scooter. It was an old white Suzuki Jimmy, some sort of dwarfish SUV, and everything about it was inept and sluggish. Much like its former owner. Cormac looked forward to dumping it and getting into his own car. They were closing in on his house on the Lisburn Road. His plan was to get his Police Service of Northern Ireland ID out of his safe and his police issue Glock 17 along with a few boxes of ammo. The PSNI ID would cut through any bullshit hospital red tape and get John's gunshot wound seen to quicker. Cormac still had the pistol from the safe house but it didn't have a full clip and he wasn't sure how well cared for it had been. He wanted his own, reliable piece.

Mattie was in the back seat. He propped up his injured father and winced along with every pain-ridden moan that slipped from between John's clenched teeth. Cormac watched Mattie's young face in the rear-view mirror. The kid looked utterly lost. Cormac trawled his mind for some words of encouragement, wisdom, comfort... anything. Nothing occurred. It wasn't a typical enough set of circumstances to warrant cliché.

"We'll get your da sorted, Mattie. Don't worry."

The kid didn't acknowledge him.

Cormac lived in a mid-terrace house. Parking at his front door during office hours was never a guarantee. He slowed the Suzuki a little at the start of the terrace and sought out a gap wide enough to dump the piece of shit. He made momentary eye contact with a hard-faced man in a blue work van. His passenger played with a mobile phone, unaware of the driver's sudden interest in Cormac. They were parked just a few doors down from Cormac's house, the van's nose pointed out towards the road for a quick exit. All the better to get the drop on somebody.

His house was being watched.

Cormac neither sped up nor slowed down. He needed time to think. At the end of his terrace he took a right and entered the network of housing estates just off the Lisburn Road. He took a right and a left and another right, found a barley legal parking spot on the corner of the street and killed his engine.

"Is this where you live?" Mattie asked.

Cormac shook his head. "There's somebody at my place." He checked his mirrors. It didn't look like the blue van had pursued them. But they might not have been the only ones set to watch his house. How had the bastards closed in on him so quickly? They weren't cops, Cormac was sure of that because he'd caught them on without even trying, but O'Neill's crew had no way of knowing that Cormac's actual home was in South Belfast. He'd joined O'Neill's crew with the back story that he'd come from Newry, a border city with a growing Dissident Republican support network. His softer South Down accent had lent strength to this, as had the backing of a colleague deeply immersed in the investigation of the Real IRA.

Maybe he'd read too much into the look that passed between him and the man in the blue van. A lot had happened and his adrenaline levels were tweaked. Paranoia may have gotten the better of him. Still...

He reassessed his situation. He was basically on the run with a beat up kid and his bleeding father in tow. It was too big a risk to go to the house and hope that his gut instincts were off. They rarely were and going against them would most likely get him and his charges in even deeper shit. And if he took them to the hospital, could he be sure that his handler had his back if he needed to call through a favour or three? The information on his likely whereabouts had to come from somewhere. If somebody at the station had ratted him out to O'Neill and his men he couldn't risk reaching out for that particular lifeline. He'd get Mattie and John somewhere safe first and then see what they had to say back at HQ.

Cormac restarted the Suzuki. "We have to go somewhere else."

"Where?"

"A friend's house."

He looked into the back seat at what he was about to bring to Donna Grant's doorstep. She would be less than thrilled.

Jeremy Quentin, the Q in PHQ Publicity, stood up as the final slide of the PowerPoint presentation faded from the screen, and offered his junior colleagues a quick clap. The three bright sparks seated at a little round table by the huge office window lapped up the praise. Then the two young men of the group high-fived. At least the young lady had the wit to look embarrassed for them.

Lydia groaned internally as Jeremy cleared his throat. Was there more to this fucking circus?

"I could talk some more about what PHQ can offer you, RC," Jeremy said. "But I won't."

Thank Christ.

"I think our presentation said everything that needed to be said. What do you think, RC?"

Rory looked to Lydia and crossed his eyes, then back to Jeremy with his business face on.

"Aye, I thought it was class, like. How'd you get my picture onto that aftershave ad?"

"Photoshop, RC."

"Magic." Rory fiddled with a lever under his chair and it sank with a pneumatic hiss. "One small criticism, though... I don't know what you did with the aul' airbrush, but I looked a wee bit like a fruit. Do you not think so?"

Jeremy shot a glance at one of his cubs; a young man with thick glasses and a mane of cartoonish spiked hair. The Photoshop wizard, Lydia assumed.

"That was by no means a finished piece, RC. Consider it a mock-up. Just a thrown together image to give you a taste of what—"

"Chill out, Jeremy," Rory said. "I was only slegging."

Jeremy's brow knotted. "Em..."

"Slegging means taking the Mickey," Lydia offered.

Jeremy's lips parted in a quick and easy fake smile. "I see. Irish, is it?"

"Belfasty," Rory said.

"Oh? Is that a thing?"

"Oh, aye. Some people call it Norn Iron spake, but Belfasty's more… specific, you know?"

"Fascinating." Jeremy's head bobbed for a little too long. "So, anyway, we've said our bit. We'd love to work with you, RC. And now you have an idea of what we can do for you if you do sign with us. I guess the ultimate decision is yours. You tell us what you want and we'll hammer out the details with Lydia."

"You mean LG, here?" Rory asked.

Jeremy paused for a second then he raised a long, slender finger and waggled it. His well-practised smile returned. "Ah, more *slegging*, eh?" He turned to his people. "We'll have to watch this one, folks."

The young lady's giggle seemed a little too shrill to Lydia's ear but Rory gave her a look of interest. Cool as a Trebor mint, the PHQ girl flipped through a file on the table in front of her and pretended not to notice Rory's attention.

"Okay, Jeremy," Lydia said as she stood up. "Thank you for that. We'll be in touch, then."

Jeremy spread his arms. His palms turned out as if he wanted a hug. "You're leaving already? I thought we could all head out for a spot of dinner."

"Sorry. No rest for the wicked, right, Rory?"

"Yeah. Another time maybe, J-man."

Jeremy crossed the office floor and grasped Lydia's hand in both of his. He pumped her arm with too much enthusiasm and leant in close. She caught a whiff of his aftershave. Subtle. "Are you in talks with somebody else?"

"Of course," Lydia said.

"McGoldrick?"

"Maybe."

"The old Scot, eh?"

"Like I said, *maybe*. We'll be in touch soon."

Jeremy turned to shake Rory's hand and found an empty space. Lydia looked over at the little round table where Rory had pulled up a chair beside the trendy young thing who had pretended not to notice him. Her blonde hair was short and carefully shaggy. Corporate punk. She wrinkled her nose when she smiled and something about her reminded Lydia of Tinkerbell, the fairy from Peter Pan.

"Quick on his feet, isn't he?" Jeremy said.

"It's why City paid so much for him."

Rory took a business card from the blonde, squeezed her hand and whispered something in her ear before he left the table. As whatever he said registered, her hand went to her mouth and she blushed.

"Looks like you made that worth your while," Lydia said while they waited for the lift.

"You mean the girl?" Rory yawned. "Ach, you know me when I get bored."

"Pretty distraction."

"Aye, she gave me her number."

"Of course she did. You meeting her tonight?"

"No, sure me and you have plans, don't we?"

Lydia felt as if she'd lost a golden opportunity. If he went out with the corporate punk it would make her task for the kidnappers easier. She swallowed the lump in her throat and prayed the moisture in her eyes didn't show.

"They were pretty loose plans, Rory." Her voice came out a little higher than she'd expected. She dropped the pitch and tried to soften her words. "If you think your luck's in with this one, don't let me stop you."

"Not at all. I'm looking forward to a chilled out night. Don't know why we haven't done something like this sooner."

"Probably the fact that I'm a wife and mother got in the way."

"Well, you're *a free woman* tonight."

They stepped into the lift and Lydia considered Rory's statement. A free woman. Had she ever been trapped? She might have often felt that way, especially when Mattie was younger, but he'd come into the world on her terms. He hadn't asked to be born. How could she consider that entrapment?

Mattie loved her unconditionally, a concept she'd heard about but hadn't experienced in her own childhood. It surprised her how much he needed her and how much she needed him and how much satisfaction that dynamic brought. She'd fretted over her son turning thirteen, imagining an overnight transformation that replaced her sweet little boy with a smelly, surly teen, but that hadn't happened. He had gotten a little quieter, maybe. More thoughtful. And more intriguing.

Rory bumped her hip with his and knocked her out of her reverie.

"Hey, where are you? Cloud Cuckoo Land?"

"Sorry, Rory. What were you saying?"

"Those guys seemed all right. Do we really have to go to this next meeting?"

"Rule one, Rory. Never accept the first offer."

"Fine, but if there's another presentation like that one I'm going to fake explosive diarrhoea."

"McGoldrick's old school. I don't think he knows what PowerPoint is."

Donna wasn't in. It came as no great surprise to Cormac. She worked unsociable hours at the hospital. Combined with his own random work pattern and unsettled life-style it was little wonder that they couldn't keep it together as a couple. It'd been a couple of years since they'd broken up but Cormac still knew her number off by heart. A small blessing since he'd been denied access to his mobile phone along with the gun and ID he had stashed in his safe.

He'd gone to the garage across from the Malone Road apartment building to use their payphone. There was no queue. Even with the high population of univer-sity students in the area. It seemed that a mobile had become one of life's essentials, not just a luxury. The conversation had been cold and efficient. She didn't even register surprise that he was calling her in need of a favour. Maybe she'd have more to say in person. Her part of the phone call had been a series of affirmations. "Yes, I can get off a little early. Yes, I can bring some stuff with me. Yes, I can be subtle."

She was probably playing it cool in case anybody overheard her.

Mattie and John were asleep in the back of the Suzuki. Cormac craved a steaming hot coffee. Nothing fancy, just some decent instant in a polystyrene cup. A splash of milk and maybe half a sugar. Just to get the heart pumping. He reached out and fiddled with the car stereo again. Settled on a local phone-in talk show.

The current caller spoke with a thick North Antrim accent that made Cormac want to punch the wind-screen. Shrill indignation and gap-toothed whistles, like an old kettle. He had a beef with the local hoods, who were probably three quiet kids and a BMX bike if the caller was as backwater as he sounded. But it wasn't the voice or the stupid things he said that twanged on Cormac's last nerve. It was the wheezy inhalation he took between sentences. Each one came as regular as a pendulum swing creating a monotonous rhythm in the speech.

Cormac thumped the volume knob with the side of his fist and the radio powered down. What he really needed was some sleep but he couldn't see it coming any time soon. A burst of rain drummed on the roof of Paddy's car. He felt the little white motor stuck out like a sore thumb and he wasn't exactly a hundred miles away from his staked-out house on the Lisburn Road. If the feelers went out, it wouldn't take a fantastic stroke of luck to happen upon him. Getting rid of the little shit-box would be top of his to-do list once he got Mattie and John into Donna's apartment.

A silver Seat Leon pulled into the car park just a tad too quickly. It jerked to a halt in the space next to Cormac's – nose in where he was facing out. He didn't get a good look at the driver through the tinted windows but the blare of an ABBA CD put all doubts to rest. It was Donna, and if her less than smooth driving was anything to go by, she was pissed off.

"Would he be willing to get his teeth fixed?"

Rory smiled at McGoldrick and tapped one of his incisors. "They're not broken."

McGoldrick was dressed in khaki chinos and a striped green polo shirt, ready for the golf course as usual. He ran a little hand through his thick white hair. It flopped back into a perfect side parting. "Is this kid for real, Lydia?"

Lydia wished she'd listened to Rory and skipped the meeting. McGoldrick was a rude little bastard at the best of times but something seemed to have crawled right up his backside that day. And what if the kidnappers called? She wanted to know if John and Mattie were still safe.

"Lydia," McGoldrick's bark pulled Lydia out of her murky thoughts, "I'm talking to you, hen."

She shook her head. "Rory's not Beckham, Mr McGoldrick. And not everybody wants one of the pretty boys. Asking Rory Cullen to fix his teeth would be like asking Wayne Rooney to pin back his ears."

"It'd take more than that to give Rooney the Hollywood look," McGoldrick said. "Rory's almost all the way there. He's a handsome kid. Great skin, good hair but he's got woeful teeth."

"Here, you," Rory said. "I'm standing right here, like."

"Kid, shut it. The grownups are talking."

Rory stood up. "I liked Jeremy better. Let's go back and seal the deal with him."

McGoldrick popped up from his leather chair. It rolled back on its castors and butted the wall behind him. He straightened his back and stood his full five foot five. Spittle flew from his mouth as he shouted at Rory. "Don't push my buttons you little shite. Sit your arse back down. I'll tell you when this meeting's over."

Lydia threw her hands in the air. "What the hell's going on, Mr McGoldrick? I've come here as a favour to give you a chance to woo my client and you're acting like he stole the cream out of your coffee."

"What's the matter, kid? Can you not fight your own battles?"

Rory unbuttoned his suit jacket and let it fall off his shoulders onto the floor. He popped his cufflinks and started to roll up his sleeves. "Fine, then. Come on and have a go, mate. But I'm not going to go easy on you just because you're a little old fucker."

McGoldrick nodded and rounded his huge walnut desk. Lydia jumped up to intercept him before they kicked off and Rory got himself arrested. McGoldrick looked past Lydia at Rory and flashed his dentures for the first time since the meeting began.

"The kid's got balls."

"He's Northern Irish," Lydia said. "I'm told it comes with the territory."

McGoldrick shook Lydia's hand, his grip a little too firm. "I like him."

"Glad I meet your approval, you old fart. Does this mean we're not going to dig the heads off each other?"

"And damage that pretty face?" McGoldrick said. "How will we make each other rich if I leave you looking like a gurner? Of course, if I knocked out a few of those teeth it might be an improvement."

"Don't take this meeting as a foregone conclusion," Lydia said. "Nobody's signed anything yet, Mr McGoldrick."

"Oh, yeah, I forgot." McGoldrick laid a hand on his cheek and rolled his eyes in a surprisingly effeminate way. "Jeremy Quentin wants a piece of this. How will I ever compete with that slick bastard?"

"How indeed?" Lydia asked.

"Five phone calls I made this morning. Two sportswear labels, a hair product brand, a car company and a video game developer. Three of them have pretty much dropped their knickers for the kid and the other two are ready to play ball."

"Fuck," Rory said.

"'Fuck' is right, kid. While Jeremy and his munchkins were dicking about with projectors and presentations I was playing the field. There's no substitute for good old-fashioned juice in this industry, no matter how many computer whizz kids you employ."

"How do you know what Jeremy was doing?" Rory asked.

"I play dirty," McGoldrick said. "Something you know all about judging by your record at Chelsea last season."

"What about the details?" Lydia asked. "You got a percentage in mind?"

"My number crunchers are working on that. They'll have a contract for you to consider by close of play today. And I'll be expecting an answer some time tomorrow. The older I get the less time I want to waste pussyfooting."

"No problem. We'll be in touch with you tomorrow, Mr McGoldrick."

McGoldrick walked them out of his office. His PA waited on the other side of the door, armed with a notepad and pen. She asked Rory for his autograph and led him to her desk. While the PA gabbed with Rory, McGoldrick laid his hands on Lydia's shoulders and kissed the air at both sides of her face. Then, with his hands still resting on her shoulders, he looked Lydia deep in her eyes. His face turned to granite.

"You're up to something, aren't you?"

Lydia gently removed McGoldrick's hands from her shoulders, gave them a friendly squeeze and let them go. His arms fell to his sides and Lydia noticed his short fingers curl into fists.

"I don't know what you're talking about," Lydia said.

"Don't insult my intelligence. I know you were working L'Oreal. And even though you went at it like a sledgehammer to a walnut, you were actually getting somewhere. Why would you throw all that work away on what seems to be a whim?"

"Maybe I had an epiphany? I wasn't doing Rory any favours in that area of his career. Figured we'd both make more money if I outsourced."

"I don't believe you. We'd have been in talks long before now if you were that clever."

"But look how eager you are now that I've held out this long. All suspicious but ready to snap him up anyway."

"Don't get too cocky, hen. I know a good deal when I see one, so I'm going to welcome Rory into my fold even though I'm sure you're not one hundred per cent legit. But consider this a friendly warning. When I figure out your angle, and I will, you'd better hope that it doesn't hurt our friendship. I could do your career a hell of a lot of damage."

Lydia's career was the least of her problems, but she gave McGoldrick a suitably grave nod before she turned away from him.

McGoldrick continued to speak to her back. "I've got my eye on you now, Lydia. It's only a matter of time before I figure out what you're up to."

CHAPTER 8

I wouldn't marry one of those girl-band singers. They're fit and all that but I imagine you'd be marrying the whole band. And not in a good way. There'd be no chance of a ménage a six, like. That'd probably knacker you anyway.

Rory Cullen, *Cullen: The Autobiography*

Donna Grant snipped away the bindings from Mattie's broken fingers. Her designer glasses had slipped down her nose a little and Cormac had the urge to push them back up for her. Maybe even mop her furrowed brow. She looked different. Prettier, maybe. Was it the new hairstyle? Shoulder-length curls with blonde highlights that framed her face in a more flattering way. Perhaps she'd lost weight and her cheekbones had become more prominent. Or was it just that he'd allowed her fine and delicate features to be blurred by the two years since he'd last seen her?

She held up a length of black string. "Are these laces?"

Cormac turned his palms upwards. "I had to

improvise."

Donna tutted and reached out to stroke Mattie's face. "You must be in agony, darling."

"I'm all right," Mattie said. "Better than Dad at least."

Donna had worked on John's gunshot wound before attending to Mattie's fingers. He'd been fed a painkiller and antibiotic cocktail then cleaned, stitched and bandaged. Cormac had talked him into lying down in Donna's bed once the codeine serene had kicked in.

"Your da's in good hands, kid. Donna's a terrific doctor."

Donna smiled at Mattie and when the kid looked away she switched her gaze to Cormac, her eyes like diamond-tipped drill bits. He resisted the urge to smile at her.

"Rest your hand on this before I strap those fingers back up again." Donna pushed a bag of frozen peas across her kitchen table. "Do you want a glass of juice or anything?"

"Yes, please."

Donna went to the fridge built into the glossy white shaker kitchen. Cormac noted the toast crumbs on the worktops, the dishes in the sink and tea stains on the cupboard door under the spot the kettle sat on. He thought about a playful reprimand for her characteristic sloppiness but decided against it. It was probably too soon to get cute with her.

She took a carton of orange juice from the fridge and half-filled a pint glass. Mattie took it eagerly and swallowed most of it in one go. He went to put the glass down and stopped. He let it hover an inch above the tabletop and tried to look over a cereal box sat in the centre.

"Do you have a coaster, or something?" he asked.

"Aren't you well trained?" Donna said. "I don't bother with that kind of thing. Just put the glass wherever's handy."

Mattie looked a little guilty as he sat the glass down among the existing coffee rings. Donna flicked on the TV, visible from the kitchen table due to the open planning in her apartment. She set the remote down beside Mattie's good hand.

"I'm just going to have a quick smoke while your hand numbs a bit." Donna said. She drew a ten-pack of Silk Cut from her velour tracksuit bottoms. "See if you can find something decent to watch."

Mattie smiled at her. "Thanks."

"Join me for a cigarette, Cormac."

Donna knew he didn't smoke but her look warned Cormac off declining her invitation. He followed her out of the French doors in the living room onto a tiny balcony with a wrought iron guard rail. The second floor apartment had a decent view of South Belfast.

Cormac looked out onto the Malone Road. "Nice place you—"

"What the fuck is going on here, Cormac?"

"Mattie and his father needed some help."

"And who the fuck are they?"

"I'm kind of looking after them for a bit."

"Well, you're obviously doing a bang-up job."

Donna lit her cigarette and drew viciously on it. She blew smoke in his face.

"Why do so many doctors still smoke? Surely—"

"Fuck off."

"Look, I'm sorry to bring this to your doorstep, Donna. There was nobody else I could turn to."

"How did you even know where to find me? I've

moved twice since… since I last saw you."

"You know what I do. It wasn't that difficult to—"

"Keep tabs on me?"

There was no point denying it. That was exactly what he'd done. He leant on the guard rail and watched a herd of students plod their way from the Queen's halls of residence towards the university. Donna speed-smoked her cigarette and crushed the butt under her trainer. She flipped open the pack and pulled out another, then she thought again and slid it back.

"Why can't you take them to the hospital? The boy should have an x-ray. And if he doesn't need surgery, he's a definite case for physiotherapy. Sooner he gets it properly sorted the better. As for the father… Jesus, what a mess."

"We don't have time for all that. Not right now."

"So you figured you could call on me for an express service?"

Cormac stood up straight and rounded on Donna. He fought to keep his voice level. "I've never asked you for anything before now. And this isn't even for me. You could do me this one favour, considering…"

Donna licked her lips and fiddled with the lid of her cigarette packet. "You're laying the guilt trip on me, then? Old reliable."

"Look, I don't want to get into anything with you now. If you'll just look after Mattie I'll get the hell back out of your life."

"And what about that gash on the back of your head?"

Cormac patted the blood-crusted hair around the wound. "The bleeding's stopped."

"It still needs to be cleaned. Couple of stitches wouldn't do you any harm either. I lifted a whole load of stuff from the hospital after you called, extra needles and thread included."

"Whatever you think." He realised that he sounded like a sulking teen and wanted to kick himself for his inability to show a bit of gratitude.

"Come back in, then. I'll see to you after Mattie."

Back inside, Mattie had settled on a music channel. He tapped his good fingers in time to a hip hop beat. Underneath the table his leg jittered with pent up nervous energy.

"How's the hand feel?" Donna asked.

"Freezing."

"Well, let's get it sorted, then."

"Can I use your phone?" Cormac asked.

"Go ahead." She waved her hand towards the living room area. "It'll probably be on the coffee table."

"Okay." He moved towards the table and stopped. Looked over his shoulder. "Oh, and, thank you."

She treated him to a stiff smile.

Cormac found the phone underneath an empty Doritos bag. He took it out onto the balcony and dialled the number he'd memorised before the start of his most recent assignment. As it rang, he held onto the guard rail for support.

The handler didn't waste any time on niceties. "Where the fuck are you, Kelly?"

"In Belfast."

"Specifically."

"A friendly place. Things went a bit pear-shaped, sir."

"Fucking right they did. We've found the body in the safe house."

"But I didn't call that in yet."

"Big brother's been watching."

Cormac's grip on the guard rail tightened. "What the fuck for?"

"Insurance against a holy fuck-up like you managed to land us with."

A light drizzle started to fall. It dappled Cormac's face but did nothing to cool the burning in his cheeks. If they knew he'd been involved in a kidnapping, they should have stormed the safe house and extracted the family. His default brief was always simple: don't break cover. It was up to the powers that be to make judgement calls based on the available information.

"Did you manage to keep the hostages alive, Kelly?"

"The father and son are with me. Frank Toner got away."

"Uninjured?"

"So far as I know. Any word on O'Neill and the rest of his goons?"

"He's gone to London with two cronies. The Brothers Grim. We believe they're going to touch base with Martin Rooney at some point. It's the opportunity we've been waiting for."

Rooney was a big player in Cormac's case. They were building evidence of a link between the London-based cocaine dealer and Ambrose O'Neill's crew. The kidnapping had cropped up in the middle of the multi-agency investigation and sent everything arse over tits. It had been sprung on Cormac as the new boy in O'Neill's crew and if he'd had a means to communicate with his handler he'd have demanded the Belfast gangsters arrest for kidnap and blackmail that night. Instead, he'd battened down and set his objective at keeping the Gallaghers alive. A decision, he was sure, his handler would have to officially commend him for when they next met. Unofficially... it should have been all about the Rooney case.

The handler continued. "And they're keeping as tight a watch on Missus Gallagher as our counterparts on the mainland are on them. We're going to have to work on locating Big Frank."

Mainland. It was this sort of effortless referral to England that still divided the catholic cops from the old protestant boys. But as usual, Cormac didn't raise an objection. He hadn't the inclination for all that mast-nailing shite.

"Do you know why they targeted this family?"

"Of course," the handler's voice barked down the line. "I need you to come in for debriefing. When can we expect to see you, Kelly?"

"A couple of hours."

"Hours? Are you lost?"

His handler, "Big Brother", was acting as if he'd lost track of him. Something gnawed at Cormac's gut. He deliberately withheld his position.

"Gallagher and his kid need some medical attention."

"Oh, for fuck sake. Are they badly hurt?" It wasn't a question born out of concern.

"One of the crew broke a couple of the kid's fingers—"

"We can see to that here."

"And the father had a through and through gunshot wound. Lower abdomen."

The handler clacked his teeth. The sound burrowed its way from the earpiece right into the centre of Cormac's brain.

"We'll have a doctor and an ambulance waiting for him. Just get here."

"They're both in safe hands now. What's the rush? I'm handling the situation."

"You're not a doctor. You're not qualified to make…" The handler took a deep breath. "Fine, we'll see you in two hours."

Too easy. Something was up.

"What about the woman? Lydia Gallagher? The kid's going to want to speak to his mother."

"Don't call Missus Gallagher. O'Neill's lost a lot of leverage but he's still got close tabs on her. We'll ensure she's safe. But for now we'll have to take a step back and see if O'Neill has the balls to go through with his plan now that it's gone out of control."

The handler cut the call. Cormac stood on the balcony for a few more seconds and let the drizzle soak into his hair. When he felt calm enough to face Mattie and Donna he went back inside. Mattie held up his freshly strapped hand.

"She's a lot better at this than you are."

Cormac smiled at him. "Well, she is a doctor."

"Only just," Donna said. "Now, come over to the sink so I can get started on you."

"The kitchen sink? Is that hygienic?"

"Don't worry. I've got anti-bacterial washing liquid."

Mattie reached out and grabbed Cormac's arm as he passed him.

"Are you going to call my mum after this?"

Cormac patted the kid's shoulder, self-conscious that Donna was scrutinising him.

"We're just waiting on word from the station that the bad guys are taken care of. But you'll all be together soon. I promise."

###

Soho Square. The name would always hold illicit connotations in Lydia's mind. When she'd first moved to London the Soho area still hadn't quite shaken its reputation as a sex industry hotspot. But with every visit to the city centre square she was a little disappointed to see nothing more out of the ordinary than upmarket offices, trendy pubs and obstructive road works. She raised an arm to shield her eyes from a cloud of dust kicked up by a nearby jackhammer jockey. Rory placed a hand on the small of her back and ushered her away from the door to McGoldrick's office. She imagined the old Scot looking down at them from his window and quickened her pace just enough to break contact. If Rory noticed her mild rebuke he didn't show it.

"Come on," he said. "I'll buy you a drink at The Toucan."

She spoke to him over her shoulder as they walked. "An Irish theme pub? Are you serious?"

"They do a decent pint."

"John says they charge an arm and a leg for bad Guinness in those places."

"You're worried about paying an extra fifty pence on the pint after the deal you've just worked out? Wind your neck in. It's time to celebrate."

"My head's really banging, Rory."

"A decent drink's better than a couple of paracetamol. We'll be fifteen minutes. Half an hour, tops."

Lydia ran a hand through her hair. The constant rumble and whine from the road works clamoured. McGoldrick's parting words rankled. A chill wind nipped the dry, cracked skin at the corners of her mouth. Rory wasn't going to give up on the idea of a celebratory drink. There was no point arguing. She turned sharply and stopped at a pedestrian crossing, ready to lead the way to The Toucan. Something bounced off the side of her face.

She had just enough time to realise that she'd cut off a hurried pedestrian before a man in a black woollen hat stepped around her and stormed off without a word. Rory found his voice as the hunched figure hurried down the street with his hands jammed into the pockets of a black military-style jacket. Lydia cringed when Rory cupped his hands around his mouth.

"Watch where you're fucking going, mate."

"Rory, leave it." She checked the inner pocket of her business suit jacket to make sure it hadn't been dipped. The phone was still there. "*I* bumped into *him*."

"Aye, but the bastard didn't even take a second to see if you were okay."

"It's London."

Rory took a deep breath and Lydia braced herself for his next yelled insult. He exhaled with a sigh.

"Thanks, Rory."

"Come on, I want a drink."

She let him take the lead this time. He walked with his arms locked out by his sides and his fists clenched. His vibe wasn't lost on those in his path; couples parted, tourists swerved, and fat city-pigeons fluttered. An illogical way to rage against the ill manners of a pedestrian, but that was Rory through and through.

Imagine what he might do to somebody who really crossed him.

Lydia pushed the thought down deep where it was lost in a boiling pot of stronger emotions.

The Toucan was predictably full and yet nobody seemed to recognise Rory. Unusual, considering the column inches dedicated to his career and personal life in the Red Tops. But then, this wasn't exactly the local working man's boozer. During office hours on a Friday, the bulk of the trade came from tourists who sought the real English experience... in an Irish theme pub. The navvy descendents from the nearby road works had a few hours graft left in them before they could invade the place with their dusty tongues hanging. Lydia hoped to be on her way back to Teddington by then.

They found a spot at the bar just wide enough for two stools, though Rory chose to stand. Lydia adjusted herself on the high stool and wished for longer legs. Her feet hovered an inch above the horizontal pole that served the vertically blessed as a footrest. She crossed her ankles and tried not to fidget.

"Hiya, love. A pint of Guinness and a glass of rosé when you've a minute, please."

Rory's Northern Irish accent cut through the pub's background noise like a nuclear icebreaker ship. It attracted bemused smiles from some of the other patrons, though it had little effect on the barmaid. Lydia noted the piercing blue eyes and sickeningly beautiful sculpted cheekbones. She guessed that the girl was Polish. Would put good money on her being of Eastern European origin at the very least. Then she felt a tinge of guilt at weighing her up on such a flimsy premise.

The rosé came first; the Guinness glass stood half-empty under the pump in the way that Irish, Northern Irish and third-generation-removed-Irish men seemed to think so important. Lydia reached for her glass, raised it, paused and sat it back down. Her gut contracted. Rory, mildly puzzled, frowned.

"I'll wait for you," she said.

He crimped one side of his face. "Aye, dead on."

Lydia didn't know for sure if he was being sarcastic. She could have asked but feared where the question might lead. After her meeting with McGoldrick she didn't want to risk another confrontation. Another few taps and the wall she'd built up would tumble.

"Do you want anything to eat?" Rory asked.

"I'm not hungry."

"Well my stomach thinks my throat's been cut."

"Feel free to order something for yourself."

"That'd be weird."

She looked at her glass again. Considered downing the lot in one go. Then maybe she'd order another and tell the possibly-Polish chick to leave the bottle. Something classy like that.

"I need to go to the loo," she said.

Rory shrugged then turned to smile at the barmaid as she delivered the topped-up pint of Guinness.

"What part of Ireland are *you* from?" he asked.

The barmaid leant forward a little as if to share a whispered secret with Rory. Lydia tensed her shoulders in expectation of a much deserved rebuke.

"I'm from the county of Poland," the definitely-Polish chick said. "What part of Scotland are you from, love?"

She made "love" sound like *luff*. Lydia smirked, as much at her own insecurities as the barmaid's sass. Neither Rory nor the Pole paid her much heed as she dropped off the barstool and scoped for a sign leading to the bathroom.

She spotted white text on a green-lit background. *Toilets*. And directly below the little rectangular sign, a man sat at a table on his own. He wore a black military-style jacket and a black woollen hat. Lydia gawped. He waved. She won a brief but gruelling battle with paralysing dread and then moved towards him, step by oh-so-slow step.

The blue van jerked off the road and into the car park in front of Donna's apartment like it had almost missed the turn. Cormac had taken a seat by the doors out to the little balcony, instinctively setting up a watch. His handler hadn't called him back and the passing time made him edgy. The pair of thugs that got out of the blue van made him edgier still. One of the thugs – older than the other one by some years – looked at a piece of paper in his hand, then tucked it into the back pocket of a pair of faded jeans. Cormac lost sight of them as they moved towards the front door.

"Are you expecting anybody today, Donna?"

"Like who?"

"You haven't got a plumber coming around or anything, have you?"

She shook her head.

"Take Mattie into your bedroom. Put something against the door and don't come out until I call you."

"What's happening?" Mattie asked.

"I'm not sure yet, kid. Just go keep an eye on your da for me."

Donna took Mattie's hand and led him to the bedroom. Cormac weighed his options. Go and face them in the hallway or draw them in to the apartment. He expected the doorbell to sound. There was a security pad on the door that could be buzzed open from a little speaker phone in the hall.

There was a knock at the door to Donna's apartment. Somebody else had let them through. Those communal security doors were utterly pointless. In any case, the decision was out of Cormac's hands. He'd have to face these heavies in the apartment.

Cormac made a conscious decision not to draw his gun. It went against his training and his instincts, but there was something in him that wanted to resolve the situation in the safest possible manner. There was too much at risk with Donna, Mattie and John trapped in the bedroom. Besides, he was low on ammo.

The door crashed open, the night latch useless without a Chubb lock to back it up. Cormac held his ground, just a few yards from the doorway. If they had guns he was prepared to dive for cover along the couch. The heavies stepped in, not overly concerned about cover. One of them wore a low-slung tool belt, a claw hammer hung at each hip. He'd plaster dust on his boots and undistinguishable tattoos on his forearms. His face was ruddy and weather-beaten. His partner was dressed for the gym: tracksuit trousers, trainers and a hooded top. He was younger but just as broad as Bob the Builder.

"Did you think we wouldn't find you, dickhead?" Sporty Spice asked.

"You two need to get out of here now," Cormac said. "Consider this fair warning."

Sporty Spice turned to Bob. "This man must have been dropped on his head when he was a child. Do you hear him, like?"

Bob shook his head. "Taking the fucking piss." His voice had a forty-a-day rasp.

Good, Cormac thought. *He'll be easy enough to handle... so long as the hammers stay in his belt.*

"Big Frank sent us. Get the aul' fellah and the kid and c'mon," Sporty Spice said.

"I'll hang about here for a while yet. I've a few

questions you two could answer for me before you go, though."

"I think he's a cop," Bob said.

"Wise up," Sporty Spice said. "Sure Frank told us who he is. Kelly's a good fenian name."

"Look at him. Fucking undercover, so he is."

Bob was smarter than he looked. Cormac would have been shot weeks ago if this one had been put on the crew.

"Let's keep it civil, lads," Cormac said. "No need for name calling."

Bob drew a hammer and handed it to Sporty Spice.

"I'm not looking for trouble, lads."

"I bet you're not," Sporty Spice said.

Cormac bit back his temper and continued. "Okay, so me and Frank have a couple of loose ends to tie up. I'll come along with you guys on my own. Then things don't have to get stupid."

"Aye, he'd be pleased as fuck with that arrangement," Bob said.

Cormac rounded the sofa. It didn't look like the heavies were carrying guns. Decommissioning had made them a little tougher to distribute around the greater Belfast area, though it was still a possibility they had a pistol or two concealed. He kept his hands visible and took a step forward; almost within Sporty Spice's hammer-swinging range. "Any other way isn't going to go well for you two."

Bob squinted. The cogs were beginning to spin behind those eyes. Cormac allowed himself a few seconds of hope. He was handling the situation, tense as it was, with nothing more than—

Sporty Spice lunged forward and swung the claw

hammer in a big downward arc. Cormac scrabbled backwards, dodged the wild swing but bumped against the back of the couch. He relaxed his muscles and tumbled backwards. His body flopped onto the seat cushions and he rolled onto the floor. As he rose onto one knee Cormac snaked his hand into his coat and closed it around the grip of the Glock 17. He drew the weapon and stood. Supported his right wrist with his left hand. Levelled. Grinned. At this range he couldn't miss. Sporty Spice knew it too. The young thug had the hammer held above his head, cocked for a lethal strike. It froze there.

Bob's husky voice grated; "Back up, wee lad."

Cormac spared the older man a quick glance though his aim on Sporty Spice didn't falter. Bob looked worried. He didn't want to have to report back an almighty fuck-up to his superiors. The man knew the score. He'd the calm carefulness of experience. Cormac reckoned he could work with that. The other eejit, though, he could be a problem. The raised hammer began to visibly shake. Lactic acid or a ruse, Cormac couldn't be sure. Either way they weren't going to be locked in the stand-off for much longer.

"Do as he says," Cormac jabbed his Glock at Sporty Spice. "Lower that weapon very slowly and step the fuck back."

"Why don't you lower yours?"

"Mine's a gun, dickhead. Who's going to come off worse?"

Bob offered his two cents. "You know, if he was going to shoot, he'd have done it by now. Might be worth a go, son."

Sporty Spice twisted at the waist to look over his shoulder. "You want to swap places?"

Cormac took advantage of the distraction and kicked out at Sporty Spice's floating ribs. The blow rocked the thug backwards. Cormac took a backhand swing at him and caught the side of his head with the barrel of the Glock.

Bob pushed past his injured partner. He held his left hand up as if to ward Cormac off; his right hefted his claw hammer. Cormac considered shooting him but opted to save the ammo. He darted forward, clattered into Bob and made a grab for the shaft. Bob reeled backwards. Cormac stuck close and went with him. They hit the wall adjacent to the open front door. Bob's back absorbed all the impact. His stinking breath clouded Cormac's face. The hammer came down. Cormac raised his left arm. Slipped it inside Bob's. The attack slid away like rain off a roof. Cormac sank his forehead into the older man's reddened face. Cracked the nose. Felt a wild surge of joy. He drew back his head to butt him again. Then something wrapped around his legs.

This was Sporty Spice's half-hearted effort to re-enter the fray.

The younger thug attempted to lift Cormac but he couldn't break his stance. He grappled for Cormac's hips, intent on throwing him to the ground. No chance. The blow to the head must have shaken something loose. The big lump had abandoned his hammer and just wasn't fighting smart. Cormac turned in his opponents rubbery hold and took advantage of his position. He used one free arm to grab a handful of his attacker's ear and the other to pistol-whip the back of his head. Sporty Spice went limp and Cormac let him fall to the ground. He lifted a foot to finish him but Bob wouldn't stand for it. The older man shoved Cormac from behind. Cormac tottered a few steps to recover from almost tripping over Sporty Spice. He turned to face Bob.

Blood poured steadily from the aul' fellah's busted nose but his eyes were clear. Cormac edged backwards. The push had landed him back in the middle of the room. Bob closed the fighting space in two strides. Cormac's patience ran out. He raised his gun.

"I *will* shoot."

Bob spat blood. "No you won't." He plucked a Stanley from a loop on his tool belt. Thumbed the switch and bared a wicked triangular blade.

CHAPTER 9

Money is killing this game. I'd play for three square meals a day and a roof over my head if that's all it paid. Fucking love those Ferraris, though.

Rory Cullen, *Cullen: The Autobiography*

The man in the black military-style jacket indicated that Lydia should sit on the barstool opposite his. Her rubbery legs folded a little too quickly and she laid her hands on the round table for support. It wobbled under her weight and rocked the amber contents of a pint glass. She settled on the worn cushion and rested her clasped hands in her lap. The man fixed his eyes on her breasts.

She could smell blood. Feel the too-recent memory of when stained fingers traced the line of her jaw. But this wasn't the bastard who'd touched her at the holiday home. His bare face lacked the telltale claw marks Lydia had inflicted. It could have been the second intruder from the night before but she didn't think so. She'd sensed a terrible wildness about those two and, from their voices, had pinned them as a little younger than the stranger sat in front of her. He looked about forty. His sunbed tan did little to conceal the pockmarked skin on his cheeks. Momentarily lost in some lechery, he gnawed on his lower lip and Lydia caught a glimpse of gleaming white teeth.

"Who are you?"

He looked up at her face but Lydia could take no comfort from the shift in focus. She tried not to imagine what went on behind his greedy eyes.

"I'm just a messenger, darling."

His east London accent surprised her. She'd expected broad Belfast tones.

"I'm here with a friend." She tilted her head back towards the corner bar where Rory chatted to the Polish barmaid.

"Yeah, looks like he's keeping a real close eye on you. But don't fret, darling. I'm only here for a quick natter. We'll be done before your valiant knight's done chatting up that foreign bint behind the bar."

She wanted to lift his glass and throw its contents in his face. But the need to hear something, anything about her family suppressed the urge. She nodded, *Say your piece, then.*

"The men you're working for want you to wrap things up today. They want access to the house in Teddington. Do what you have to do to get them in."

"What about my—?"

"No questions, darling. It's a simple instruction." He paused for a few seconds, daring her to speak again. "Very good. Now, if you've held up your end of the bargain, all will be well. If not... you probably know what to expect."

The man flashed his ridiculously white teeth and got out from behind the table. He winked at her, downed his pint and left.

Lydia sat on and tried to digest what she'd just been told. She needed to get Rory back to his house and... Then what? She hadn't found a kink in his security system yet. Would she be able do that without Rory breathing over her shoulder?

She felt a hand on her back and almost upended the table.

"Whoa, take it easy, Lydia."

"Rory, for fuck's sake, you near put the heart in me sideways."

He gave her a look. "Jesus, my ma used to say that. Did you pick that one up off John?"

She looked away.

"What are you doing over here anyway, you big freak? Staring at the wall like some headcase. They'll be after you with the butterfly nets if you're not careful."

"I'm not a third wheel kind of girl."

"You took off so I could score with the barmaid? Very considerate but I was just being polite. Jesus, do you think I try to bed every woman I meet?"

"I don't give it any thought at all, to be honest."

"Ach, don't get all sniffy about it. God you've had something up your hole for the last few days. Would you not just relax and smile for a bit? These moods of yours are bringing me right down."

Rory held out his hand. Lydia took it and hauled herself off the stool. She didn't look at his face. Her words were directed at his chest.

"Will we finish up our drinks, then?"

"What about one more for the road?"

"Make it a half one, will you? I could do with a few hours at the computer back at yours."

You're going to have to shoot this bastard.

It was the last thing Cormac wanted to do. And it wasn't just down to his ammo shortage. He'd already killed one of O'Neill's men. The man's cousin no less. It was a safe bet his cover was fucked. But Bob – with murder in his eyes and a Stanley knife in his hand – would make for a decent consolation arrest. He might even get a lead on Big Frank Toner out of it.

Sporty Spice was still sprawled out on the floor with no sign of recovery. Bob stood alone against a bigger, stronger, armed opponent. There was only one way it could go. But Cormac had to rely on the aul' fellah coming to the same conclusion.

"Last chance, big man. Put your weapon down."

Bob pounced. His blood-smeared face twisted as he loosed a primal snarl. Cormac skipped backwards and jerked his head back. The blade whistled past his face.

Cormac readied himself for the next swipe. It didn't come as quickly as he'd expected. Bob had over-extended himself, his first attack too clouded by anger to be anything but clumsy. The older man tried to plant his feet to attack from a stronger stance. Cormac took his opportunity and sidestepped Bob to move into the open-plan kitchen. He felt a new energy course through him. More fighting space, a choice of weapons, a moment to breathe.

He reached out with his free hand and snatched a knife from the block on the countertop. The ten-inch blade was water-stained but plenty vicious. He tucked his gun away and adjusted his grip on the knife so the dull edge of the blade rested against his forearm. Bob approached slowly. Cocky. He bounced the Stanley knife from one palm to the other. Must have watched a few too many American street gang flicks in his youth.

"You drew blood first," Bob rasped, and pointed a thumb at his busted nose. "It wasn't me."

Not exactly versed in Rambo movie trivia, though.

"That's not the line, dickhead."

Bob shrugged off the accusation. "Whatever, son. You're still fucked."

There was rust on the Stanley blade. Cormac looked beyond the emboldened and approaching Bob. He dropped his jaw and widened his eyes.

"Jesus, Mattie, *don't*."

Bob took the bait and turned to see what the kid was up to. Cormac slashed the back of Bob's right arm. Skin split and tendons severed. The Stanley blade fell to the floor. Bob yowled like a beaten dog. Cormac kicked the Stanley blade under the fridge then grabbed Bob by the back of his neck and ran towards the American style fridge in the corner of the kitchen area. Forehead met brushed steel. It wasn't enough to knock the tough aul' bastard out. He squawked as loud as his smoke-damaged lungs would allow.

Cormac pulled back and shoved him forward again, looking for the knockout. Something went in Bob's neck. *Shit*. He'd silenced the aul' fellah for good.

CHAPTER 10

Hooligans... They're just wankers.

Rory Cullen, *Cullen: The Autobiography*

Lydia raised her hands to her ears, prepared to cup them. Rory held the champagne over the kitchen sink and popped the cork. The little wooden bullet shot up, butted the ceiling and plummeted to the floor. A dribble of foam ran down the elegant glass neck and trickled over his fingers. He sat the bottle down beside the flutes on the worktop and licked the traces of bubbly from his knuckles. Then he retrieved the cork from the floor and took it to a cutting board on the worktop. As Lydia poured, Rory cut the cork into two identical halves. He wrote the date on each piece and handed one to Lydia. He pinned the other half to a notice board hung on the back of the kitchen door adorned with at least twenty other dated and neatly lined champagne souvenirs.

"That's some collection," Lydia said.

"I've had a lot to celebrate."

Lydia wanted to shove her champagne flute into his face.

The champagne frothed in the glasses as Rory dropped a strawberry into each one. He tilted his towards hers for the obligatory clink. The little red berries bobbed in their drinks.

He affected an effeminate stance. "Fruity."

She granted him a polite smile. It felt like a hard day's work.

Bubbles popped and tickled Lydia's nose as she sipped. The ice-cold drink rolled down the back of her throat and she relished its cool trail. But her pleasure was short-lived. Guilt crowded in and blackened her glimmer of cheer. How dare she enjoy anything while her family suffered? Her second sip turned sour on her tongue.

Rory tipped his glass upright and emptied the champagne and strawberry into his mouth. His cheeks bulged as he tried to chew the berry without spewing the bubbly. He swallowed the whole lot down, hooted and burped.

"Fuck yeah. I'll have another one of those," he held his glass out to Lydia.

She poured him another drink and plucked another strawberry from the top of the punnet. It bobbled around the rim of the glass and fell to the floor. They both lunged for it and their foreheads met with a snooker break clack. Lydia stumbled backwards and Rory caught her by the wrist. He kept her on her feet but splashed them both with his drink.

"Shit, sorry," Rory said.

"Ow, Rory you utter bastard!" Lydia rubbed her forehead.

"Jesus, take it easy, Lyds. It was only an accident, like."

"Lyds?"

Rory opened his mouth. His tongue ran along his lower row of crooked teeth. He pushed his jaw forward. It was obvious he wanted to say something else and

Lydia was ready for him. Ready to unload all her pain. But Rory let her down. His face eased into an awkward smile.

He set his glass by the sink and then stepped up to Lydia to examine her forehead. Rory cupped her face in his hands and tilted her head back to examine the damage under the cluster of spotlights. Her heart sped up.

"It's a wee bit red, but I don't think it'll bruise. Sorry, Lydia."

Rory's hands lingered on her face and Lydia raised her eyebrows. He smirked.

"Want me to kiss it better?"

She pushed him. Hard. He shrugged.

They took the bottle, the strawberries and their glasses to the kitchen table and sat opposite each other. Lydia was glad of the physical barrier. She could still feel the warmth of his palms on her face. The day before, a man in a balaclava, with blood on his hands, had traced the line of her jaw with his fingertips and Rory's touch had invigorated the hangover from that intrusion. She forced down a slug of champagne.

"That's the girl," Rory said, "have a top-up."

Lydia raised her glass to meet the mouth of the bottle. The bubbly sloshed into the flute and foamed. She necked half of it before Rory could offer a strawberry. There were no placemats on the table so she set her glass back on the existing ring of moisture she'd left on the unfinished Mexican pine.

"So, are we going with the old bastard or the slick guy?" Rory asked.

"The old bastard."

"Dead on. I like him, but if he mentions my teeth again, I might have to set him straight." He threw a slow motion hook into the air. It passed over the top of the bottle.

"McGoldrick's veins are full of piss and vinegar. He's a good man to have on your side, so long as you've a thick skin. Powerful isn't the word for it."

"So what am I going to do with all this money?"

"What all you boys do. Squander it on cars and WAGs."

"Yeah, I suppose a chunk of it will go on that. But I don't want to end up skint after my legs go. Too many eejits have done that. I need to invest or something."

"Don't ever say that to a journalist. It'll fuck your reputation."

Fuck. Casual swearing was one of her getting tipsy tells. Champagne got the job done pretty fast.

"I'll have to give the financial advisor a shake," Rory said. "If I can find his number."

"You're not so hot on the bills and banking side of things, then?"

"Nah. I've no interest. So long as the bank machine spits out cash every time I stick my card in, there's not much else I need to know."

Lydia raised her glass. "To the bottomless bank machine."

Rory raised his and then they knocked back their drinks. Rory poured fresh ones. Lydia fiddled with her phone. No texts. She checked the time. The hours were steadily ticking by. When were the bastards going to arrive?

"God, we got through that fast," Lydia said.

"Goes down too easy, doesn't it? Will I open another one?"

"I think I need something less fizzy. I'll get the hiccups if I stay on this stuff."

Rory sprang out of his seat and made a beeline for the drinks cabinet. "Vodka and orange juice? It'll count towards our five-a-day."

Lydia had to stay alert but a drunk Rory might be easier to get information from. And she needed to arm herself with info. Like the code to his alarm system. Maybe she could convince him to go out and pass on the information when the bastards finally called. And maybe a little Dutch courage would help her too. More alcohol seemed like the answer. Not the best but an answer nonetheless. The champagne had awakened a thirst she knew she should suppress. Or should she? Lydia gave Rory the thumbs-up.

"Make mine a double."

Cormac dumped a mug of cold water on Sporty Spice's face. The young thug gasped into consciousness. His eyes settled on Cormac's and he tried to move. Found himself bound by the strips Cormac had torn from a bed sheet. He writhed on the living room floor seemingly unaware that he was no relation to Houdini. Cormac settled into an armchair and waited for the idiot to wear himself out.

He'd ordered the others to stay in Donna's bedroom until he'd worked a few things out. John was still half out of his mind on the pill cocktail Donna had fed him and offered no argument. Mattie, pale and anxious, barely acknowledged him. Donna hadn't let him off so easily.

"What the fu…" She took a deep breath. "What have you brought to my doorstep, Cormac?"

"The kid doesn't mind if you curse."

"You're not funny."

"I'll get you protection. You'll be safe."

"Safe? I'm hiding in my bedroom because my ex has been fighting God-knows-who in my living room. You think I'm ever going to feel safe here again?"

"I'll help you find a new—"

"Get out of my sight."

"Maybe you should get John ready to go? We might need to leave here quickly."

"Maybe you should fuck off, Cormac."

And he really should have fucked off but that would mean abandoning his second dead body of the day. Self defence or not, the tally didn't sit well with him.

At last, the trussed up hatchet man gave up his struggle with a grunt.

"Where the fuck's Paul?"

Cormac blinked. The dopey bastard had given up his partner's first name without a second thought. *Amateur.*

"I left him in the kitchen."

"Is he all right?"

"He's had better days."

"My head hurts."

"A pistol-whipping will do that to you. Suck it up."

"I'm going to kill you."

"Aye, yeah."

Sporty Spice opened his mouth to share some new nugget of wisdom. Cormac slid off his chair and shoved a pair of rolled up socks into the goon's big mouth. His gag reflex sent him into a spasm. He fought too hard to pull oxygen in through his nose and his panic-stricken face reddened. Cormac slapped him hard. Distracted him from his hissy fit. Sporty Spice's teary, hate-filled eyes narrowed. He started to breathe normally.

"Give the shite-talk a rest, big lad," Cormac said. "I'll pull this gag out of your mouth in a second but all I want to hear is answers to my questions. You go off on one and I'll fucking smother you."

Sporty Spice nodded.

Cormac unplugged him.

"What's your connection to Big Frank?"

"He's a mate."

"A mate that pays you?"

"Sometimes. If something needs done, like."

"Were you here to kill me?"

"No, mate. I swear. Frank just wanted us to track you down."

"With hammers?"

"That was Paul's idea. 'Just in case,' he said."

"What's your name?"

Sporty Spice's eyes darted to the left. "Pearce."

Cormac pounded his fist into Sporty Spice's stomach. The lying bastard's legs shot up. A heavier blow might have folded him in half. He coughed and his eyes streamed.

"Tell the truth."

"It's Shane. Shane Morgan."

Both names? This fellah's softer than shite. "That's more like it, Shane. Stay honest and we'll get through this rightly. Is Frank still in Belfast?"

"I think so. He didn't say."

"What about his family."

"Don't know."

"What *do* you know, Shane?"

"A big job went wrong. It was your fault. Now Frank's trying to fix things."

"How'd Frank get in touch with you?"

"He didn't. He phoned Paul and Paul brought me in on it."

"Wait there."

Cormac went to the kitchen. He looked down at aul' Paul. *Dead* Paul. He hadn't been as tough as Cormac had first thought. A bit of a tussle – an angry one, granted, but still just a fight – and the man clocked out. Cormac averted his gaze from the unnatural angle of Paul's neck. Went hunting in the dead man's pockets. He found a battered phone in the jeans. Clamshell design. Cormac could hear grit grind in the hinge when he flipped it open. The display was dimmed by a fine layer of dust, the buttons grubby and stiff. He checked the call records. The contact name TONER topped the list of received calls.

"Very sloppy, Big Frank." He hit a button to return the call.

Frank picked up on the second ring and launched right in.

"Was our info sound?"

Cormac didn't answer. He wondered where the "info" had come from.

"Paul? Are you there?"

"Hiya, Frank."

"Who the fuck's this? Kelly? Is that you?"

"Afraid so."

"Put Paul on the phone."

"He's… what's the word? Indisposed?"

"You still at your ex's flat?"

"Why don't you come and find out?"

Frank took a deep breath. Cormac suspected a torrent of abuse was headed his way. He hung up.

Chapter 11

A footballer should never marry a girl with the potential to earn more money than them. The beautiful game attracts alpha-males. They can't cope with a woman that brings home more bacon than they do.

Rory Cullen, *Cullen: The Autobiography*

"I'm getting death threats, Lydia."

Rory's voice, usually a little too loud for most situations, was barely audible. He sounded like a pubescent boy confessing to some shameful deed. A drunk pubescent boy. He sat at the Mexican pine table, a half-empty glass of vodka with a dash of orange juice within hand's reach. Lydia willed him to reach for it again. He was three or four drinks ahead of her and his were much stronger than hers. She'd seen to that, topping up his glass regularly. Outside, the evening cold descended and the natural light faded. The gang would make their move under the cover of darkness. It made sense. She could almost feel the bastards approach.

"Death threats, Lyds."

Lydia held her tongue. Waited for him to tell her the full story before reacting. Death threats to footballers were not uncommon. Fervent fans, high-rolling gamblers, scorned glamour models... off the pitch the high-profile players trod a minefield. Most of them led to nothing, just the product of frustration or obsession in the majority of cases. But it only took one crazed fucker to cause a major problem – just one opportunist to follow through and end a life.

"Most of them have been hand-delivered to my door."

Shit. Major problem.

"The last one came with a bullet."

A bullet. The favoured theatrical accompaniment to a Northern Irish death threat. John, in his hideous habit of making light of his country's past, had joked about sending bullets to his mother-in-law in his speech on their wedding day. His side had laughed. Hers shared an almost tangible awkwardness. She should have taken that speech as an omen.

Lydia's mind revisited the scene at the holiday cottage. Balaclavas, harsh Belfast accents, a well-practised ease about the whole situation. She didn't know if the men who held her family were IRA, UV-whatever or simply Northern Irish gangsters. It didn't matter. They had guns and they had kidnapped her family.

"How long has this been going on?" At the back of her mind, Lydia blamed Rory for her family's situation. If he'd acted faster, spoken to somebody about the threats before now, would the bastards have moved on to her?

"A few weeks now."

"And you still thought it was a good idea to go to Belfast?"

"To get out of this house for a week or two?" Rory swirled the dregs of his booze, sniffed at the rim of his glass and set it down on the table. "I thought it was a *great* idea."

If you're too fucking stupid to make the connection between bullets and Belfast, maybe.

Lydia buried her hands in her hair and rested her elbows on the table. She stared at her unfinished vodka and orange juice and concentrated on not puking.

"What'll I do, Lydia?"

She spoke to her glass, afraid she'd explode if she looked at him. "Fucked if I know."

"I shouldn't have left Chelsea."

Lydia curled her fingers. Her nails dug into her scalp and threatened to break skin.

"Those bastards are crazy," he said.

"Your old team?"

"No, no, no. The fans. Well... no, not the *fan* fans. The dirty, stinking bastards that pretend to be fans but are just after a ruck. Hooligans, you know? And I really let them have it in my book. Said they were wankers and scumbags. The fucking *firm*. They're—"

Lydia thumped her hands down onto the tabletop. Rory's bullshit ceased.

"Wise the fuck up, Rory. You realise you're talking about the football bogey men, don't you? The *Headhunters*? I mean, come on. Is that who you think tracked you down to hand deliver bullets? Cut through the media hype and all that's left of that gang is a bunch of pot-bellied lager louts that can't even get into their team's grounds anymore. Head-*bangers*, more like."

Rory's face reddened. "I suppose you think the IRA's gone away too."

"How can you even compare...?"

Balaclavas, shotguns, kidnapping. *Her* kid. Mattie. John... It all mounted in her mind. Weighed her down. Lydia wanted to vault the kitchen table and strangle the shit out of Rory. Bang his empty head off every wall in the house. Squash his eyes into the back of his skull with her thumbs and kick out his crooked teeth. Her temperature rose and her breath hitched.

And she puked into her drink.

Mattie screwed up his face like Cormac had just offered him a shit sandwich. "You left him alive?"

He was looking at Shane, still tied up and struggling on the floor. Donna was helping John to the door. They were headed for Donna's car at the front of the building but it was slow going. Mattie had hung back a little, to check out the result of the earlier commotion no doubt.

"Yes, he's alive." Cormac didn't draw Mattie's attention to the dead body in the kitchen area. He couldn't tell for sure if the kid could see aul' dead Paul from where he was standing. The breakfast unit might have obscured the view. "That's a good thing, Mattie. I don't want to have to kill anybody." *Wasn't Paddy an exception?* "And when I do have to I'm not particularly proud of myself. Whatever these guys might have done, they're still people, mate."

Mattie looked unconvinced but Cormac stepped down from his soapbox. They needed to move. He motioned for Mattie to leave. They checked on Donna and John's progress from the landing. The injured man cursed with each movement. They were only halfway down the stairs. Cormac willed them on. He hopped from foot to foot for a few seconds but knew it was pointless to tell them to get a move on. Donna was being sensibly cautious with a badly hurt patient. There was no way Cormac could rush her on. Then he had a thought. He left Mattie on the landing and returned to the apartment.

Shane had managed to get to his feet. With his ankles and wrists still bound, the effort had done him little good. He looked helplessly at Cormac. Cormac couldn't resist. He went to Shane and swept the legs out from under him. The hogtied thug hit the ground hard. Cormac knelt beside him and patted down his pockets, in search of a mobile phone.

"You may as well lie there until Frank comes, Shane. Get some rest."

"He's going to kill me." Shane's voice was thick with self pity.

"Nah, mate. That'd be a waste of manpower. He'll put you straight to work."

"Do you think so?"

Does this eejit actually want you to comfort him? Cormac found the phone and scooped it out of a zippered pocket in Shane's tracksuit trousers. He stood up and took a step away from Shane. "Well, yeah. Big Frank's going to need all the muscle available to him. Especially since aul' Paul's dead." Cormac relished the horrible shock on the prone man's face. *Fuck you, you low rent hood.*

"You killed Paul?"

"Did you not think he was awful quiet, Shane?"

And at that, big, hard, hammer-wielding Shane burst into tears.

Cormac was stunned. Shane's reaction seemed so pathetic and weak. Childish, even. Surely the man knew that his chosen line of work carried the threat of fatal consequences? Most of the career criminals Cormac had encountered had a vacuum of spirit in common that years of living by a brutal code had instilled in them.

But this big lump, trussed up and crying on the floor, must have been new to the game. Maybe he was still getting to grips with the rules. For a moment, Cormac wondered if it wouldn't be a kindness to put him out of his misery after all. It was a thought that strengthened his resolve to let Shane live.

Cormac used Paul's battered phone to call Shane's immaculate, top of the line handset. He set Paul's on the mantelpiece then found a hold option on Shane's to mute the phone and held it to his ear.

"Tell you what, Shane. I'll light a candle for your boyfriend next time I'm at mass."

Shane spat a glob of watery snot at Cormac's shoes. "Fuck off."

The exchange came through loud and clear. Cormac nodded to himself and slipped Shane's phone into the breast pocket of his jacket.

"All right, Mattie. Time we were leaving."

He'd sensed Mattie hovering at the door. The kid was transfixed by the weeping wreck on the floor. At the sound of Cormac's voice, he snapped out of his wide-eyed stare and nodded tightly. His mouth had shrunk to a puckered slit, like he'd bitten into a lemon.

They left the apartment building and Cormac got behind the wheel of Donna's car – the silver Seat Leon. Donna was in the back with John. She asked him if he was in much pain and he hissed a barely audible response through his teeth. Mattie got in to the passenger seat and spared his father an over-the-shoulder look of concern.

Cormac took Shane's phone from his coat pocket, tapped a button to switch to loudspeaker mode and set it on the dashboard. The crude bugging device picked up Shane's continued struggle for freedom. The bound thug had been too busy crying to notice Cormac's setup so there was a good chance they'd get an early warning of Big Frank's arrival.

Somebody had leaked information about him to these animals and Cormac needed to find out who he could trust.

CHAPTER 12

I don't really get why my transfer fee was so controversial. Clearly I'm worth every penny. In any case, I'm sure some other player will top it at the next transfer window. That's football.

Rory Cullen, *Cullen: The Autobiography*

Lydia reread the text message.

"*Callin in 2 mins. Make sure u can talk.*"

She stood in the hallway and cocked her ear. Rory was in the living room watching one of his Chelsea matches from last season. The volume blared. He'd never hear her voice over the racket.

Her mobile phone screeched out that ridiculous Lady Gaga chorus. She wouldn't be able to listen to any of the mad bitch's music again. The Pavlovian response would be too much. She thumbed the green button.

"We're here. Get the door opened."

She recognised the voice. It was the man who had greeted her at the cottage with a sawn-off shotgun and kicked off the nightmare.

"How—?"

The line was dead.

Lydia put away her phone and took a brief moment to steady the shakes. When she had a handle on herself, she went to the living room.

Rory was perched on his sofa, primed to spring to his feet and yell instructions and abuse at the recorded match playing out on his jumbo-sized TV. He didn't register Lydia's presence until she stepped into his line of sight. She gave him a nervous wave and he craned his neck to look around her. Then he realised what he was doing and shifted his focus to her.

"You all right, Lydia?"

She needed to get the security code. Keep it simple.

"Yeah, I just need to get something. Where's the nearest pharmacy?"

"Probably Kingston Street. It's dead easy to find too. Just follow the road that runs along the side of the house. You'll practically bump into the shop front."

"Great, thanks. Um, you want anything while I'm out?"

"There's a minimarket right beside the pharmacy. Maybe you could pick up a bottle of *vino* for later? Or more vodka."

"Certainly."

Lydia stepped out into the hallway. She felt like she'd gotten away with something, then Rory called out to her.

"Oh, here, you need me to disable the alarm."

It's going to work! "Or you could just tell me the code..."

Rory's backside hovered inches from the cushion. He thought for a second then lowered himself back onto the sofa.

"Twenty-two, ten, nineteen-forty-six."

"Somebody's birthday?"

"George Best's."

Rory's attention was divided between her and the TV, with the TV enjoying the lion's share. She could almost feel him drift away as she tapped in the numbers. The system started to bleat.

"What have I done?"

Rory paused the recording, heaved himself off the sofa and went to the number pad. "You've just hit a wrong number or something. Let me try..." His fingers found the right sequence and the beeping stopped. He went to the door and opened it for her. Stepped aside to let her pass.

Lydia looked out into the front garden. Two men in biker gear approached, their tinted helmet visors down. They had guns. Lydia whimpered.

"What's wrong, Lyds?"

Rory looked beyond her, cursed and shoved the door shut. He grabbed her by the back of her coat. One of the men hit the door. It moved but held. Without the bolts engaged, it wouldn't hold for long, though. And with the alarm deactivated there'd be no automatic emergency call to the police.

"Upstairs, quick."

She hesitated and Rory jerked her coat.

"Move, you stupid bitch. We have to go."

They were headed towards a dead end, but Lydia allowed him to drag her backwards. It was all going to end, one way or another. She was too tired to fight.

"What are you waiting for? We need to move."

Cormac shot Donna a glance in the rear-view mirror. She held up a bloodstained hand then dropped it back out of sight. He looked over his shoulder to see Donna's hand pressed against her patient's abdomen. John Gallagher's wound was bleeding through the stitches and dressing. The car's interior light timed out and they were shrouded in twilight. Cormac nodded slightly towards Mattie for Donna's benefit. She shook her head. His ex didn't think he should tell the kid in the front passenger seat that his da was bleeding out in the back of the car.

Cormac clacked his teeth together a couple of times. He needed to jar his brain back into motion. "If we go to the City Hospital, can you get us through any bullshit questioning?"

"He'll be seen to right away. Just get us there."

Cormac listened to the improvised phone-bug. It picked up Shane's heavy breathing. The thumps and bumps of the thug's struggle with his bindings had ceased. If he'd any sense he was saving his energy and coming up with a decent explanation as to how he'd let his partner die and his quarry escape. Cormac handed the phone to Mattie.

"Look after this for me, kid. If anything gets picked up on it, a voice, somebody else coming in to the apartment, whatever, you make sure I hear it, right?"

Mattie, face rigid like he was afraid to look flattered or nervous, held the phone's speaker a few inches from his ear. Cormac winked at Donna in the rear view mirror. She averted her glare; no sign of forgiveness. He started the engine and slipped the Seat Leon into first. Then he spotted a dark hatchback with its full beams on pull a ridiculous manoeuvre on the Malone Road. In the process of overtaking a little red Micra it barely missed a City Bus pulling out from a stop on the other side of the road. Horns blared. The car, a black Ford Focus, indicated left. It was coming into the car park.

"That'll be our Frank, then," Cormac said.

He quashed the urge to speed out of his parking

space and peel off in the opposite direction. That would be the best way to draw attention to them. He held back and hoped the Leon's slightly tinted windows and the darkened winter sky would provide them with enough cover.

"Come on, Cormac."

"Just a minute, Donna. We need to be cool here."

Cormac drew the Glock out of his pea coat and rested it on his lap. If Big Frank did see him, he'd have no option but to shoot. But with an armoury consisting of a half-empty clip, he would need to make each shot count.

Big Frank screeched to a halt at the door of the apartment building. He jumped out of the car with his usual lack of finesse, almost tripping over his own feet in his rush to the door. The gorilla didn't waste time with the security system. He pulled a Desert Eagle hand cannon from the waistband of his jeans and pumped three rounds into the lock. The kid flinched but held his tongue. Cormac could hear the hurried whisper of Donna in prayer. Then Frank was in the building.

"Hold the phone up to my ear, Mattie."

Cormac nosed the Leon out of the car park entry way and held tight for a break in the traffic. No need to panic. They'd be gone before Big Frank figured out the situation. The phone crackled into life.

"What the fuck happened here? Where's Paul?"

Shane's voice was clipped and steady. He'd prepared his response. "You didn't tell us we were going after a fucking cop."

"Where the fuck's Paul?"

"He's dead. The cop killed him."

Big Frank roared and there was a sickening thump. Shane started coughing.

"Keep your mouth shut about that, you dickhead. Ambrose O'Neill doesn't get taken on by sneaky peelers, all right?"

Shane's wheezy response was muted by the frantic hoot of a car that swerved around the Leon's front end. The driver stopped for a few seconds to point his finger and make an angry face. Cormac motioned him on with a dismissive wave.

Frank was talking again. "You know you were out of line, don't you, Shane?"

"Yeah, no sweat, Frank. Sorry."

"Just watch your mouth, okay? Now did Kelly hurt you bad?"

"I've a sore head, but I'll live."

"Good, because I need your help. We'll have to move aul' Paul when I'm done cutting you loose."

"Ah, Frank, don't make me lift him. He was my godfather."

"Was he? Ach, bollocks... Right, look, that's okay. Leave him there for now. I'll call somebody else."

"Thanks."

"I'll hunt down this Kelly fucker and make sure you get your chance at a bit of payback, okay?"

"Fucking right. He's only just left too."

"Why the fuck are we still here, then? Come on. What car did your man say the dirty doc drove?"

"Silver Seat."

"Hold on..." Footsteps then the swish of a drawn blind. "He's right fucking there! Come on you slow bastard."

The line of traffic broke and Cormac pulled out onto the road. He tried to plot out the journey ahead. Once he got to University Avenue he could hang left and cut through to the Lisburn Road and get John to the City Hospital.

Cormac broke the lights at the bottom of the Malone Road. John cursed and groaned in the back when they took the left too hard.

"Sorry, mate."

"Just fucking drive, Cormac," Donna said. "I'll hold him as steady as I can."

The ugly but iconic hospital building loomed in front of them. Cormac registered the pedestrian crossing ahead. Red. Not good. But he could see a break in the two lanes of oncoming traffic that blocked his path onto the hospital entrance. The Leon's engine roared and Cormac pumped the horn. He whipped up the handbrake and relied on the reactions of the well-seasoned Belfast drivers. Joyriders had nothing on this move. Horns blared and headlights flashed like strobes. But they made it through. Cormac risked a glance at the chaos he'd left in his wake. The Ford Focus sailed through the gap in traffic Cormac had created. If nothing else, Shane was a decent driver. Cormac would have to up his game.

"These bastards are too close to risk stopping here, Donna. They've already proved they're not afraid to pull out the guns in public. I'll try to lose them on the way to the Royal."

Belfast's other major hospital was close enough that Cormac could have them there in five or ten minutes if he continued to drive like a lunatic. He flipped on his hazard lights and dropped into third gear. The Leon's engine roared and catapulted them through the hospital grounds. They came out onto the Donegal Road and cut off a speeding Audi. The Audi's driver leaned on his horn and then whipped out into the oncoming lane to attempt to overtake Cormac. He drew level with the

Leon and lowered his window. Signalled that Cormac should do likewise. Cormac waggled his Glock at the uppity prick.

"Fuck off, mate."

Angry-man in the Audi slammed on his brakes and almost caused a pile-up.

The Focus was just a few cars down the line and closing fast.

Cormac bullied a filthy Hyundai Getz out of his path. The student-type driver waved his middle finger with an admirable degree of apathy as the Leon edged past. Cormac didn't think this young fellah deserved the same fright as the Audi guy. He set the gun back onto his lap, waved an apology and sped on.

Up ahead, a long row of glaring red brake lights. No exit in between. The Focus was five cars' lengths behind and showed no indication of slowing. Cormac braked hard. The Glock slid off his lap and disappeared under the dashboard.

"Ah, no."

He swerved to the left and mounted the kerb just before the Focus rear-ended him. Big Frank was too slow on the draw. Missed a split-second opportunity to put a bullet in Cormac's face. They sailed past. And as Cormac rolled to a stop, other cars filled the space between the Leon and the Focus like Tetris blocks. A cold, sticky sweat sprang out on his forehead and trickled from his armpits over the corrugated curves of his ribcage.

With all the CCTV, traffic-watch webcams and speed cameras posted along the stretch of road on which he'd just travelled, the cops had to be on their way to see what the fuck he'd been playing at. Police interest in their vehicle would feed back to the wrong people at high speed. His handler could renew the efforts to drag him in. He pricked his ears for the squall of PSNI Land Rover sirens. Nothing, but that was little comfort. Their arrival was inevitable.

Up ahead, the Focus was penned in by other cars. Cormac popped on his hazard lights and played chicken with the oncoming traffic. He drove past the trapped Focus to a discordant orchestra of car horns, revved engines and yelled death threats. Big Frank tried to get out of the car to shoot at them as they passed but he couldn't pull himself together quick enough. They swerved back into the correct lane as the traffic lights changed and Cormac guided the Leon towards Broadway Roundabout. The huge arty structure in the centre of the roundabout, nicknamed 'The Balls on the Falls', was lit up by flood lights. The Royal Hospital lay on the other side. But a glance in the rear-view mirror showed that Shane had negotiated the tailback and was on the move again. Cormac realised he wouldn't be able to lose their pursuers in the short distance to the hospital. He had no choice but to dig his heels in and face down the thugs.

CHAPTER 13

Why the hell would you name your kid after the city he was conceived in? You think that child wants to be reminded that his mum and dad love to shag every time he hears his name? It's a good job those dopes can afford to pay for some quality therapy.

Rory Cullen, *Cullen: The Autobiography*

Lydia's chest hitched. They were at the top of the stairs and the front door had just been kicked in. The men in the biker gear were on their way to get them.

Rory pointed to his room. "In here."

"And what? Hide under the bed?"

Rory dashed in and she followed. From the landing she heard the front door slam shut. They went to Rory's room. He opened his sock and condom drawer and scooped out a nasty looking hunting knife and what looked like a kid's toy gun. Then he went into the bottom drawer and took a little box from beneath a jumble of boxer shorts. Clicked it into the business end of the gun-type thing, flicked a switch and handed it to Lydia.

"Aim for the chest and pull the trigger, okay?"

The weighty plastic thing had a stubby pistol grip and a trigger that was set in what would normally be the stock of a handgun. The edges were rounded but the overall appearance of the object was blocky, like a mobile phone from the eighties. A yellow badge on the side labelled it as an X26. This meant nothing to Lydia.

Then she noticed the butt of the grip was embossed with something. She traced her finger over the words. TASER X26 MADE IN U.S.A. She didn't ask him if it worked through leather.

Down below, there was a brief and mumbled exchange between the intruders and then the creak of motorcycle boots on stairs.

Lydia went to Rory's bedroom window and swept open the curtains. Looked for an escape route.

"There's a trellis here, Rory. Will it hold us?"

"Wise up."

Rory stood in front of the door, knife in hand and poised like a gunslinger. Lydia scrambled over the bed, the taser held high, careful not to set it off, and stood beside Rory but had no idea what to do. She grabbed Rory's wrist with her free hand.

"They probably have guns. Maybe you should drop the knife?"

"Will I drop my trousers and bend over for them as well?"

"I'm serious, Rory. Just give them what they want. Maybe they won't hurt us."

The bedroom door burst open. Lydia hid the taser behind her back. One of the bikers stood in the doorway. He hefted a handgun to head height. Aimed somewhere between Lydia and Rory.

"Where's your safe?"

Rory raised the knife. The biker chambered a round and settled his aim at Rory's chest.

"Put the knife *down*, Rory," Lydia said.

Rory didn't respond. Lydia saw the muscles push out the skin around his clenched jaw and realised he'd been scared stiff. The knife was up but going nowhere. The gunman didn't know that, though.

"Listen to her, Cullen."

Lydia saw Rory's brow crease. He began to shake. She sidestepped away from him. The gunman spared her a quick glance but kept the gun trained on Rory. Her grip tightened on the taser. She had to do something. But the biker, body armoured in leather, head cased in thick plastic, offered no target. She cursed. Levelled the taser and pulled the trigger.

The biker jumped a little and turned his gun on Lydia. She shut her eyes tight. Waited for the bang. The last thing she'd ever hear. It didn't come.

She opened her eyes and saw that both bikers were now in the room. They held their guns by their sides and towered over Rory. He lay on the bed, his body wracked by an electrically induced seizure. Two thin wires ran in spring-like loops from his upper arm to the taser in Lydia's hand. She dropped the X26 and the cartridge popped out of the muzzle. Rory's violent shakes stilled. He lay on the bed, dazed and confused. The first biker into the room reached out and took the knife from Rory's loose grip.

The second biker turned to Lydia. "Fuck me, I knew you were working for us, but that might have been taking things a bit too far."

"Just get what you came for and go."

"Better do as she says," said the first biker. "If that's how she treats her friends, like."

"I was saving him from getting shot."

"Whatever helps you sleep, love."

The second biker found the safe in Rory's wardrobe. He lifted it out and gave it a cursory glance.

"It's a combination lock."

"I doubt your man will be thinking clearly enough to provide the numbers for a while yet. Just take the whole thing. We'll drill through the lock."

"How the fuck are we going to transport this on a motorbike? It weighs a tonne. You'll have to wake him up."

Rory moaned and said something unintelligible.

The first biker bent at the waist and put his ear to Rory's mouth. "Say that again, Cullen."

He moaned again.

"He's telling me to take his motor. The keys are hanging up in the hall."

"Fair enough. I call the car. Fucking hate that bike."

"There's a bunch of bank statement and credit card bills in the kitchen beside the microwave," Lydia said. She wanted them to get everything at once and ensure her family's safety.

The men barely spared Lydia a glance as they strutted out of the room and chuckled to each other on the way down the stairs. She went to Rory and hovered over him, ready to help as soon as he asked her to. If it took him three hours to recover from the taser then that's how long Lydia would stand there. She looked at the nasty little electrodes she'd shot into his arm and shuddered. Reached out to stroke his face.

He looked completely sapped, but had just enough energy left to turn away from her.

Cormac held his position, on his knees behind the open door of the Seat Leon. He scanned the road through the rolled-down window for a target. The damp cold from the grassy surface of Broadway Roundabout seeped through his jeans and little lumps of grit bit into his kneecaps. He pumped a couple of bullets into the air. Heard a few screams over the rumble of car engines and the bass-thrum of car stereos.

Big Frank and Shane had abandoned their car and taken cover behind a minibus in the now gridlocked traffic. The vehicles couldn't move forward for rubberneckers trying to figure out why the Ford Focus was empty and flashing hazard lights. Cormac wasn't sure if Big Frank was still behind the high-sided Mercedes or if he'd squirmed down the line of cars to get an easier shot. Either way, Cormac couldn't sit around and see how things developed. He had to get moving.

"Over here, Frank!" Shane's voice squalled above the motorist hubbub.

Frank's automatic pistol cracked. Blackbirds on a power line fluttered, squawked and shat. Cormac moved away from the Leon, he didn't want to return fire in case a stray bullet took out one of his passengers. He headed towards a highway maintenance van. It was a white Ford Transit with a luminous orange and yellow Battenberg strip on each side and a rack of hazard lights on the roof. He flattened his back against it and tried to put a bead on Big Frank.

He felt a presence by his side.

"What now, Cormac?"

Mattie had slipped out of the Leon and followed him, quiet as a dormouse.

"Fuck's sake, kid. You should have stayed in the car. Your da needs you."

"He's got Donna. I should help you."

"Just stay close to me, all right?"

Cormac tested the van's door handle.

"Are we going to nick it?"

Cormac took more than a little satisfaction from

bashing in the driver side window with the butt of his Glock. The shattered glass that fell onto the seat was easily removed. Cormac yanked the cover off and dumped it on the ground.

"Can you hotwire this?" Mattie asked.

"Nope. Not without a laptop. We're going to have to push it."

"What's the point in that?"

"No time, mate. Just put your back into it."

Cormac reached into the cab and flicked a switch that set the orange hazard lights spinning in their little Perspex bubbles. He released the handbrake and shoved the van into the lanes of traffic behind it. Mattie helped, though most of his energy seemed to have been channelled into a giggling fit.

"This is crazy," the kid said.

Cormac peered along the side of the Ford Transit. Cars at the head of the two farthest lanes had stopped to let the van out. A man in a Honda Accord pretended he couldn't see the oncoming maintenance vehicle and continued on his merry way. He lost his rear fender.

"We hit one!" Mattie's voice squeaked in euphoric enthusiasm.

"It's not like he couldn't have seen it coming. Some people deserve a good prang."

The van lost its momentum but managed to create an obstruction across an essential lane-and-a-half of the roundabout. He'd laid the seeds of chaos. Horns started to blare and drivers rolled down their windows to yell abuse at nobody in particular. Cormac and Mattie stood close to the van. They wouldn't be the first thing Frank saw when he eventually got close to the roundabout and from Cormac's vantage point he'd be able to get the drop on the ugly big bastard. He was back to playing the feline role in the cat and mouse game.

Cormac was pretty satisfied with his ad hoc strategy. Then he heard the first of the police sirens. Their blue flashing lights were visible on the horizon. They were barely minutes away. He couldn't wait. Made a snap decision to break cover and go at Frank from the higher ground. He could only hope that he'd created enough distractions to give him a fighting chance in a head-to-head.

But before he could tell Mattie to stay put, Big Frank's square head came into view. His movements were slow and less clumsy than usual but he walked with no regard for cover. Cormac already had a clear kill shot but he held back on it. The moron was no good to him dead. Big Frank edged closer and then Shane bumbled into the frame. From the cover of the highway maintenance van, Cormac traced their movements down the sight of his Glock, alternating his aim from one to the other. When they got to the opposite edge of the road the van blocked, their self-preservation sense should have been on full alert. But still they shambled about, determined to find their man.

Cormac put a bullet in Shane's left shoulder. The hapless thug crumpled.

Big Frank held his arms out just above waist height and moved away from his fallen partner as if he was treading thin ice. Cormac took aim, held his breath and fired. The bullet tore through Big Frank's calf muscle. He toppled like a felled tree.

Cormac stepped out from behind the van. "Toss your gun, Toner."

The automatic pistol skated along the road surface. Big Frank knew the score now.

"You *are* a cop, then." Big Frank's voice was

strained but not quite angry.

Cormac didn't confirm. He motioned for Mattie to stay behind the van and crossed the three lanes. Then he stood over Frank; aimed his Glock at the big square.

"I didn't believe it at first, but you must be," Frank said. "I'd be dead by now if you weren't."

The sirens encroached. The uniforms would be on top of them in half a minute.

"We've no time at all here, Toner. Can you walk?"

"Hobble, maybe."

"It'll have to do. Get up."

"And if I don't?"

"You can take your chances with the boys in green."

Big Frank struggled to his feet. It was like watching a mountain form. He pointed at Shane. "Are we taking him with us?"

"Will he talk?"

"Course not."

Shane had bled like a stuck pig and was close to passing out. But with the right attention he'd live. "Leave him, then. They'll take him to the hospital."

"And where are you going to take me?"

"Out of here for a start." Cormac pointed towards the silver Leon. "You'll be riding in the boot. Might be a tight squeeze but I can't trust you to play nice with the other passengers."

The cops were a stone's throw away but were impeded by the traffic chaos Cormac had created with the Highway Maintenance van and they would only meet more obstacles when they got to Broadway Roundabout. He'd get his ragtag crew to the hospital even if he had to ram his way through every car in the way.

It was just a matter of time before all the shit caught up with Cormac, though. That was the way of it. And by then, how much more would he have to answer for?

CHAPTER 14

Pop stars are always going to come off better in the red tops and the glossy housewife magazines when things turn to shit. Get yourself a nice glamour model.

Rory Cullen, *Cullen: The Autobiography*

How do you topple a mountain?

"Don't you love your family, Frank?"

Cormac studied Big Frank's craggy features. He just needed a small shift. Anything. But the square-headed goon had reverted to the old school interrogation technique. *Pick a spot on the wall and say nothing.*

"Because you're losing a lot of blood, mate. It'd be a shame for you to bleed out so close to the Royal."

Nothing but a fixed scowl.

After leaving the chaos of Broadway Roundabout, Donna had volunteered to go on to the hospital with John Gallagher. She'd explained that it'd be easier to get John seen to quietly if Cormac, Mattie and Big Frank weren't with them. That suited Cormac. He wanted some time with Big Frank, and though Mattie probably shouldn't be a witness to what Cormac planned, he didn't want to argue against Donna's logic. He was lucky enough that she'd taken on responsibility for John.

They'd found a prefab hut at a small building site on the perimeter of the hospital grounds. Cormac had used a length of sewer rod from the site to force open the rusted cage in front of the door. Two brisk kicks at the flimsy deadbolt and they were in. Cormac swept unwashed teacups and dog-eared copies of The Sun and The Daily Star off a canteen table and set up a make-shift interrogation room. Mattie kept watch through a dust-smeared window for unwanted attention and Cormac and Big Frank took their places at opposite sides of the table. Cormac's gun sat where the recording equipment should have been. Big Frank's wrists were crossed behind the back of his chair, trussed up with cable-ties. It was a human rights barrister's wet dream.

In such an unofficial and illegal situation, Cormac couldn't help but think back to the RUC days. Too many lifers he'd encountered during his career in the PSNI harked back to their Special Branch heyday with a fond twinkle in their eyes. Usually after the fourth or fifth drink at the Christmas bash. Festive nostalgia.

Whatever Frank could tell him, Cormac didn't have the time for sleep and food deprivation. And he certainly didn't have the psychotic inclinations for stress-positioning or the infamous waterboarding technique. With a damp cloth and a bucket of water he could effectively threaten to drown Big Frank in a tried and tested practice handed down from the British Army to the RUC in the late sixties. Big Frank was already cable-tied to his chair. If Mattie held the damp cloth over the captive brute's mouth and nose, Cormac could pour a steady stream of water over his face for a minute at a time. It'd soften the bastard up all right, but even thinking about it brought Cormac dangerously close to his sadistic predecessors' murky level.

Surely there's moral leeway when you know *the fucker's bad to the bone.*

"Frank. Who told you where to find me?"

Nothing.

"If you tell me, I'll let you go and have that leg seen to. But if you don't cooperate, well, I might aim for the knee next. Maybe put a couple in your thigh after that. Then your hip. It'd only take a few well-placed shots to book you a spot on a wheelchair for the rest of your life. But who am I telling, eh, Frank? A man with your experience. I heard that you were a real punishment aficionado before they kicked you out of the Provos in '88. How many teenagers did you cripple for life with your bats, hammers and guns? Do you remember how they screamed? Called for their mummies? All those joy-riders and drug dealers taught a lesson at your hands. Imagine the happiness in their hearts if they could see you trundle along the Falls Road on your own set of wheels."

Cormac stood up and placed his palms on the tabletop. Leaned forward and tilted his head back so he could look down his nose at Big Frank. Allowed his right hand to inch ever-so-obviously towards the gun.

"Come on, Frank. Save us both a bit of time. I just want to get this kid back to his mother. But I can't call in for help until I know who I can trust, or more importantly, who I can't."

Big Frank's gaze never faltered from the damp-stained wall.

Cormac thought about bartering for the info. He could have offered Big Frank an opportunity to disappear if he agreed to play ball. Told him he could go and take his family on the run, with a guarantee that he wouldn't be pursued. But Cormac didn't want to throw that down too soon. Big Frank might perceive it as a position of weakness on Cormac's part.

"Shoot him, Cormac."

Mattie's voice was low, not much more than a whisper, but it cut through the hanging silence like a chainsaw. The kid wanted nothing but pain for this man who had kidnapped and humiliated him. And Cormac couldn't blame him. But he had to play this clever. Shooting Big Frank while he was armed was one thing, and totally justified in Cormac's mind, but to start pumping lead into him to extract information... It was another line in the sand. Cormac already had blood on his hands. Fat Paddy and aul' Paul, both dead. Sporty Shane injured. And he'd answer for each one of them at some point, with a hand on his heart that none of the three incidents could have been avoided. But there was no way to justify emptying a clip into a man tied to a chair; neither to his seniors nor himself. There'd always be payback in those small hours when the sins of his past visited his half-sleep dreams.

"Go on, Cormac. Shoot him."

Cormac reached for the gun. Hefted its serious weight. Big Frank broke off from his staring match with the wall to glance at the Glock. Mattie's heartfelt urgings for blood had brought with them a new atmosphere in the prefab hut. Cormac drew out the theatre of the moment. Snapped back the slide to chamber a round.

Then Mattie kicked off.

The kid darted from his post at the window and scooped one of the dirty mugs from the floor with his good hand. Before Cormac could react, Mattie smashed the mug into Big Frank's cheekbone. The mug shattered and rained bloody fragments onto the floor. Big Frank growled and bucked in his seat. Mattie dropped the mug handle and curled his fist. He walloped Big

Frank's forehead with a hammer-blow. Cormac put his gun back on the table and went to Mattie. He wrapped his arms around the kid's waist before he could swing another punch. Hauled him backwards. Mattie's feet kicked out with the indignant strength of a beaten mule. He connected with Big Frank's chest and toppled him over. Cormac was driven backwards by the recoil force. He dropped Mattie in his struggle to maintain balance. The kid darted back towards his target.

"Mattie, stop!"

Mattie leapt into the air and landed both Converse-clad feet on the side of Big Frank's head. A sharp crack echoed. Mattie fell backwards. Cormac held his breath. The kid had broken the fucker's neck. Jesus Christ.

Then Big Frank groaned and rolled onto his back. It wasn't his neck that had snapped. The wooden chair he'd been tied to had given way in the ruckus.

Mattie pushed himself up off his backside and onto his feet. He was about to go for another double stomp. Cormac grabbed the kid again. He bucked like a live wire as Cormac hauled him backwards.

"Fuck's sake, Mattie. You're going to kill him."

"You think I don't want to?"

"Not if you want to find out where your mother is. Think straight, kid."

Mattie's taut frame softened a little. Cormac loosened his grip and lowered the bloodthirsty thirteen-year-old to his feet. Stood on full alert for a few seconds in case the kid attempted a second volley. Big Frank coughed and moaned.

"You all right, Frank?" Cormac asked.

He snuffled and spat. "Fuck yourself."

At least he was talking. Maybe Mattie had done

some good. Cormac retrieved his gun from the table and edged towards the beaten lump. He was conscious that Big Frank had a greater range of movement now that the chair he'd been tied to was in bits. Knowing the bastard's form, an attack wasn't just likely, it was imminent.

"Sorry about that, Frank. Teenagers today, eh? They're bloody ruthless."

"I'll kill you both."

Big Frank spat again and from his new vantage point, Cormac could see that there was a lot of blood in his gob. Wee Mattie had done some job on him.

"Look, mate. I'm sure you're in a lot of discomfort now, so I understand you getting a bit cranky. I think you could cut the kid a bit of slack, though. You did take him hostage, like. And his da took a bullet over the whole mess."

Big Frank choked up a guttural sound that might have been a chuckle. "Game wee fucker, isn't he? Punch like that, you can tell he's half Irish."

Is this progress?

"Come on, Frank. Tell us who gave me up. It's gone beyond a choice now. You're in bad shape."

Big Frank closed his eyes and nodded. Cormac allowed his shoulders to sag. The finish line was in sight. Get rid of Big Frank, contact the mother, hole up somewhere and sleep.

Big Frank's body jerked like a sidewinder snake. Cormac skipped backwards a second too late. Big Frank rolled into his shins and rocked his balance. He felt the pull of gravity but rather than resist, he tried to use it to his advantage. Cormac bent one leg and dropped his knee into Big Frank's ribcage. The pressure of the blow pounded through flesh and muscle. A whistling whine blasted through clenched teeth. Ribs cracked. Cormac tucked his head in, led with his uninjured shoulder blade and tumbled off the big lump. He rocked forward onto one knee and twisted to point his gun at Big Frank.

It had been a last ditch effort. As much about satisfying pride than entertaining any sort of hope of escape. Wincing shallow breaths, Big Frank was spent.

"You're a stupid bastard, Frank."

"Nearly got you, Kelly."

In your fucking dreams, mate. "Aye. Close one. Can we get on with this now?"

"What's in it for me?"

"For a start, I'll not give the kid five minutes alone with you. God knows what I'd come back to."

Mattie folded his arms and looked away from Cormac's conspiratorial wink.

"Give me something real, Kelly. This fuck up of a job has cost me any chance of earning in the future. And I'll probably end up dead. I need to look after my own."

"All I can offer you is a head start. Cooperate now and I'll not put forward any information about where I last saw you or what shape you're in. You'll have time to get patched up under a false name and go to wherever your family is."

"You'll not put forward information to who? Your colleagues at the station?"

Cormac tucked his gun into the shoulder holster. "Ambrose O'Neill. No doubt I'll see him before you do. And that's who you'll need protection from the most."

Big Frank used a section of the broken chair to help himself stand. He wobbled on his feet like a mutant toddler. "Fuck it, then. I'm tired. Let's get this over with."

###

Lydia had a glass of water in one hand, a packet of aspirin in the other and a tonne of guilt tied to her heart. She took the stairs one by one, edging slowly to Rory's bedroom like a child dragging their feet on the way to the principal's office. It'd been fifteen minutes since she tased him and although his sporadic jolts and jerks seemed to have subsided, he still hadn't said a word to her. She hoped the water and painkillers would make a decent icebreaker, though she'd little idea if they'd make him feel any better. What did you give a man you'd just electrocuted? It was hardly a Hallmark moment.

She stepped into the room and Rory was on his feet. He sneered at her. Lydia held out her offerings. His hand whipped out and lashed the water out of her hand. It tumbled in the air and sprayed its contents like sparks from a Catherine wheel. The empty glass landed on the carpet with a thud. It lay on its side and the remaining contents sloshed out.

"Jesus, Rory."

She bent to retrieve the glass.

"Leave it."

Rory was puffed up, his stance riddled with trademark aggression that he usually reserved for the pitch. Lydia was acutely aware of his speed and strength. And killer instinct? He'd been blooded at Chelsea FC for Christ's sake. In a heartbeat he could go through her like a diamond-tipped drill bit.

"You knew they were coming."

"Rory, I—"

"That's the only reason you decided to go to the shop, right? To let them in. You were making a fucking mug out of me."

"You've no idea what's happening here, Rory."

"Why don't you explain it to me, then? Explain why my agent, a woman who makes a tidy sum from protecting my interests, knew that my house was about to be robbed. And while you're at it, explain why she thought it would be better to get me out of the way rather than warn me or call the cops."

"I can't."

"You fucking can and you fucking will, do you hear me?"

Lydia flinched as the tail end of Rory's sentence jumped to an ear-splitting volume. He moved towards her and she backed out of the room. Her stomach cramped and she bent slightly at the waist. She raised her hands to protect her head from a possible assault. A tear rolled off the end of her nose.

"Please, Rory..."

"This another act, Lydia? I'd no idea you'd such a talent for it. You must have missed your calling."

A few more retreating steps and she stood next to the bathroom. She sidestepped through the door and attempted to swing it shut. Rory darted forward and she was jarred backwards by his force. The bathroom door clattered into the wall and cracked a tile. Then he clamped his hands around her upper arms and drove her backwards. The backs of her legs connected with the toilet and she was forced to sit. She'd the presence of mind to be thankful of the closed toilet lid. Rory towered over her, his crotch much too close to her face.

"Talk."

"You don't know what you're asking me to do, Rory."

"Talk!"

She was cornered. Pinned down. Beaten. She

opened her mouth and the whole story tumbled out. From arriving back to the holiday home to find her family had been kidnapped to the demands of the kidnappers and the real reason for their sudden jaunt back to London. She told him that the gang didn't just want some money. They wanted everything. His cars, his house, his financial information. They wanted to own him.

Rory placed a hand on her shoulder. She allowed herself an instant of hope. He understood her position. How could she not screw him over for the sake of her family? And sure it was only money. She could make more for him.

Then Rory tightened the grip on her shoulder. His face, already reddened slightly by the drinks he'd consumed throughout the day, turned crimson. He bared his teeth.

"You fucking bi—"

She whipped her head to the left and sank her teeth into his wrist. Rory yowled and let go. Lydia pushed past him, ran for the bathroom door. She felt his fingers scrabble for purchase on her suit jacket but he couldn't catch hold.

"Get back here, you bitch."

The world narrowed. Lydia concentrated on making it to the bottom of the stairs. She made it. One step, four steps, stumble, slip, run. The hall floor. She was at the front door. The night air kissed her cheeks. Encouraged her to keep running. She could leave. Escape.

No.

A hand closed over her face. Rory had her. He dragged her backwards, back into the hallway, and then she was on her back. Lydia bucked on the floor, dug her heels into the carpet for purchase. Pushed. Went nowhere. Rory pinned her down, one hand pressed down just above her breasts. His other hand wrapped itself around her throat.

Oh, no, oh, no, oh, no.

It was over. He was going to kill her. Over money. Something so stupid and meaningless and yet the most important thing for this man at that moment. Worth killing over. And this was how it would end for her.

Blood rushed in her ears and she could just about make out the panicked animal noises she made as she tried to draw in air. The edges of her vision darkened.

Rory, stop.

And then he did.

Lydia sucked in a lungful of sweet, sweet air. Her exhalation a howl. He'd come to his senses. Thank God. Rory had realised he'd been swept up in madness. Jesus. Lydia blinked away her tears and tried to focus on her client. Would this make them even? Could she trust him now that he'd toed such an insane line? Where could they go from this point? Surely this wasn't the kind of thing they could joke about in a few weeks.

Her vision sharpened and she realised there was a man standing behind Rory. He loomed over the kneeling football superstar. A little man with grey hair dressed in a naff tracksuit. He held a gun to the back of Rory's head.

"Mrs Gallagher?"

Lydia was struck by his accent, old school BBC. "Yes?"

"Mr McGoldrick sent me. And it looks like you owe him a thank you card for it. The name's Stephen Black, by the way. Very pleased to meet you both."

CHAPTER 15

I score goals and I love women and drink. So, yeah, I guess I am like George Best. But I plan to take care of myself and make the most of this life. I'm too blessed to piss it all away.

Rory Cullen, *Cullen: The Autobiography*

Cormac drove onto the miniature roundabout at the City Cemetery gates on the Falls Road. The solid white circle painted on the tarmac reflected the orange haze from the streetlights dotted along the road. Since it was quite a few hours after rush hour, Cormac didn't have to contend with the kamikaze manoeuvres of black taxis piloted by ill-tempered drivers. He came off the round-about onto the Whiterock Road and pushed Donna's motor just a little over the speed limit. Mattie sat in the passenger seat and fiddled with the radio dials. The boy couldn't find a station to settle on and the constant hopping set Cormac's nerves on edge. But he held back on giving the boy grief about it. They were minutes from their destination.

"Wow, the radio over here sucks. It's all talk and country music. Where's the good stuff?"

"Check the glove-box. Might be some CDs in there."

They ignored the occasional thump and yell from the boot of the car. Cormac had delayed his promise to Big Frank. He couldn't really let the psycho gorilla go to the hospital while Donna and John were there. Not unless he could provide some extra protection for them.

Cormac turned off the Whiterock Road into the Ballymurphy estate. He hit the speed bump at the entrance too hard and cursed under his breath as he braked. Mattie was bucked in his seat and dropped a Faithless CD he was trying to slip into the car radio. The shouting from the boot increased. He'd have to keep that idiot quiet.

"It's gone under the seat," Mattie said. "I can't reach it."

"Don't worry about it. We're here now."

Cormac drove past a couple of terraced blocks and turned left. Mattie shifted on his seat to get a better look at the faded Republican mural on the corner of a house on their right. Cormac stifled a sigh and eased the Leon up a slight incline. He mounted the curb outside a semi-detached house on their right and yanked up the handbrake.

"I won't be long," Cormac said.

"Can't I go in with you?"

"No. I've a feeling this guy's going to be prickly enough. Don't worry. You'll be safe here. Just don't open the door to any smartarse kids, all right? Friend of mine lost his car once when a wee hood told him he'd a flat tyre. He got out of his car to check it and the kid jumped in. *Vroom*. Eat my dust, and all that shite."

Mattie snorted. "That's a pretty good one, though."

"Yeah, they're dead innovative, aren't they?" He patted Mattie's shoulder awkwardly. "I won't be long. Just sit tight."

Cormac found a chamois leather cloth in the door compartment, got out of the car and went to the boot.

He yanked it open and cracked Big Frank a good one on the jaw. It didn't knock him out but the square-headed thug was dazed enough to allow Cormac to stuff the chamois into his mouth. He slammed the lid closed and thumbed the key fob. The car flashed hazard lights and the locks slid into place with a clunk. Cormac took a deep breath before he dragged his feet up the short garden path to the front door of the semi.

The doorbell's chime started out strong then became a distorted stutter on the second push. Cormac took a step backwards and waited. He cleared his throat so his initial greeting wouldn't squeak. *This is a mistake*, he thought.

Declan Canavan's bulldog features filled the little square of glass set high in the PVC door. He screwed up his face as if a swarm of wasps had flown up his trouser leg. Deadbolts and Chubb locks disengaged. The door opened and Canavan beckoned Cormac in with a curling finger.

"Hurry up, you fucking imbecile," Canavan said. "Before someone sees you."

Cormac stepped out of the cool night air into the stuffy confines of Canavan's lamp-lit hallway.

"Close the door behind you, Kelly."

Cormac's eyes traced the bulky mix of muscle and fat that jostled together under the back of Canavan's T-shirt with each heavy step. He followed the squat brute into his kitchen at the back of his house. A laptop whirred on the table top. Canavan sat in front of it and closed the lid. He directed Cormac to the seat opposite. Cormac stood behind the chair and laid his hands on the backrest. He didn't intend to stay long.

"How goes the cause, Canavan?"

"Don't be cute, son. What do you want?"

"A favour."

"You haven't returned my last one. And if the reports I'm hearing are right, that particular act of generosity might bite me in the hole yet."

Cormac leant forward, pressed down on the back of the chair. "You've heard something, then?"

Canavan shook his head. Heavy jowls shifted into a canine grin. "What are you like, Kelly? If you ever come into money, that's the time to share the wealth. Keep all this trouble to yourself."

"I need your help."

"And I need peace to do my own job."

Cormac looked over Canavan's head. A picture of the island of Ireland in a cheap frame hung on the wall behind him. A banner in green font circled the map. It said "In Defence of the Nation". Below it the number "32" stood out in black. It was a reference to the thirty-two counties of Ireland. North and South united. Dissident Republican shite.

"Have you or any of your *boys* heard from Ambrose O'Neill in the last few hours?"

"I've heard nothing. If the boys have, it hasn't got back to me yet."

"Can you find out?"

"No."

Cormac blinked. "Why not?"

"There are more important things at stake here. If you've fucked up your assignment, I'm very sorry about that, but it's not my problem. You've gotten as much help as you're going to get from me. I got you into the gang, for fuck's sake, and God knows what I have to deal with now that O'Neill has obviously gone against me to toss you to the side. I'm washing my hands of you."

"Stop acting like getting me into the crew was a personal favour. You were ordered to help me out."

Canavan drummed his fingers on the lid of his laptop. "Right, well, I'll await further orders from on high. Fair enough? Until then, get the fuck out of my house."

"I think there's a leak at HQ."

"We're done here, Kelly."

Cormac felt the weight of the Glock against his ribs. His hand twitched but he restrained it from reaching into his pea coat. Instead, he snagged his wallet out of his back pocket and drew a receipt from one of the slots. He took a pen from Canavan's table and scribbled down the number of the phone he'd taken off Sporty Shane.

"It's in your interests as much as it is mine if there's something rotten going on. Look into it and let me know what you find out."

"You're giving me orders now? I've got ten years on you, pup."

Cormac wanted to spit into Canavan's big jowly face. But he swallowed back a sour mouthful of saliva and asked for his next favour.

"I need ammo. Maybe a better gun." He took the Glock from his pocket and set it down on the tabletop. "I've no idea how reliable this one will be. The crew's hardware was a little on the shitty side."

"Aye, guns are a wee bit rarer round these parts since decommissioning." Canavan reached for the Glock and examined it in the low wattage light. "Bit of a fixer-upper all right." He pointed the gun at Cormac. "But I'm sure it still works."

Cormac stared into the muzzle. He was unfazed by Canavan's antics. The guy had always been a bit of a prick.

"Can you help me or not?"

Canavan set the gun down.

"You're a pain in the hole, Kelly. But I'll help you one last time. After this, we're quits, right? Don't even ask me for a stick of chewing gum."

"Just get me a decent shooter, mate."

###

Lydia coughed then said, "Who are you?" Her throat was raw and her speech husky.

"Stephen Black."

"Yes, you told me your name, but who are you? Are you a policeman?"

"Oh, dear lady, no. A common police officer? God forbid. I'm a security consultant, currently in Mr McGoldrick's employ."

Lydia eyed the pistol still aimed at Rory's head. Its barrel elongated. Lydia's movie-gleaned knowledge of guns recognised it as a silencer.

"Do security consultants usually carry guns?"

"The expensive ones do." He closed over the front door. "Now, what are we to do with Mr Cullen?"

Rory's hands were latticed on top of his head. He looked over his shoulder, through the triangle created by his crooked arm. "Stop pointing that gun at me for a start."

"Can we trust you to behave yourself?"

"Yes."

"Good." Stephen Black tucked the gun into a shoulder holster and zipped his tracksuit top over it. "It'd be a shame to shoot such a valuable man."

Lydia got to her feet, slow and steady. She used

the wall for support until she could trust her balance. Rory would have killed her. The thought of it didn't seem to connect with reality. A man she'd spent so much time with. He'd sat in her office, travelled with her, had dinner with her family for Christ's sake. And all that time he had the potential to strangle her to death. Lydia tried to push the thought away. She didn't know what else to do with it.

For his part, Rory merely looked confused. He was stood upright, one hand hung awkwardly by his side, the other twitched at the hem of his un-tucked shirt. The anger had washed away from his face and he was wide-eyed. It wasn't fear of being shot by Stephen Black, as far as she could tell, but a kind of childish wonder. She could almost hear the "what if" questions going off in his mind.

"I… I'm sorry, Lydia."

Lydia rubbed her neck and shook her head. She wasn't ready to talk to him yet.

"Right!" Stephen Black's voice was bright and breezy. "Shall we get you two to Mr McGoldrick's office, then? He's very keen to talk to you."

"What about?" Lydia asked.

"I suppose you'd be best to ask him. At this moment in time, I'm merely your driver." He jangled a set of car keys. There was a Vauxhall keyring attached. "I'm parked out front. Cullen, you'll be in the passenger seat. I think Mrs Gallagher needs a little time to herself. Rest her throat and such."

Rory didn't move.

"Chop-chop, Mr Cullen. And don't forget to lock up. There are some dodgy characters in this world. Even in a street as upmarket as this one."

CHAPTER 16

Okay, some of us do think we're above the law. But it's not often we push it too far. I mean, short of shooting an intern with a pellet gun, most of what we get away with isn't that serious. We're just a bunch of lads messing around. There's no harm in that, for the most part.

Rory Cullen, *Cullen: The Autobiography*

Mattie pumped up the stereo and nodded to the beat. He'd retrieved the Faithless CD from under the seat. The music was too loud, the high-end snare piercing Cormac's eardrums while the bass thrummed deep in his chest. He looked sideways at Mattie, intended to ask him to turn the noise down to a bearable level but the words stuck in his throat. The kid looked almost happy. Cormac was reluctant to snatch that little bit of escape from him. Surely he could bear the relentless drum and bass for a few tracks.

Mattie laid his forearm across his eyes. Now the kid was crying. Cormac averted his gaze. Mattie turned down the music and tapped Cormac's upper arm.

"Can you pull over for a second?"

Cormac mounted the kerb just before the exit from the Ballymurphy estate. Mattie opened the passenger door and puked. He coughed and spat a mix of mucus, saliva and bile onto the footpath. Cormac reached out to rub the kid's back then withdrew his hand. He felt awkward and useless. Leagues out of his depth.

Then Mattie straightened up in his seat. He flexed his damaged left hand slightly and hissed. Like he was trying to blame his broken fingers for the vomit and tears. Without a word, Cormac started the car. Maxi Jazz's smoke-ravaged vocals assaulted them until Mattie reached out and reduced the volume to a background rumble. Cormac pulled out onto the Whiterock Road.

"I'm sorry," Mattie said.

"You've nothing to be sorry about."

"Yeah, right."

Cormac shifted gears. Wracked his brains for wise or comforting sounds. He had nothing.

"It's the pain," Mattie said.

"Are Donna's pills not doing anything for you?"

"I'm not talking about my hand."

"Oh. Right."

"It's like I need to punch something but I can't." Mattie fidgeted like a speed freak as he tried to explain. "Something's eating me up inside. I don't know how to stop it. There'll be nothing left of me if I don't stop it but I don't know how."

Cormac's grip tightened on the wheel. Mattie had no idea what was happening to his mother and his gut-shot father had been dumped in a hospital in a city he didn't know. The stress was getting to the poor kid.

"We've done it, though. We just have to get you back to your ma, Mattie. You'll be back in London in no time and this'll all be a shitty memory."

"My dad could die, couldn't he?"

Cormac shook his head. "He's a strong guy, mate.

And the wound's definitely not fatal. The worst can happen to him at this stage is a nasty infection and that's the truth. He'll pull through."

"Cormac?" The name didn't roll naturally from Mattie's English tongue.

"Mattie."

"My dad wasn't much use, was he?"

Cormac hesitated. Weighed his options and decided to be as straight as he could with the kid. "You're being a little hard on him. There wasn't much he could have done."

"He could have gotten us out of there. Why didn't he put up more of a fight? He always tells me I need to be tough. But when it came to it, he couldn't stand up to those bastards."

"Just try not to think about it for now," Cormac said.

"Wow, great idea. Why didn't I think of that?" Mattie opened and slammed shut the glove box. "Easy-fucking-peasy, right?"

Cormac bit back a reprimand about respecting other people's cars. He probably owed him a free pass. Accident or not, he *had* shot the kid's father.

In happier times, Donna used to tease Cormac about his apparent inability to feel the softer emotions. And like most teases, even from those who care the most, there was more than a grain of truth in it. Cormac sometimes worried that his capacity for empathy was subpar to that of his modern, sensitive contemporaries. That he was some sort of anachronism born into the wrong decade. He didn't cry at funerals – not even his father's. Babies held little fascination for him. And he'd never fully opened up to a companion. Donna had gotten closer to him than anybody else, but there'd always been a blank wall between them. Something that made it impossible for them to truly connect. And although he was incapable of it, he sensed that Mattie needed an emotional connection with somebody. Somebody he wasn't embarrassed to cry in front of. Somebody he didn't feel the need to act tough for. Somebody other than Cormac.

He owned up. "I really don't know how to make you feel better, Mattie."

"I don't want to feel better." Mattie snuffled. "Just leave me alone."

Cormac noticed a small cluster of shops on the road. One of them was still open, the vulgar glow from its fluorescent sign intruding on the darkening atmosphere. An off licence. He double parked on the road and waved a visibly disgruntled taxi driver past him.

"Mattie, forget I'm a cop for a minute."

"Okay..."

"Have you started drinking yet?"

"I'm thirteen."

"Never?"

Mattie shook his head.

"Right, I reckon this is a good time to start."

Cormac unfastened his seatbelt and reached for the door handle.

"Wait," Mattie said. "I'll be okay. I'm sorry."

"I'll concentrate better if you can settle down a bit. You've been through a lot. Consider this medicine. Let me worry about getting you home."

Cormac took Mattie's silence and confused expression as consent and got out of the car. He felt like he'd solved a problem. Applied a temporary fix at least. And for the most part he was able to ignore the disapproving little voice at the back of his head. The one that sounded an awful lot like Donna.

Stephen Black ushered Lydia and Rory towards the old Scot's office. Lydia sensed Rory stiffen as the older man's hand pressed against the small of his back. She was glad of his discomfort. Her shock at Rory's actions had given way to a smouldering rage on the journey to Soho. *How fucking dare he?* Stephen Black pushed the thick double-doors just below the minute brass plaque with MCGOLDRICK engraved on it. He looked Rory up and down before gesturing for him to enter. Rory scratched his thigh, posture disjointed, his ballsy suave temporarily misplaced.

Stephen Black turned to Lydia. "Normally I'm a 'ladies first' kind of chap but I think I should keep an eye on this fellow for now. Please excuse the deviation from etiquette."

Lydia followed the men. McGoldrick looked up from a newspaper. It was a Red Top and he had a highlighter pen in his hand. The little bastard still trawled for libel cases himself. Like he didn't have a room full of lawyers to do that spade-work for him.

Lydia couldn't resist a jibe. "This how you spend your Friday nights, Mr McGoldrick?"

The old Scot didn't even have the decency to act ashamed. He capped the highlighter and twiddled it between his stumpy fingers. Stephen Black moved to the corner of the office, his attention fixed on a bookcase filled with tomes that McGoldrick liked to admit he'd never read. Lydia took another look at him, this time with clearer eyes and in better light. The man's tracksuit was so wrong, like a hoodlum in a tux. Lydia could see argyle socks between the cuff of his trousers and the tops of his trainers. Whippet thin, grey-haired, Mediterranean swarthy.

"Why did you ask me here, Mr McGoldrick?" Lydia said. "Really."

"Didn't Mr Black fill you in?"

"Your security consultant? He said he'd leave it to you."

Lydia took the central visitor's seat at McGoldrick's desk and waited for the others to arrange themselves around her. Rory sat on the chair to her left and Stephen Black stood behind him, leaving the chair to the right empty. The old Scot held court.

"Let's not drag this out, Lydia. I know you're in trouble. What can I do to help you?"

"Why was your man watching me?"

Stephen Black spoke, his voice just above a whisper. "Maybe you should tell him about Mr Cullen's indiscretion first?"

McGoldrick ran his hands through his thick grey hair. It flopped back into its well-trained side parting. He leant back on his leather office throne. The recline mechanism hissed.

"What's he talking about?"

"You first."

"I was suspicious about your intentions when you came to me earlier and asked for help with Rory's sponsorship deal." He nodded towards Stephen Black. "So I had you followed."

"Your security consultant tails people?"

"He has many talents. And when it comes to money, I don't fuck around. I figured there had to be some sort of angle. But I wasn't expecting to hear what my associate reported back."

Rory leaned forward in his seat. He was sucked in by McGoldrick. Lydia couldn't blame him. Physically, McGoldrick was the smallest person in the room and yet he commanded it like a king. He continued:

"John and your kid, Mattie, got kidnapped yesterday and you found out about it that evening. You came to London this morning and visited me this afternoon. When you left here you spoke to a man at The Toucan pub. It didn't look like a social exchange."

Stephen Black clicked his fingers.

Lydia turned to look at him despite her resentment. "Don't click your fingers at me, Mr Black. I'm not a waitress."

"Terribly sorry. I simply thought it was an opportune time to interject with this." He passed her a canvas wallet fastened with zips and Velcro. Very similar to the one Mattie used for his school dinner money.

She hesitated before opening it. The edges were frayed and she could see a shiny credit card-sized outline. It unfolded into three panels, each one containing a clatter of plastic. A little see-through pocket displayed a driving licence. The photo in the corner was of the pockmarked, sunbed-tanned creep who'd delivered the message at the pub earlier. She folded the wallet back up and tossed it onto McGoldrick's desk.

"Where'd you get that?"

Stephen Black flexed his fingers. The gesture was effeminate but seemed to be without irony. "The art of pocket picking is alive and well in London. Surely you've seen the street signs?"

"You're a wee bit dodgy if you ask me, mate," Rory said. "How can we be sure you're on our team?"

"*We're* not on the same team anymore," Lydia said.

"I'm fucking sorry, all right? It's not like I was going to kill you or anything. It was just like that what-do-you-call-it... temporary insanity or something. I would have stopped before that English wanker came in and started playing the hero."

Lydia waved him away.

"Seriously, Lydia. Have you never seen Spooks on the TV? Those MI5 bastards are slippery as fuck. And he looks just like one."

"I think the kid's got your number, Black," McGoldrick said.

"Not quite bang on, but close enough for government work, as they say." Stephen Black had the wallet again. He drummed his fingers on the back of it.

Lydia tried to look unimpressed by the little party trick. He must have taken it from the desk when Rory had distracted her. Hardly an act of Derren Brown proportions but he'd done enough to convince Rory that he was some manner of spy.

He's sneaky, Lydia thought. *A bit off-kilter, too.*

McGoldrick tapped his desktop with the highlighter pen.

"I don't understand why you would care, Mr McGoldrick."

"I'm a businessman, Lydia, not a monster."

To many he fell somewhere in between businessman and monster, depending on how much money was at stake. But she'd always treated him with respect, and he returned the favour. She could do him the courtesy of hearing him out.

"Okay, Mr McGoldrick, I appreciate the offer. But what good are you to me now? They've got what they wanted so now I get my family back."

"Oh, really? Have they called you yet to tell you

where they've been keeping them?"

"It's only a matter of time…"

"Lydia, these people are criminals. They might have no intention of returning your family."

"If you really think that, then it's definitely time to call the police."

"Fucking right it's time to call the police," Rory said. "You should have called them from the start."

"Shut up, Rory," Lydia said.

"So what's it to be, Lydia?" McGoldrick asked. "Personally, I fancy Mr Black's chances. He'll get to them quicker than the police and he doesn't have to follow any of their daft rules."

"I need time…"

"Time's running out, hen. Let's go now."

"Go where?"

McGoldrick sat back. He looked to Stephen Black for an answer. The little man stroked his chin. Then Rory piped up.

"I might be able to help there."

"All suggestions are gratefully received," Stephen Black said.

"They stole my car," Rory said. "My old iPhone was in it. It's got a shitload of music on it so I left it plugged into the stereo when I got the new model last month. Couldn't be arsed transferring all the files, you know?"

"And that's relevant because…"

"Because, I've got this app, you see. A fucking GPS tracker! It's meant to help you find it if it's lost or stolen. So if we know where the phone is, we know where the pricks who stole my car are."

There was a moment of silence then McGoldrick slapped his hand off his desktop. "Let's get fucking moving, then."

CHAPTER 17

I've been dealt a fair amount of red cards. I get passionate some-times. Some people can't handle that. Pansies. Remember when real men played football? I miss that.

Rory Cullen, *Cullen: The Autobiography*

Mattie slurped on the big bottle of WKD Cormac had bought for him. The kid was as likely to get a buzz off the additives that coloured it blue and hid the taste of booze as he was off the actual alcoholic content. But it was a good distraction for him. Medicinal almost. Cormac hardly felt guilty about it at all.

"What now?" Mattie asked.

"Back to the hospital to check on Donna and your da."

"And then?"

"We phone your ma and figure out how to get you guys reunited."

Mattie regarded his bottle for a moment, shrugged and took another sip. Obviously he felt that he was unlikely to get into trouble over it.

"But what about the rest of the gang, Cormac?" The kid still wasn't getting his name right; splitting the syllables in the wrong place – *Core-mack*. "Will they get arrested?"

"Oh, yeah, wee man. Don't worry about that. We've plenty on them now. They'll all go down hard, so they will."

"Heh. 'So they will'."

Cormac realised the kid was taking the piss. He cleared his throat. "Aye... so they will."

"Sorry, couldn't resist."

Cormac thought he detected a little slur in Mattie's voice. The kid was barely a quarter into his bottle, though. He'd hardly be feeling the effects already.

"Do you think Mum is okay?"

"Aye, definitely. These guys are professional enough to know that she'd be no use to them if they hurt her. She's completely safe."

He said it without hesitation and injected plenty of confidence into his tone. Whether or not he actually believed it was irrelevant. There was nothing he could do about it if Lydia Gallagher was in trouble; it was beyond his power. But the kid just needed some assurance and that he could provide.

Mattie took another slurp of WKD.

"Maybe take it easier on that stuff," Cormac said. "Slow and steady."

"Yeah, yeah. No worries. It's not really doing anything for me anyway."

There it was again. The slightest of slurs. He'd underestimated the strength of the alcopop. Or the kid's resistance to it. It'd been some time since his own first experience with booze and back then there was no such thing as the brightly coloured kiddie drinks that had gotten popular in recent years. He'd split a bottle of white cider with a mate. Thought he was doing well until he tried his first cigarette on the same night. Emptied his stomach onto the footpath. His mate, Kevin Murtagh, had looked after him that night. Made sure he got cleaned up before he went home, filled him full of Polo mints to cover up the stink of cheap booze and tobacco. Kevin Murtagh... thinking about his child-hood chum still hurt.

Kevin had been a good friend. Fun, loyal and wild; everything you needed to enjoy your teen years. But he'd come from a republican family and it was inevitable that he would get caught up in the bullshit. He'd signed up with the Provos at a young age and Cormac had turned his back on him. Cormac's family had been devastated by "IRA activities" when his father had been killed during an attempted bus hijacking. For his best friend to align himself with the same organisation had been a slap in the face. But Cormac would always regret not showing up at Kevin's funeral to pay his respects. The young Provo had been turned by Special Branch and when he was found out for it, his "comrades" nailed him to a tree in South Armagh and emptied a Webley revolver into his face. In the following months, wracked with guilt and white hot with fury, Cormac dropped out of university and signed up to join the RUC.

Cormac tightened his grip on the steering wheel and tried to force the memories back into the little com-partment at the back of his mind. He couldn't have all those old hurts come back. There was a lot to be done and he needed to be focussed. His revenge would continue to be delivered in small doses in every case he worked. The dark idea of putting a bullet in Big Frank's head was chased away. It wouldn't bring the satisfac-tion it promised.

"You okay, Cormac? I can hear you grinding your teeth."

Cormac relaxed his jaw and forced a smile. "Yeah, no worries, kid. It's just something I do when I'm thinking too hard, you know? My wee brain gets cross with me if I push it."

"Hmmm."

"Right, there's the hospital. Let's see how your da's got on."

"We haven't pieced together all the whys and where-fores just yet. But we do have a few leads."

Stephen Black's eyes met Lydia's in the rear view mirror as he spoke. He was behind the wheel and Lydia sat in the back on the passenger side. Rory fidgeted beside Lydia, his wrists bound with cable ties until he proved he could "play nice" as Stephen Black had put it. The Premiership superstar seethed silently. McGoldrick rode up front. There was no telling how long Rory's stolen Land Rover would remain at the address they'd tracked it to through his iPhone GPS app. It could end up in a shipping container to Nigeria in a matter of hours and their trail, the only thing they could grasp at, would go cold.

And so the four of them had piled into Stephen Black's dark blue Vauxhall Vectra. The finely tuned engine purred and hauled them about the London streets with impressive bursts of raw power. And there was a greenish sheen off the windows that suggested to Lydia they might be bulletproof. She figured it had been a police vehicle at some point in its life. And now it belonged to… well, whatever this posh little guy driving it was.

"But I did a bit of digging on the nasty fellow you met at that awful Irish theme pub," Black said. "Brendan Rooney. London Irish. Known to the police as a loan shark and criminal handyman. He's served a year here and there for some minor convictions. Bottom of the food chain type of fellow, you know?"

"So how does he wind up running errands for a gang of Belfast kidnappers?" Lydia asked.

"How indeed. That's where things get rather interesting. Brendan Rooney may not have risen rapidly through the hierarchy of the London criminal fraternity, but he's connected to a man of great influence among that unsavoury lot. His cousin, Martin Rooney, is quite the shady entrepreneur by all accounts. Sex, drugs, rock and roll, money laundering. His portfolio is quite impressive."

"And the relevance of this is…?"

"Oh, don't worry Mrs Gallagher. I won't waste your time with extraneous information. You see, Martin Rooney was an IRA sympathiser in the eighties and early nineties. He donated money, housed terrorist operatives and sang rebel songs at weddings. But as the Rooney cocaine empire grew, his association with the conservative Irish Republicans diminished. They were pushing their anti-drug dogma and he was enjoying the profit too much to let his political inclinations get in the way. He kept in touch with a few soldiers from those good old days, though. I suspect that one of those long-standing contacts kidnapped your family."

"Why?"

Stephen Black shrugged. "Let's not speculate. I don't have a complete picture right now but I'm confident that we'll get to the bottom of this lickety-split, without breaking any of the kidnappers' rules concerning police involvement."

"How long before we get to Peckham?"

"Five or ten minutes."

"And what are we going to do when we get there?" Lydia asked.

"I think we should keep an open mind on that front. Best we have a good nosey at the setup and then maybe formulate a plan of action if we deem it advantageous."

Lydia twisted the cap off a bottle of sparkling water she'd taken from McGoldrick's office. The bubbles fizzled on her tongue and tickled her nose. The sensation, coupled with her stress-induced hypersensitivity, brought tears to her eyes. She wondered if this move was a risk too far. Could anything really be gained from a bit of I-Spy with these animals? It wasn't as if they were on their way to uncover the location where her family was being held captive. The exercise was essentially the lion tamer sticking his head in the lion's mouth.

"We shouldn't do this," Lydia said.

"That's just your nerves talking, Lydia," McGoldrick said. "Don't worry. Our man here is the best. He'll do his thing and be gone before these arseholes get so much as a sniff of him."

"I really am quite good," Stephen Black said.

"It's all right for you two to tell me to chill out and go with the flow. It's not your family that'll get killed if things go pear-shaped. No. Forget it. Turn back. I'll just wait for their next call, okay?"

"Lydia," Rory said. "I'll back you one hundred per cent if you really want to bail on this, but don't be too hasty. You've got the upper hand for the first time since these bastards came for your family. It could all amount to nothing, but do you really think you can sit back and let things play out, knowing you had a chance to try *something* and you chose to pass it up? You're just not built that way."

"Well said, that man."

"Shut up, Stevie, will you?"

"That *was* a great speech," Lydia said. "But again, it's easy to dish out advice when you've nothing on the line."

"Well how about this, Lydia?" McGoldrick said. "What if you do jump through every hoop? Play the good little pawn and give them every single thing they want. What then? Do they release your family, shake your hand and say thank you for all your hard work? Or do they decide to put you on to the next client? And another one after that? Where does all the shite end?"

"That won't happen. These people are after Rory for some reason. Once they've got what they want, they'll be done with me."

"They're after money, Lydia, pure and simple," McGoldrick said. "And Rory Cullen's their latest meal ticket."

McGoldrick's tone had a real edge to it and once again Lydia wondered why the old Scot wanted to get anywhere near the whole mess. It wasn't personal and it didn't really take anything out of his pocket. Rory's potential earning power wouldn't be affected if he got cleaned out. And no matter how McGoldrick played it, Lydia didn't believe he had an altruistic bone in his body. He'd an angle to work, she just hadn't figured out what it was yet.

"Look here," Stephen Black said, "we're just a stone's throw away from where our friends are holed up. Seems foolish to turn back now. I assure you, Mrs Gallagher, you have nothing to fear. I'll just perform a brief recce, report back to you and then we can decide what to do next. A little game of peek-a-boo, so to speak."

"We might not get another chance," McGoldrick said.

She could feel their anticipation. They wanted action. Craved it. It was a Venus and Mars thing. In their minds they were presented with a problem and now they had a slim chance at a solution. A terrible weariness descended on her and at that moment all she wanted to do was be still. This was a new kind of helplessness. She'd been at the mercy of the kidnappers for too long and now these men, well meaning as they might or might not be, wanted to tackle the situation. Try to fix things. She didn't have the energy to fight them any more.

The Vectra rolled into a parking space on a residential street. Stephen Black turned off the engine.

"We're here, Mrs Gallagher," Stephen Black said. "Rory's Land Rover is parked nearby, if his GPS signal is accurate. I'd wager that the quarry is in that most attractive block of flats to our right. Say the word and I'll get to work."

Lydia gave the four-storey building a once over. White PVC windows, red brick balconies, rusted satellite dishes. There had to be fifty homes crammed into it.

"The words needle and haystack come to mind," she said. "How are you meant to find them?"

"I've a hunch that the black Land Rover by those saplings is Mr Cullen's."

She spotted Rory's car among a small fleet of less conspicuous hatchbacks and saloons. It'd been parked in a space that was almost sheltered by a plot of shrubbery and three young trees. A couple of teenage boys dressed in branded sportswear eyeballed the Land Rover from the doorway of the closest ground floor flat.

"And I'd bet that those young rogues over there have been paid by somebody to see it comes to no harm." Stephen Black rubbed his hands together as if to warm them. "A higher bidder could easily extract a little inside knowledge from them."

"What do you say, Lydia?" McGoldrick asked. "You going to sign off on a little detective work here?"

She doubted they would take heed of her if she said no. It was time to relent.

"Do what you want, Mr Black. Just make sure you do it well."

CHAPTER 18

*I was surprised to see so many of my contemporaries on Twitter.
I didn't think a lot of them could read, never mind figure out how
to use a computer.*

Rory Cullen, *Cullen: The Autobiography*

Lydia watched the man tumble over the low balcony wall and plummet. It looked so slow and maddeningly preventable, like a vase toppling from a shelf. He'd crashed through the front door of the flat Stephen Black had broken into just a few seconds previously. Lydia had thought it reckless behaviour on the ex-spook's part but held her tongue. The lights had been off and Stephen Black had spoken to the dodgy-looking youths from the ground floor before venturing up to the flat they'd pointed to. She assumed that they'd told him the place was unoccupied and he'd decided to investigate. No such luck.

She felt a strange lightness in her lungs as she traced the man's descent from the top floor of the block of flats, like millions of little hands were pushing her diaphragm upwards. And she must have heard the crack of every broken bone on impact. She briefly wondered if a man could survive a four-storey drop. Then the screaming began. The faller wasn't dead but it sounded like he wanted to be.

"Oh my God," Lydia said. "Who's that?"

McGoldrick looked over his shoulder. "Don't worry. He's no friend of ours."

She wanted to vomit but her stomach was empty.

Stephen Black emerged from the flat, silenced pistol in his right hand, pointed at the starless sky. His head whipped from left to right before he stepped forward and looked over the balcony at the screeching man below. It was hard to tell for sure from their vantage point, but Lydia suspected the little mystery man was smiling. He turned and went back into the flat.

"What the fuck is the mad bastard doing?" Rory asked.

"His job," McGoldrick said. "Don't worry. He'll be fine."

"Fuck *him*," Lydia said, "what about my family?"

Rory reached out his bound hands to take hers. She flapped him away. *Fuck your consolation, Rory.*

"This is all about your family," McGoldrick said.

"You sure about that, McGoldrick?"

The old Scot didn't react to the jagged edge in Lydia's voice. His whole demeanour was boardroom cool.

"That guy's no daftie, Lydia. He'll get what he needs here then cover his tracks. We've just taken the first step towards getting your husband and son back."

She clenched her teeth against a tide of abuse. Better to store it up and allow an eruption at a more opportune moment. Most likely in a violent manifestation. The recipient was still to be determined, but at that moment, McGoldrick and Stephen Black were high up on her list. She reined in the rage like only a protective mother could. Watched the flat's door.

The man who'd fallen from the balcony had stopped screaming. It didn't bode well for him. Then it registered with Lydia that none of the residents of the block of flats had gone out to see what had happened. They'd probably written it off as a gang stabbing and didn't want to get into the middle of it.

Less than a minute later, Stephen Black sprang from the shadows with a backpack slung over one shoulder. He raced along the balcony towards the communal stairway and spiralled downwards. Then he was out in the open. He went directly to the silent man on the ground, regarded him for a heartbeat and pointed his elongated pistol at him.

The muzzle flashed. *Phut. Phut.* Stephen Black's victim jerked twice. Rory made a choked noise. A failed scream. Lydia accepted his hands when he offered them for the second time. McGoldrick seemed unfazed by the coldblooded murder.

Stephen Black got into the car and handed the backpack to McGoldrick. The swarthy little man twisted in the driver seat to look at Lydia and Rory. His eyes were bright and wide, his face radiant, his breath slightly hitched. He could have been out for a brisk walk around the park.

"I think we'll get a lot out of that little manoeuvre," Stephen Black said. "Got a bagful of goodies."

"You killed that man," Lydia said.

"It was a mercy killing. He'd have died of internal injuries sooner or later after his nasty drop."

"It's not like the guy jumped off the balcony, though," Rory said. "You must have pushed him."

"Self defence, I assure you."

"We can talk about this later," McGoldrick said. "Get us out of here."

Stephen Black gunned the engine and drove out of his kerbside parking space with all the lackadaisical calm of a Sunday driver.

"Did you kill the other one too?" Lydia asked.

"Beg your pardon?"

"I met two men in biker gear earlier and the same two men came to Rory's house to steal the safe. Was the other one in the flat?"

"He was well hidden if he was."

"So it's only a matter of time before the second guy sends word back to Belfast about this…"

No attempt at assurance was offered.

"You realise that you two are responsible for whatever harm comes to my family now, don't you?"

Rory wiggled his hand out of Lydia's tightened grip. The men in the front said nothing.

It took them fifteen minutes and three separate sets of directions to locate Donna in the hospital. The Royal was basically two buildings meshed together, one modern and one ancient, and some of the floor numbers didn't even match up. Take the stairs to the second floor in the new building and you could find yourself on the sixth when you navigated your way to the old one – without mounting a single step.

John Gallagher lay shirtless on a cot, his wound sewn up but not dressed. Yellow dye stained the area around the stitches. Donna stood by his side. She made an adjustment to John's IV drip then faced Cormac.

"How's he doing?" Cormac asked.

"Surprisingly well. The wound's clean and he's been pumped full of antibiotics and painkillers. In a few days, maybe a week, we can think about sending him to a hospital across the water, get him closer to home."

"A week? I don't think that's a good idea. O'Neill's men will be looking for us."

"What can I tell you? He needs time to recover."

"But surely he'll need to disappear before people start asking you awkward questions."

"He's had surgery, Cormac. The awkward questions have begun. No doubt the police will be along soon to find out who he is and why he's been shot."

"They've called this in?"

Donna shrugged. "I didn't ask them to, but..."

"We have to leave now."

John moaned and shifted in his cot.

Donna's brow furrowed. She spared her patient a quick glance then returned her focus to Cormac: "That's not happening."

"O'Neill has somebody feeding him information from my unit. If they're even half-awake and John's name comes up in a police report, the goon-squad will be here ahead of whatever pair of uniforms they send this way. You want to explain to them what's best for your patient?"

"Fuck's sake, Cormac."

"What can I say, Donna? We need to get moving." Cormac waved his hand at the IV and heart monitor setup. "How much of that stuff is portable?"

"We can't just wheel him out of—"

"This isn't a discussion. Gather up whatever you need. Mattie can help you carry some of it. I'll scope the way ahead. We're leaving this minute."

"In what? We can't fit all this stuff in my car."

"I'll get something sorted. Meet me at the Falls Road entrance."

"Cormac—"

He didn't have time to argue. The door swung shut behind him and cut off Donna's protests. He headed directly for the set of lifts at the end of the narrow corridor. The disinfectant smell of hospital intensified. His footsteps were impossibly loud. He tried to tread lighter without sacrificing speed.

Cormac got to the lift without incident. He mumbled prayers and threats until the door pinged open. Inside the lift he jabbed at the buttons and willed the piece-of-shit to hurry the fuck up. Every second lost lessened their chances of getting out. The lift juddered to a halt and Cormac entertained images of a dozen cops fanned out on the other side of the sliding doors, weapons drawn. The metal slabs drew back to reveal a porter with an empty trolley. Cormac nodded at the little man in the blue uniform and breezed past him. No cops at the information desk. He jogged to the automatic doors ahead of him. Cold air whooshed in from the street. He stepped outside and scanned the main road.

No cops.

He didn't like that feeling. Relief over the absence of his colleagues. It made him think that he'd crossed a line and there was little chance he could turn back.

Cormac shook his head as if to dislodge his doubts. He had to concentrate on the task at hand. They needed to transport an injured man without causing him further damage. Hijacking a car was out of the question...

An ambulance pulled up to the kerb in front of him. It seemed like a no-brainer. Cormac reached into his jacket and curled his fingers around the handle of his Glock. He stepped up to the passenger-side door and tugged it open. A pair of beefy paramedics gaped at him, too shocked by his sudden intrusion to form words.

"I hate to have to do this, lads."

Cormac pulled out his gun.

Stephen Black parked his Vauxhall Vectra under the overhang of the very strange architectural decision that was the Peckham Library. The building was shaped like a top-heavy Tetris block; a chunky L-shape turned on its head. Load-bearing beams supported the upper floors, defiant of gravity. The library was closed for the night but Lydia had to question Stephen Black's logic.

"This isn't really an inconspicuous place to park, is it?"

"There's a lot to be said for hiding in plain sight," he said. "Don't fret. We won't be here very long. Fascinating building, though, isn't it?"

"What's in the backpack?" Lydia asked.

McGoldrick unzipped it and reached inside. He pulled out a laptop and a mobile phone.

"I imagine we'll find some pertinent information on those," Stephen Black said.

McGoldrick booted up the laptop and gave it to Stephen Black. It loaded quickly and he started to flick through various programs.

"Looks like they've already emailed your information to somebody, Rory old chap."

Rory cursed. "They didn't hang around, did they?"

"No, but at least the damage can be somewhat

contained now. We'll concentrate on the more pressing matters first." He looked pointedly at Lydia. "And you can get some financially-minded people to sort out this rotten mess in the next few days."

Stephen Black went back to the keyboard.

"What are you doing now?" Lydia asked.

"Availing of the rather excellent Wi-Fi connection this area provides. It's amazing what you can find out about somebody who hasn't the wherewithal to delete their internet browser history."

"Anything useful?"

"In the right hands, this could provide an entire legal case. In the short term..." Stephen Black rattled out another burst on the keyboard. "Does the name Ambrose O'Neill mean anything to either of you?"

It didn't.

"Well judging by the email activity here he's quite central to all of this. I'll run his name by some contacts and see how he might be linked to our cocaine king, Martin Rooney."

"How long will that take?" Lydia asked.

"More than a few minutes, less than a few hours I would imagine. I'll make the call in a moment. Could you hand me that mobile phone, please?"

McGoldrick passed him the handset.

Stephen Black thumbed a few buttons and clacked his tongue off the roof of his mouth. "No numbers in the contact list. Just a few in the recent call log." He handed the phone to Lydia. "Any of these yours?"

"Yeah, the top one." She noted the time of the call and handed the phone back to him. "They used this to call me before they raided Rory's house."

"I'll arrange a trace on the other numbers in the log. Maybe we'll be fortunate and one of them will lead us to your family."

"You can do that?" Rory asked.

"Quite easily, yes."

This is all a little too good to be true, Lydia thought.

"Now, if you'll excuse me, time is of the essence." Stephen Black opened his door and moved to leave the car.

"Why can't you make the call here?" Lydia asked.

"In my line of work discretion is paramount. It's best if I conduct certain things out of earshot." He waggled his fingers in a limp-wristed wave and got out of the car. Then he marched swiftly to a curved bench beyond the shadow of the library's overhang.

Rory loosed a blast of air through pursed lips. "He's good isn't he?"

"The best," McGoldrick said.

Lydia watched him through her window. He gesticulated with his left hand as he spoke on his own phone, the other handset balanced on a thin thigh. "I don't like him."

"That's all right," McGoldrick said. "He'll help you anyway."

"Why?"

"Because I'm paying him to."

"And again, I have to ask, why would *you* do that for *me*?"

"I just want to help you get your family back, Lydia. Is that so hard to believe?"

Lydia left the question unanswered. Whether or not McGoldrick's motives were true, at that moment trusting him was her only option.

Chapter 19

I suppose talent has a lot to do with success. But you can't rely solely on it. I find the more I practice, the harder I train, the more talented I get.

Rory Cullen, *Cullen: The Autobiography*

Declan Canavan's face filled up the little square window set in his front door. Cormac gave it a second for the disgust to register on the fat man's face then he tapped the glass with the muzzle of his Glock. The door opened and Canavan dragged Cormac into the hallway, his meaty hands clamped on Cormac's shoulders. Cormac pressed his gun into one of Canavan's jowls.

"I don't have time to fuck around, Canavan. Let go of me."

"Get that gun out of my face before I shove it up your hole."

Cormac twisted in Canavan's grip then laid his free hand on the big bulldog's sternum and shoved. Canavan stumbled back a few steps. Cormac pointed his gun to the floor as a show of good faith.

"I need your help."

"Fuck off, Kelly. You've already worn out your

welcome here."

"I'm not asking. You're going to help me whether you like it or not."

"No, I'm going to turn you in. You think I haven't heard about your capers? Best thing you can do is head straight to the station and give yourself up."

"I'd be more worried if you'd thought to answer the door with a gun in your hand. I've got the drop on you without even trying."

"And what if one of the boys shows up here? That's you fucked."

"You better hope that doesn't happen. I'm willing to take you down with me."

Canavan pointed a thick finger at Cormac. "That's me and you done, dickhead. You've run out of credit with me."

"Shut the fuck up and listen to me."

Cormac spoke fast. He told Canavan that John Gallagher was in the back of an ambulance parked a few streets away. Cormac had driven him to the closest place to the hospital that he could think of. It wasn't ideal but he knew that Canavan wouldn't turn them away. They needed a place to lie low until Cormac could get in touch with Lydia and figure out what to do next.

"Are you stupid?" Canavan shook his big head in exasperation. "I recommended you to O'Neill. This is the first place he'll check when he comes looking for you."

"He's not going to start a war with you."

"Don't be so fucking sure. The man's a headcase."

"The clock's ticking. What's the best way to do this?"

"Well, not by driving a big fucking ambulance up to my door, that's for sure." Canavan rubbed at his chin; jiggled his jowls. "We'll go get them in my jeep and park up in the alley out back. There's no real lighting there so we'll get them into the house without drawing too much attention."

"That's the spirit, big man." Cormac tucked the Glock away. "C'mon."

The Lady Gaga ringtone shrieked for attention. Lydia wanted to throw her phone out the car window. Private number. It couldn't be good news.

"Answer the damn thing," McGoldrick said.

She thumbed the green button, held the mobile to her ear and closed her eyes.

"Hello?"

"I don't know how you did it, but you shouldn't have."

The Belfast twang of the man she'd first encountered on the doorstep of a hired cottage on the outskirts of Belfast. His voice seemed thicker, maybe with emotion. She knew the voice, though his ski mask was the only visual memory she had of him. But maybe she'd learned one more thing about him.

"Ambrose O'Neill?"

A pause. "You've just murdered your family, bitch."

The line went dead.

Lydia felt cold. She'd murdered her family. No. That wasn't real. It was the bluster of a scared bully. The silence in the car oppressed. It was as if Rory and McGoldrick had stopped breathing lest they upset her. She looked out her window at Stephen Black who seemed to be finished with his phone call but was taking a private moment on the bench.

Quiet time's up. She opened her door and sprang out of the car.

Stephen Black turned at the sound of her heels on the paving slabs. He gave her a half-smile.

"Just waiting on a call," he said when she was in reasonable earshot.

"Give me the other phone."

He tilted his head slightly then plucked the dead man's mobile from its resting place on his thin thigh. Lydia snatched it out of his hand. He had the good sense not to complain about her manners. She scrolled through the menu options to find a list of recent calls. Selected the second number on the list. It was picked up on the second ring.

"Who's this?"

The same Belfast twang. Ambrose O'Neill. A name to pin on her horror. "Lydia Gallagher."

"Don't waste your breath begging. My people will track your husband and kid down again within the hour. And when I get back to Belfast I'll take my time killing them."

A raging burst of dizziness mushroomed in Lydia's head. *Track them down again?*

"You don't have my family…"

"Like I said, Lydia Gallagher, it won't take long to get them back. Belfast's a small city and we know all the hiding places."

Lydia was reeling in her mind but her deal-making instinct to remain cool kicked in. *Keep him talking until you figure this out.* She went Belfast. "Me and *my* people will track *you* down first, dickhead."

"I underestimated you once, love. I won't make the same mistake twice."

He hung up on her again. She almost smiled.

Stephen Black watched her, his expression catlike in bemusement. "A new development?"

"They don't have my family."

"Did they escape or were they rescued?"

"I'm not sure. If the police had them, they'd have been in touch, surely."

"One would imagine."

She clicked her fingers. "They must have escaped on their own." Pride blossomed in her chest. *How did you manage that, John?*

"I should phone my husband." Lydia reached into her handbag for her phone then paused. "No. Wait. They might be hiding somewhere. What if his ringtone gives them away?"

"Good thinking," Stephen Black said. "I'm sure they'll contact you when they can."

She giggled then stopped herself. "Oh, God. It's not over yet, though. Those bastards are looking for them. What'll I do now?"

"Go back to Belfast. Find them first."

She was overwhelmed by obstacles. "By the time I get to the airport and book a plane... and which one should I go to? Would a ferry be faster? No, of course not. A plane... from Heathrow, maybe."

"Need I remind you that there's a ridiculously wealthy man sat in the passenger seat of my car?"

Lydia sprinted back to the Vauxhall Vectra. She yanked open the driver's door.

"Your helicopter," she said to McGoldrick. "How fast can it get me to Belfast?"

CHAPTER 20

I should probably play for the Northern Ireland international team. It'd be a gesture, you know? Like religion doesn't matter any more. This is a squad Catholics and Protestants can support side by side. The problem is, I like winning.

Rory Cullen, *Cullen: The Autobiography*

They laid John Gallagher on Canavan's bed. Donna busied herself with the IV she'd taken from the hospital. Then she examined his wound. John was barely conscious but seemed almost comfortable. Donna checked the time and opened up the brown leather case she'd filled with supplies. She selected a tub of pills and set one on John's tongue, raised a glass of water to his lips. Cormac, Mattie and Canavan stood at the bedroom door, spectators to a live hospital drama.

Since they'd gotten to Canavan's place Cormac had begun to feel edgy. He didn't want to stand still for too long but all of the moving about wasn't good for John. He didn't need Donna to tell him that, though no doubt she'd remind him of it soon enough. But they couldn't stop at Canavan's forever either. Even if O'Neill was busy across the water, as Cormac's handler had claimed, there had to be men scouring Belfast for them. Cormac had raised too much hell to slip through the cracks. And then there was Canavan's ever-diminishing patience.

"He's bleeding on my sheets."

"Ask him to stop," Cormac said.

Donna threw a withering glance their way.

Mattie tugged on Cormac's sleeve. "I think we should call my mum now."

Cormac nodded. "Lend us your phone?"

Canavan huffed air but lumbered off to fetch his handset.

"You know your ma's number, kid?"

Mattie's eyes widened. He shook his head.

John mumbled something. Cormac moved closer to the bed, asked him to repeat himself.

"There's a business card in my wallet." John croaked the words. "Back pocket."

Cormac looked to Donna for permission.

She nodded slowly. "Just be gentle with him."

Cormac slid his hand underneath John without jolting him and drew out the wallet. He flipped it open and went through the cards. John didn't clean his wallet out very often and it took half a minute to find the faded business card.

"Pass me a phone, please."

He said it to nobody in particular but Donna was the first one to hand him a mobile. Cormac tapped in the number and handed it to Mattie.

"Don't spend too long chatting, mate. I need to get stuff sorted out with her."

Mattie held the phone to his ear and paced the patch of carpet at the foot of the bed. One of the floorboards creaked with metronomic regularity.

"Mum?"

Mattie squished up one side of his face and held the handset a few inches from his head. Cormac could hear the excited shriek of Lydia Gallagher's voice. It tapered off after a few seconds and Mattie got his chance to speak.

"We're in a safe place now but dad's pretty hurt... Yeah, I'm fine." He looked at his taped-up fingers and shrugged, decided not to worry his mother with the horror tale. "We'll see you soon. There's a policeman here who wants to talk to you, sort out how we're going to get home. Chat later, yeah?"

Cormac took the phone from the kid. His mother was still gabbling and Cormac had to interrupt her.

"Missus Gallagher, my name is Detective Cormac Kelly. It's good to get in touch with you at last."

She sniffed back a sob. "Whatever you've done to save my family, thank you."

"We need to figure out how to get you guys back together now. Are you still in London?"

"Yes, I'm about to fly back to Belfast, though. I can be there in a few hours."

"I think we'd be better off getting your family back to England." He didn't want to go into his concerns about PSNI involvement in the kidnapping unless she needed further convincing. "I'm happy to accompany them, though it'll probably take more than a few hours to figure out the safest route."

"I might be able to help you with that."

Lydia scanned the night sky for McGoldrick's helicopter. It'd taken them a few hours to organise the pick-up and a dropdown point. The old Scot had decided that they'd be best avoiding the heliports in London to bypass air traffic control and awkward questions from security. Time bandits. He'd directed them to the London Golf Club, just south of the city in Kent, where he was a long-term member with benefits. Lydia, McGoldrick,

Stephen Black and Rory stood a few paces away from the helipad, silent in the eerie calm of the otherwise deserted course.

The helipad, basically a raised patch of land on the edge of the course, looked smaller than Lydia would have imagined. Marked out in white paint, the H in the centre of the circle looked like it would serve as parking bays for a pair of Land Rovers. The surrounding circle seemed too small for safety. She shuddered at the thought of a rotor-blade severing stray limbs.

"Shouldn't we ask somebody to turn on the lights?" Lydia asked.

"We'll wait until the helicopter's in view," McGoldrick said.

"What, you're worried about the electricity bill?"

"No, hen. It's just the way they do it here."

McGoldrick seemed distant; his voice didn't reach its usual booming level and he hadn't made eye contact with Lydia since they'd got to the golf club. It made her uncomfortable. They were at the end of this nightmare, at last, but now that they were standing still, she couldn't quiet the nagging voice at the back of her mind.

Can you really trust McGoldrick?

She had to trust him, though. Without McGoldrick, his money and his contacts, she would probably still be online booking flights for John and Mattie. Who knows what could have gone wrong in that time?

Lydia tried to ignore her doubts. Her boys were on their way home. As soon as she saw them – hugged them, kissed them – she would call the police and report the kidnapping. Between her story and Detective Kelly's they'd be able to arrest O'Neill and his men. And all would be right with the world again.

"Maybe I should call Detective Kelly?" Lydia

directed the question at McGoldrick.

"No point. The pilot will have asked him to turn off his phone. Relax. They'll be here soon."

She tried to. It wasn't easy. Stephen Black looked as distracted as McGoldrick and Rory was obviously feeling very sorry for himself. His head hung low and his hands were behind his back, still bound by the plastic ties Stephen Black had trussed him up with. Lydia actually felt for the spoilt prick.

"Could somebody cut Rory loose? I doubt he's going to attack me now."

Stephen Black raised an eyebrow and McGoldrick shrugged.

Rory looked up, his eyes wide. "Yeah, guys. Come on. I'm busting for a slash here."

"I don't want you going into the club," McGoldrick said. "You'll draw too much attention."

"Fuck's sake, aul' fella. Nobody's going to notice me."

"You're not going in there."

"I'll piss by those trees, then." Rory pointed to a cluster of oaks in the rough. "Come on."

McGoldrick turned to Stephen Black:

"Will you take him?"

"I most certainly will not. Need I remind you that I'm not a wet nurse?"

"And your job isn't exactly unionised. You do what I tell you."

"No, I agree to certain tasks and you pay—"

"Shut up. Shut up now." The words were out before Lydia had even formed them in her mind. She felt like an overwhelmed mother at the supermarket. Embraced it. "I've had enough. Just cut the ties and let the man go into the trees. What's he going to do? Climb one and start flinging shit? He knows you're armed and that he's safer with you. Stop treating us like morons."

McGoldrick and Stephen Black looked at each other for a couple of seconds. The ex-spook was the first to smile.

"You make a fair and wonderfully animated point, my dear. I'll get to it directly."

Stephen Black reached into the sleeve of his awful tracksuit top and pulled out a knife. The blade was short, serrated and more chilling than a shark tooth. He slipped his index finger into a steel ring and spun the mini dagger like a gunslinger playing with his revolver.

"Picked up this lovely souvenir in the Philippines. A cheeky little chap tried to take my finger off with it."

"Come on, man. My back teeth are floating now."

Rory turned and started walking backwards. Stephen Black met him halfway and the knife cut through the plastic ties like they were spider webs. Rory gave his wrists a quick rub then jogged towards the rough.

"You're welcome," Stephen Black called after the football star. He slipped the knife back up his sleeve.

Rory turned once to give the ex-spook a quick wave of his middle finger then vanished behind a thick tree trunk.

"He's got quite an amusing attitude that one," Stephen Black said to Lydia. "I'm sure he's an absolute joy to work with."

"I've met worse."

"And he brings in a pretty penny, I suppose."

"He's doing okay."

"Well, when you've paid off your husband's debts, I think I'd quite like to work with you."

Lydia looked him up and down. He'd managed to

scare, insult and impress her all at once.

"You don't know anything about my family, whatever your 'research' tells you. And I highly doubt that I'd need your skill-set at any point in my future."

"Don't be too hasty, Mrs Gallagher. It would have been very useful to have me on your payroll *before* your family got kidnapped."

"Oh, fuck off."

McGoldrick snorted. His toothy grin hid behind his tight lips when Lydia wheeled on him.

"And you can fuck off as well. Did you tell this prick about John's gambling?"

"Don't get uppity with me, hen. I'm helping you out here. You know I'm not the gossiping type."

"I don't really know what you are, Mr McGoldrick. And the longer I stand here the dumber I feel. We're acting like the law doesn't apply to us. We should have phoned the cops hours ago."

"You want your family dead, do you? Whether or not you think the law applies is irrelevant. I'm getting things done. Things ordinary people can't do. So how about you show some fucking gratitude you stupid wee lassie?"

"Steady on, old bean." Stephen Black stepped in front of the red-faced Scot. "You'll do yourself an injury. Think of your blood pressure."

Stephen Black's head jerked backwards and McGoldrick's fist moved through the space it had occupied.

"If you ever try to hit me again, Mr McGoldrick, I will kill you. Fair warning. I'll take your money but I won't take your shit."

McGoldrick unclenched his fists and lowered his arms to his sides. He looked old and confused, like he'd been told off by a nursing home employee. Lydia wondered how many more years the guy would live, collecting money all the way. He'd afford the best care for himself in his final years, no doubt, but in the end he would die too. And it looked as if the thought was working its way through the old bastard. He forced a cough and his Adam's apple bobbed. Lydia could almost see the pride go down his throat.

"What's going on, lads?"

Rory was back. He looked worried.

"Oh, just a little bit of admin," Stephen Black said. "Everything has returned to the status quo."

"That's good, Stevie. Because you might want to do a wee bit of security work down by those trees I just watered. Pretty sure I saw somebody lurking about."

"Ach, it was probably just a fox, lad," McGoldrick said.

"Aye? And do foxes smoke around these parts? Because I could smell cigarettes down there too."

"Kids, then. Sneaking off for a wee smoke's not a crime yet."

"Maybe you should check it out," Lydia said. "We could have been followed."

Stephen Black looked at McGoldrick and rubbed his jaw. "We weren't followed. Did you arrange for anybody to meet us here?"

"Apart from my helicopter pilot? Who else would need to know?"

"Indeed." He drew his silenced gun from the inside of his nylon jacket. "I think I'd be better served right here, Mrs Gallagher. Wouldn't want to perforate a fox unnecessarily. And we have the higher ground, after all."

Lydia nodded at his gun which he held pointed to

the ground. "So you think somebody's out there?"

"Just playing it safe, my dear. Try not to fret."

"I can hear something," Rory said. He pointed to the sky. "Is that a star or a helicopter?"

###

In a private helicopter over the Irish Sea, Cormac did the unthinkable. He slept. Donna and Mattie were sat opposite him in a pair of seats facing the cockpit, and John was to his right. A slim gap between the two rear-facing seats provided access to the cockpit. The rhythmic *chooka-chooka-chooka* beat of rotor blades and the constant drone of the engine soothed Cormac. The bird's eye view of nothingness and hours of constant activity teamed up to sap him of all energy.

There was nothing constructive to be done in the helicopter cabin. Nothing to react to. Donna's attention was on John. The injured man sat bolt upright in his seat, barely conscious and in obvious pain. Cormac didn't want to distract Donna from her watch of the patient. She seemed to be keeping him alive with an intense stare. And Mattie was busy burning every detail of the experience into his memory. The kid's head moved constantly; his eyes flitting from the seats, to the windows, to the back of the pilot's head and every point in between. He looked a few years younger, obviously confident that with Cormac and Donna looking out for him and his father, nothing could go wrong.

The occasional lurch of the vessel as it steered its course failed to unsettle Cormac. He closed his eyes. Vague dreams, disjointed images, the half-conscious jolts as his head lolled, ceased only when the engine dropped a note. His stomach flip-flopped with the helicopter's descent. He tried to focus but his brain wasn't ready to cooperate. His lids drooped. Eyes stung.

Donna nudged him. "I can't believe you slept through that."

"Ugh."

"It was so awesome," Mattie said.

"We're here?" Cormac asked, his brain still flagging.

Donna leaned forward in her seat to check on John's pulse; concern etched deep in her face. "The pilot says we're just about to land."

Cormac looked to his left. There wasn't much to see in the night sky; some lights below them but nothing that looked like a helipad. Cormac leaned to his right and looked over his shoulder, into the cockpit.

"Can you see your landing spot, mate?"

The pilot pulled one of his ear cans back and asked Cormac to repeat himself.

"I can't see a helipad. Is it safe to land?"

"Don't worry, officer. I've landed at this club hundreds of times. Mr McGoldrick comes here regularly. I barely need the co-ordinates, never mind bull's-eye lighting."

"Who is this McGoldrick guy?"

"My boss."

The pilot slipped his headphones back in place and flipped some switches. Cormac had no idea what they were for. It felt wrong to be so dependent on somebody he didn't know at such a great height. But a helicopter licence wasn't exactly criterion for his job. Neither was his instinct for mistrust and suspicion, but that certainly helped him out more than once. He checked his shoulder holster and stroked the cold comfort of his Glock. His mind started to shake the muzzy feeling of recent sleep. The power nap had sharpened him a little.

The helicopter descended.

Cormac rolled his shoulders. His sweat-dampened shirt peeled away from his back. He tapped his feet to get the blood flowing in his legs again. Cormac didn't like how the pilot had cut short their conversation. He wanted to know more about McGoldrick and his connection to Lydia Gallagher. And he wanted to know why the whole situation had gotten so complicated. Surely a man with his own helicopter could have paid the family's ransom and then some?

"Fuck this."

Cormac unbuckled his harness and stepped through the narrow opening between his seat and John's. He heard Mattie ask Donna what was going on but she didn't have an answer for the kid. Cormac settled into the empty co-pilot seat. The pilot looked at him, his teeth bared.

"What do you think you're doing, you idiot? This isn't some taxi-bus. We're *flying*."

"I've never sat up front in a helicopter before. Thought I should seize the opportunity."

"Get the—"

"Don't be upset. I just want to chat. What's your name?"

The pilot tried to stare Cormac down. He hadn't much experience interacting with serious crimes detectives, then. After a few seconds, his eyelids shuttered and he shook his head to pass off his submission as an attempt to take the higher ground.

"Capt—"

"Not your title. Not your surname. What do your friends call you?"

"Nathan."

"Okay, Nathan. Tell me exactly what you've been asked to do here."

"Take Mrs Gallagher's family, and you, to Mr McGoldrick."

"And then?"

"I'm free for the next few days. I'll probably do something with the wife and kids."

"Don't get cute."

"I don't know what you want from me. My job is to fly the helicopter when and where Mr McGoldrick asks me to. That's it."

Cormac stared deep into Nathan's bloodshot eyes. The pilot's defiance had given way to fear, but it didn't seem like he was lying.

"All right, then, big lad. Let's set this whirlybird down. How long before we get our feet back on the ground?"

"Just a few minutes. You can see the lights from the clubhouse up ahead." Nathan pointed out the front window. "We'll touchdown a fair distance in front of that. They'll light up the helipad when we're a little closer."

"Why wait?"

"Mr McGoldrick said he was trying to avoid attention. News reporters, perhaps? There are quite a few celebrity members at this club."

"Bullshit. There's no story there. Even with a foot-baller in tow, that doesn't make any sense. This doesn't feel right."

"Just look out for the lights and relax, officer. Please."

Cormac clenched his jaw shut and took a deep breath through his nose. He couldn't see a thing. Then there was a flash. And another. The source was unmistakeable.

"Somebody's shooting down there."

The helipad blinked into existence. Cormac could make out the silhouettes of people running across it. He pulled the Glock from his shoulder holster.

"Get lower but don't land."

"I—"

Cormac pushed the muzzle of his gun into the pilot's cheekbone.

"I'm your boss now. Just do what you're told."

CHAPTER 21

Of course there are gay men in football. Jesus, what year do people think this is? And I'll tell you something else. It's not just the pretty boys who're lurking in the closet for fear of their careers. Some of these lads are boot ugly.

Rory Cullen, *Cullen: The Autobiography*

Lydia edged towards Rory. He was still looking up at the helicopter and hadn't noticed that Stephen Black had his gun trained on McGoldrick. The old Scot raised his hands. Lydia nudged Rory in the ribs and nodded towards the standoff.

"Ach, balls," Rory said.

Lydia had to agree.

"What the fuck do you think you're doing?" McGoldrick asked.

"Protecting myself. I'm pretty sure Mr Cullen didn't see a smoking fox down by those trees. So what's the story?"

"You can't shit a shitter, eh?" McGoldrick's mouth stretched in an effort to smile. "Just so you know, I had no choice in this. Once you threw that Belfast boy off the balcony things got messy."

"I see. You've been keeping as much from me as you have from Mrs Gallagher, then."

"You were told what you needed to be told."

"Evidently not. You're suggesting I've brought some sort of reckoning upon myself."

"It's just business."

"Ugh, what a dull cliché. I'd have expected more from you, McGoldrick."

"What's happening?" Rory asked.

"Our friend here has devised some sort of welcome party for us, I suspect. How many of them are out there, McGoldrick?"

"You'll see soon enough." McGoldrick backed off a few paces, not quite daring to look away from the ex-spook. "I'd suggest you save as many bullets as you can, though."

Stephen Black sighed and shot McGoldrick. The silenced bullets tore into the old Scot's thighs. Two growing blotches of red stained his chinos. He screamed, staggered and sank to the ground.

"I have plenty of bullets, Mr McGoldrick."

The lights around the helipad flickered to life. Lydia's mind was hijacked by shock. Her vision sharpened but she felt a little dizzy. The sudden intrusion of electric light lent a dream-like quality to the scene. Rory went to McGoldrick's side and looked to Stephen Black for guidance.

"He'll be able to walk with your help. Hobble, at least. Take him towards the car park." He turned to Lydia. "Stay close to me. Things are likely to get messy now."

"But my family..." Lydia pointed at the helicopter.

"You'll have to let Detective Kelly take care of them for now. Come on."

Stephen Black darted across the illuminated helipad, Lydia close behind him. He led her to some long grass and a cluster of saplings. From the shadows, they watched Rory struggle with the old Scot.

"Shouldn't we protect them?" Lydia asked.

"That's what we're doing. Trust me."

Lydia was all out of trust but there was little she could do about the situation. She heard the chainsaw rev of a bike engine and looked to the trees where Rory had gone to relieve himself. The branches were lit up like a science fiction movie set-piece. A motorcycle burst from the grove and tore up the manicured grass in its path. The rider and pillion passenger hunched over as the machine accelerated. They were headed towards Rory and McGoldrick.

Stephen Black levelled his gun. Forgetting the silencer, Lydia covered her ears as he pumped his trigger finger. Sparks exploded from the side of the bike and the passenger squealed loud enough to penetrate Lydia's muffled ears. The bike skidded off course and toppled into a bunker.

"Right, come on."

Stephen Black grabbed Lydia's arm and she fought to keep her footing as he hauled her towards the car park. She raised her voice to a controlled scream to be heard over the hovering helicopter engine.

"What if there are more of them?"

"We've given them something to think about, haven't we?"

They ran until Lydia's calves burned with exertion and skidded to a halt beside Rory and McGoldrick. Rory had managed to navigate his charge through the maze of high-end four-by-fours and luxury saloons to Stephen Black's Vauxhall. The old Scot was bleary-eyed and pale with shock. Rory looked to Stephen Black for the next set of instructions. The ex-spook retrieved his car keys from his pocket and pushed the button on the fob. He flipped open the boot.

"Throw him in here, there's a good lad."

"We're not leaving," Lydia said. "Not without my boys."

"I have to be honest with you," Stephen Black said, "it's likely that my business arrangement with Mr McGoldrick is now beyond repair. My work here is done. I need to get the old chap out of here and work on disappearing for a while."

"You bastard. I can't believe you would..." Lydia took a deep breath and changed tact. "I'll pay you to help me."

"You're in financial ruin, Mrs Gallagher. You can't afford me."

"*I* can," Rory said. "Consider me your new boss, Stevie B."

"I'm very expensive."

"And you already know how much money I have. With more on the way. This could work out very well for you."

Lydia could feel control slipping from her grasp yet again. "Rory..."

"It's okay. I owe you big time, Lydia."

She didn't want the spoiled bastard's help. The temptation to throw his offer back in his face was overwhelming. But she had to think of John and Mattie. Her pride would have to take a backseat for now.

"So what's the plan?" Lydia asked.

###

Cormac lowered his gun from the pilot's face. He rested the Glock on his lap, finger on the outside of the trigger-guard.

"Don't get any ideas, Nathan. I'm still the boss-man here."

The pilot nodded, almost gratefully.

"Get me closer to the action."

Nathan pushed his cyclic stick forward and the front of the helicopter dipped. Cormac watched a motorcycle blast its way out of a cluster of trees. He could see the pillion passenger had a gun in his hand, possibly a sawn-off. Another burst of gunfire strobe-lit the shadows. The bike veered off-course and into a large bunker. The riders toppled in a tangle of limbs; their landing cushioned by fine sand.

Cormac scanned the golf course for further madness. Nathan pulled the helicopter out of its descent and looked to Cormac for the next instruction.

Donna called in from the passenger seats behind Cormac. "What's happening?"

"Somebody's shooting people down there. That's all I can see."

"Tell the pilot to take us straight to a hosp—"

Mattie cut in. "What about my mum?"

"I can't see anything, mate. We're going to have to check this out, Donna."

"John's not looking great here."

"He's going to have to hold on."

"The poor bastard's been holding on all day."

"I'm sorry, Donna. If Mattie's ma is down there she needs our help too."

Donna growled but offered no further argument.

"We're going to have to land this thing, Nathan."

"You're going to get me killed."

Cormac raised his gun off his lap. "Just do what you're told."

Nathan pushed the stick forward again and guided them towards the helipad.

"Don't land there, for Christ's sake. Give us a little distance from the gunplay."

"I haven't asked for permission to land at the other—"

"Permission my arse. Just find a nice flat spot over there." Cormac pointed out the window.

"That's a car park."

"It's half-fucking-empty."

Nathan mumbled under his breath then yanked the cyclic stick back and to the left. The helicopter turned jerkily towards the car park. Cormac heard John moan over the sound of the engine and rotors. Donna made soothing noises. Cormac slapped the pilot in the centre of his forehead.

"Take it easy, dickhead. There's an injured man back there."

Nathan clenched his jaw and his grip on the stick tightened, but the aggression seeped away from his manoeuvres. The chastised pilot guided his helicopter to a patch of car park furthest from the door of the clubhouse.

"I'm going to get crucified for this."

"Forward all complaints to the PSNI, Nathan."

The bushes at the edge of the car park shook violently in the blast of air from the helicopter's rudders. It seemed to take a life-time for the skids to settle on the tarmac. Cormac left his seat in the cockpit and knelt in front of Mattie.

"I'm going to go find your ma, all right?"

The kid nodded. His eyes were red and glossed with the threat of tears, but he held himself together.

Cormac turned to Donna.

"I want you to go to the nearest hospital with John." He drew his back-up gun from its ankle holster and passed it to her. "There are six bullets in this. Keep the pilot from getting any stupid ideas."

"Cormac, I've never shot—"

"And let's hope you don't have to start today, but it's better to have it and not need it and all that jazz."

Her face hardened in a way that told him he'd be lucky if she ever spoke to him again. He was expecting too much from her. But there was no other option and he needed to keep his mind clear to deal with the next inevitable disaster. He had no time to sweet-talk or apologise.

"When I find Mattie's ma we'll figure out what hospital you're at and meet up there."

John's voice was raspy and barely audible over the noise of the helicopter. "I want to speak to Lydia."

"You will, John. From the comfort of a hospital bed."

"No. I might not make it. Let me say goodbye to her."

Cormac looked to Donna. She chewed on her lower lip for a couple of seconds then nodded.

"I'll hold the fort, Cormac. Hurry up and get her."

"Thank you." Cormac raised his voice for Nathan's benefit. "If the pilot moves this thing so much as an inch, shoot him in the head."

###

Lydia almost smiled when Stephen Black slammed the boot of his car closed. McGoldrick thumped and roared from the inside.

"Settle down, Mr McGoldrick." The ex-spook said. "You'll do yourself an injury."

The thumping increased for a few seconds then stopped.

"Is he okay?" Rory asked.

"I don't give a shit," Lydia said. "He's a bastard."

"Fair point, Mrs Gallagher," Stephen Black said. "Shall we go see your family?"

Lydia looked towards the helicopter, now settled at the far end of the car park. She thought about kicking off her shoes and flat-out sprinting towards it, but she was hyper-aware of the possibility of more men with guns skulking in the darkness.

"Ready when you are, Mr Black."

"Very good. Keep your head down and follow me."

Bent at the waist, Stephen Black began to weave his way through the parked cars. Lydia followed close behind with Rory taking up the rear. They moved quickly, their footsteps drowned out by the thunderous noise of the helicopter. She allowed herself to think that they might actually make it to the other side of the car park.

Glass exploded from the rear window of a black BMW X5. Chunky fragments rained down on Lydia's hunched back. She screamed.

Stephen Black scuttled forward and rolled over the bonnet of a silver Mercedes. He landed on his feet, turned and propped his elbows on the car. His pistol bucked in his hand. The smell of gunplay crowded Lydia's sinuses. She scrabbled on her hands and knees around the Mercedes and stalled at Stephen Black's side. Rory followed close behind her, hyperventilating.

"We're so fucked," Rory said.

"We'll be fine, my friend." Stephen Black dropped down on one knee and ejected the spent clip from his gun. He produced a fresh one from somewhere underneath his tracksuit top and slid it home. Then he jacked the slide. "I'm not fond of getting shot. Stay close to me."

"Did you get them?" Lydia asked.

"Afraid not. They're a slippery duo."

"Do you think there are more of them out there?"

"No, they'd have engaged by now. That's not to say reinforcements aren't on their way, though. We got wise to Mr McGoldrick's move sooner than he would have liked."

"The little bastard."

"Indeed."

"I don't get it." Rory said. "What's McGoldrick after? The guy's already richer than an oil sheik."

"I'm sure we'll get to the bottom of it soon enough, old chap."

Stephen Black broke the wing mirror off the Mercedes and held it above his head. He angled it to get a sweeping view of the car park.

"Can you see them?" Lydia asked.

He shook his head. "They're probably trying to close in on us."

"We better get moving again, then." Rory said. "Stay ahead of them."

"Unfortunately, there's not a lot of cover between

here and the helicopter."

"Then we attack." Rory said. "Do you have a spare gun, Stevie?"

"Have you ever shot one?"

"No."

Stephen Black smiled and shook his head. "Then, no."

"What *can* we do?" Lydia asked.

"Either we wait for the biker boys to slip up and give away their position, or we sit tight then shoot when they make their move."

"That doesn't seem like a very good plan."

"I'll happily accept suggestions, Mrs Gallagher."

Lydia's phone blasted its Lady Gaga ringtone. She snatched it from her jacket pocket with the speed of a quick-draw gunslinger and silenced the music.

"Fuck's sake," Rory said. "Who the fuck is that?"

Lydia looked at the number on her screen. "It might just be the cavalry."

CHAPTER 22

There's no 'I' in team. There's an 'M' and an 'E' though. In fact, it's an anagram of 'ta me' as in who you should pass it to if you want to win.

Rory Cullen, *Cullen: The Autobiography*

Cormac had to pitch his voice louder than he'd have liked to compete with the noise from the helicopter. He pressed the phone tight against his left ear and covered his right with the palm of his hand. His gun was holstered. The sooner he got off the phone, the better.

"Mrs Gallagher. Your husband and son are in the helicopter. I saw gunfire before we landed. Are you injured?"

"No. Not yet."

Not yet. "Is somebody trying to hurt you?"

"Yes. We've taken cover behind a silver Mercedes. Look for a black BMW jeep-type thing with its back window blown out. We're close to that."

"How many gunmen have you seen?"

"Two..." He heard another voice at the end of the line but couldn't make out what was being said. "But there may well be more on the way."

"Stay where you are. I'll find you."

"Okay. There are three of us, just so you know.

One has a gun. You don't need to shoot him. He's on our side."

"Good to know."

Cormac hung up and tucked his phone away. He was relieved to have the Glock back in his hand. If the two gunmen were out there, they were playing it safe and keeping their heads down. And no wonder. Whoever Lydia Gallagher had hooked up with had been a sharp enough shot to hit a speeding motorbike.

Cormac hunched down to allow a painless dive for cover if the bullets started flying but not so low as to restrict his movements too drastically. He sought out the BMW four-by-four with the missing window as he hurried down a line of parked cars. Unfortunately, the rich man's playground was densely populated with a rash of expensive diesel-drinkers. He felt like he was wasting precious time on a fool's errand. Time that John Gallagher simply didn't have.

Just keep moving.

Then he saw it. A black BMW X5 with no back window. About ten cars down and one row to the right. And behind it, a silver Mercedes. Cormac inched further down the line, conscious that he'd have gotten closer to the gunmen as well. Moments later he drew level with the silver Mercedes and could see three people huddled against the side of it. Lydia Gallagher, Rory Cullen and a little grey-haired man in a tracksuit brandishing a silenced automatic pistol. The stranger was the first one to spot Cormac. He used Close Range Engagement hand signals to ask Cormac to help him cover Lydia and Rory.

Not a civilian, then.

Cormac nodded and counted off three seconds with his fingers. They both stood and fired a controlled burst of fire over the roofs of the parked cars. Lydia and Rory moved fast, not even taking the time to acknowledge Cormac's arrival.

The stranger beckoned Cormac to his side. Cormac looked into the shadows of the car park. He couldn't see anybody, but then, they were hardly likely to pop up and start waving at him. Stalling would do nothing except increase the risk of him getting tagged, though. He swept his gun in a wide arc as he momentarily left cover to get to the other man.

A flash of survival instinct urged him to duck.

Bullets whizzed over his head.

Cormac dived for cover behind the silver Mercedes. The stranger returned fire.

"I think I may have winged one of the scoundrels, Detective Kelly."

Cormac was taken aback by the man's weirdly formal English accent. It took him a few seconds to speak.

"Um, good job. You know my name, then. So what do they call you?"

"Hah, I love the cadence you Belfast boys adopt. What do they call me? Indeed. My name is Stephen Black. I'm currently under Mr Cullen's employ as a security consultant."

"Yeah? Considering recent events, he might be asking you for his money back."

"Oh, I've only just started working for him. Before that, I was hired by Mr McGoldrick."

"Who the fuck is this McGoldrick character?"

"I don't think this is the best time to catch you up, Detective. There's a good chance we've made those two fellows even angrier, and we need to be mindful of Mr Cullen and Mrs Gallagher's retreat."

With that Stephen Black loosed another burst of fire over the roof of the Mercedes. Then he hunkered down and ejected his spent clip. Seconds later he snapped home a fresh one he had produced from inside his cheap tracksuit jacket.

"Any luck that time?"

Bullets peppered the higher-sided motors behind them.

"Not enough luck, no."

"So, you're not a cop. Is this gun-for-hire business of yours legal?"

"*Gun-for-hire*, indeed. I'm a security consultant. And I think you'll find I'm very well informed of my legal limitations."

"That's not exactly the same as being legit, is it?"

"Again, I must remind you that we're supposed to be covering these civilians. Could you pull some of the weight, please?"

Cormac frowned but he raised himself slowly to a shooting position. The still unseen gunmen took pot-shots at him. They missed by quite a distance. Their muzzle flashes also gave Cormac something to shoot at. His trigger finger pumped and he sent bullets in two directions. He didn't think he'd scored a hit but the bastards would have something to think about. Cormac hunkered down again.

Stephen Black gave him an encouraging nod. Cormac wanted to hit him a dig in the jaw. There was an unmistakable air of condescension about him. Little prick.

"Let's fall back a little," Stephen Black said. "I'm quite sure that there are only two of them out there so far, but who knows what other forms of scum are skulking about. Reinforcements must be very close by now."

"I don't suppose you have any reinforcements, Mr Black?"

"Didn't think I would need them today. But you're here now so everything is rosy, my good man."

Cormac shook his head. The weird little English guy was a fruitcake. He did seem to know how to handle himself, though. Cormac had no choice but to work with him. They moved into the space between the two rows of parked cars and moved towards the helicopter. Stephen Black led the way, his progress steady. Cormac moved backwards, not easy when hunched down and moving at speed. He kept an eye out for possible threats.

"How are our friends doing?" Cormac asked, directing his voice over his shoulder.

"They seem to have stopped moving. I think they might be hesitant to break from cover and run that final stretch."

"Okay. Listen. There are seven seats in that helicopter. Counting the pilot, there are eight of us. Either you or I should stay behind and cover the ground while it takes off."

"That doesn't add up. The Gallaghers make three, plus the pilot, Mr Cullen and us. Seven."

"I have a doctor with me."

"Oh." Black paused for a second. "Who got hurt?"

"John Gallagher. Gunshot wound."

"Bad?"

"Very. He should be in a hospital bed right now."

"I see."

Cormac expected a bunch of other questions about the situation but the so-called security consultant seemed to be satisfied with the information he had. They moved another few paces before Black spoke again.

"I'll ask you to stay behind, then, Detective."

"Because...?"

"It's my job to protect Mr Cullen and, by extension, Mrs Gallagher. I'll not be able to do that remotely."

"Fair point."

Cormac thought of arguing the fact that his ex-girlfriend was in the helicopter along with the thirteen-year-old boy who'd come to trust him despite the fact that Cormac had shot his father. It didn't seem like a particularly strong argument and so he decided to let it go.

"All right. Stay in touch with me and let me know what hospital you end up in. I'll meet you there. Mrs Gallagher has my number."

"Good man. Here, take this."

Cormac looked over his shoulder to see Black's left hand extended, a car key hung from his index finger.

"The car's a Vauxhall Vectra, not far from where you found us. Just push the fob and let the lights guide you. Take it to the hospital when you're done here."

"Thanks." Cormac took the key and slipped it into his coat pocket.

They continued moving, Lydia Gallagher and Rory Cullen just yards away now.

"Something you should know about my car..." Black loosed a little chuckle, punctuated it with a snort. "There's a small Scottish man in the boot. My previous employer, Mr McGoldrick. I think you'll find him quite interesting. Get what you need from him but don't let him go. I need to spend some time with him myself."

"You've kidnapped a small Scottish man? Again, I have to question your relationship with UK law."

"Think of it as a citizen's arrest, Detective."

Cormac didn't push the issue. His own behaviour

had been less than aboveboard since the start of the kidnapping shit-storm. He no longer had the moral superiority of an agent of the justice system. His position in the PSNI had to be in serious jeopardy by now. All he could do, to satisfy his own code of ethics, was see Mattie and his family to safety then concentrate on surviving whatever came at him next.

They got to Lydia Gallagher and Rory Cullen's position.

Black's voice was cheerful. "Nearly at the end of this dreadful business now, Mrs Gallagher. We just need to get you on that whirlybird."

Lydia turned to Black, her face pretty despite the deeply worried expression. She took a deep breath and nodded. "Rory and I figured the walk from here to the helicopter would make us sitting ducks. No point getting this far only to be shot in the back."

"Very sensible. But we can't sit here all night."

"Wait," Lydia looked past Black to make eye contact with Cormac. "Thank you for looking after my family, Detective."

Cormac nodded but couldn't bring himself to speak. He wasn't sure how much gratitude she'd feel she owed him after she saw the state of her husband.

Black ushered them out into the open. He stood up straight now, a greying prairie dog on lookout duty. Cormac followed. Even hunched over he stood taller than the other three. He felt like a moving bullet shield. There was nothing he could do about that, except watch for movement in the shadows. He slipped his finger inside the Glock's trigger guard and tried to control his breathing.

The chugga-chugga splutter of a motorcycle engine kick-starting managed to cut through the noise from the helicopter. Cormac looked out into the car park and a solitary headlight burst into existence. The bike's engine snarled and the light jerked to the left. Cormac sent three bullets after it but knew he was too far away to hope for any sort of accuracy from a handgun. The bike wouldn't be long closing the distance, however.

"Hurry the fuck up," Cormac pushed Rory and the footballer picked up the pace. "Get on the helicopter now."

Lydia and Black had to run to catch up with Rory. They climbed on board. Cormac watched them long enough to see Black give him the thumbs up. He turned to face the gunmen on the motorcycle. Behind him, the helicopter engine racket increased. The motorcycle's headlight zig-zagged its way towards him, determined to create a hard target.

Cormac took a deep breath, went down on one knee and held out his gun, his left hand encircling his right wrist. He aimed, loosed a slow breath and squeezed the trigger.

"Mum!"

Lydia stepped onto the helicopter and straight into her son's constrictor hug. She squeezed back, running her hand from the top of his head to the nape of his neck. His silky hair teased through her fingers. She felt Rory and Stephen Black squeeze past her. Heard an unknown woman gasp.

"My God. It's Rory Cullen."

Lydia looked over the top of Mattie's head to the source of the voice. An attractive woman with springy hair and stylish glasses sat in one of the passenger seats.

She had a stethoscope draped across the back of her neck. A doctor. Lydia's stomach fluttered. She looked to the other passenger. John. Dressed in a bathrobe over a flimsy hospital gown, deathly pale and slick with sweat. He seemed to be unconscious.

"Oh, Jesus."

Lydia laid her hands on Mattie's shoulders and gently pushed him back. She caught sight of her son's face, badly bruised, eyes sunken, mouth drawn downwards. He rubbed at his upper arm self-consciously and she saw his fingers were bound by bandages.

"What's happened to you two?"

"It's been a rough couple of days, Mum."

Stephen Black stepped between her and her son.

"You need to sit down. We're taking off now."

The ex-spook turned away and entered the cockpit. Took a seat by the pilot. Rory led Lydia by the arm to the seat beside the mystery woman. Mattie sat down beside Lydia and Rory took the seat opposite him.

Gunfire crackled outside and became the pilot's cue to take off. The helicopter lurched and tilted and Lydia's bladder did a loop-de-loop. She closed her eyes and sank her fingers into her armrests.

Breathe, breathe, breathe.

Lydia's ordeal should have ended. She was back with her family and flying away from the danger. But her brain had been assaulted by an information overload. What had happened to her boys?

She opened her eyes and looked at John.

He must have sensed her stare. His eyelids cracked open and he forced a pathetic smile.

"Hiya, gorgeous. Good to see you."

"Oh, John. What the hell happened to you?"

"We tried to escape. I got shot in the confusion."

"Shot? Why are you not still at the hospital."

"It wasn't safe. They would have known where to find me." He took a shallow, pained breath. "Did they hurt you?"

She thought about the slaps, the manhandling and the psychological torture. Compared her physical state to John's.

"No. I cooperated."

John puffed air through his nostrils.

"I didn't."

"Neither did Mattie by the looks of it."

"You should be proud of him, Lydia. We've raised a tough kid."

Mattie beamed in spite of the grim situation that had tested his mettle. Lydia wondered about the horrors he'd been through without her there to protect him. She had to fight back the tears and push her morbid thoughts right to the back of her mind. It was time to concentrate on the present.

"We need to get you medical attention, John." She looked at Mattie again. "Both of you. I'm not taking any risks."

The mystery woman spoke up. "We're flying to the nearest hospital now." Her accent was Northern Irish but not as harsh as John and Rory's. She made it sound warm and musical.

"I'm sorry," Lydia said. "Who are you?"

"I'm Donna. A friend of Cormac's."

Lydia tilted her head.

"Detective Kelly, like."

Lydia pointed at Donna's stethoscope. "And you're a doctor?"

She nodded. "I would have advised Cormac against moving John under normal circumstances but things got really crazy back home."

"What's done is done. Will he be okay?"

"He's a fighter. I'm surprised he's still awake."

It wasn't a yes by any means but Lydia didn't want to push it. She wanted to go over to her husband, sit on his lap and squeeze him tight but he looked so delicate and tired that her weight might crush him. The bastards had taken his strength from him.

Thoughts of revenge began to surface. She'd make the bastards pay. Starting with the worst of them. The traitor.

"Fucking McGoldrick."

John raised his chin. "McGoldrick?"

Lydia hesitated for a few seconds, worried that she shouldn't encourage John to talk. Put him under further stress or sap his energy. But the doctor didn't warn either of them against it.

"McGoldrick is involved in this somehow," Lydia said.

"The greedy bastard." John shifted in his seat slightly and grunted. "I fucking knew it. He's finally stopped dipping the toe and just plunged right in."

"What are you talking about, John?"

"At the height of my... low times, McGoldrick put me on to some shady men he'd been dealing with to help me out with my losses."

"The loan sharks."

"Aye, Rooney's crew."

"What would somebody as rich as McGoldrick want with loan sharks?"

"They specialise in other areas. Drugs, racketeering, prostitution... But they also get a decent turn out of money laundering."

Lydia shook her head, still unsure of how that

related to the old Scot.

"Do you remember when the whole bung scandal exploded a few years ago? Managers, talent scouts and agents got named and shamed for accepting extra fees for signing new talent to the top clubs. Bribes to ensure a certain player ended up with the right transfer deal and on the right team."

"Who could forget it?"

"Heads rolled, that's for sure. But not all of them. The scam ran much deeper than anybody could know. It was only the stupid ones that took the fall. The braggers and blaggers. The sloppy operators. They were the ones who got arrested and dragged through the tabloid shite. But the ones who knew what they were doing? They got more careful."

"McGoldrick took bungs?"

"Took them? He pretty much demanded them on every other deal. You've traded contracts with him in the past. You must know the score, babe."

They'd talked plenty about the dodgier side to the beautiful game when they first got together. Often they'd compare notes and share outrageous gossip over a bottle of wine, never taking it too seriously. Lydia sometimes got the feeling that John's morals were a little more slippery than hers but she hadn't pressed him to 'fess up. At first it was about fearing she'd cross a line early on in their relationship. Then it was about caring too much for him to admit he might have had a darker side. She was almost relieved when she discovered his secret gambling problem. Like she knew that if that was the worst he'd ever get up to, she could live with it. But maybe she'd been kidding herself about that too.

"No, I don't know the score, John. One stupid bastard tried to pull that bung shit on me once. Some greasy little up-and-comer always on the cusp of relegation. I told him I didn't deal that way and he was lucky I didn't report him."

"Always one of the good ones... you're rare, though. Sad but true." John sighed deep. He closed his eyes and seemed to drift off to sleep. Then his lids shuttered open again. "McGoldrick kept his own nose clean by channelling his money through Martin Rooney's businesses. The fronts for his cocaine and protection income. Risky game, getting in bed with London gangsters, but McGoldrick always was a cocky fucker. Probably thought Rooney was just a greedy underling who'd be glad of the crumbs McGoldrick threw his way. But you deal with the devil and... you know?"

"I still don't understand how that led him to kidnapping."

"You've got the hottest player in the Premiership in your stable now." John pointed at a dumbstruck Rory Cullen. "Us being skint, you know they weren't after our money. Not directly, anyway. They're looking to get control of young Rory, there."

"But why?"

John shrugged then winced. "Maybe McGoldrick wants to sign him by any means. Or he's working on something with Rooney that'll earn them even more money. Rooney likes to bet on the footie, and he's better at it than I ever was. But how much better would he be if he controlled some of the greatest talent out there?"

"Match fixing?"

"It's a theory, babe."

John's smile was interrupted by a savage fit of coughing. He groaned when it passed and a thin line of blood burbled over his bottom lip. Lydia felt panic like a battering ram in her chest. She unfastened her seatbelt and rushed to John. Knelt down in front of him and grasped his hand. Donna, the doctor, was beside her. She remained on her feet and reached out to cup John's head in her hands.

"I'm fine," John said, his voice barely audible.

Donna shouted in to the cockpit. "How long until we get to the hospital?"

Stephen Black spoke over the stuttering pilot. "Mere minutes. I can see it from here."

Donna held two fingers against the side of John's neck and looked at her watch. She patted John's shoulder and said, "Good man, John. Keep on fighting. You'll make it, so you will."

John nodded and closed his eyes. Donna looked down at Lydia, still on her knees, her fingers entwined with John's.

"He'll make it," Donna lied.

"I know," Lydia lied.

line dragged him from the depths. Kept clarity. They tumbled to the ground. Came to rest side-by-side.

Cormac rolled onto his knees and brought his jammed pistol down on the gunman's helmet. Smashed through the visor. He drew his hand back and jabbed the muzzle through the gap he'd created. The gunman shrieked. Cormac scrambled to his feet and soccer-kicked the cracked helmet. Then he stomped down. The helmet cracked further. The floored man went still.

Cormac felt a thud in his chest. His feet left the ground and he landed on his back, skidded across man-icured grass. He heard the revs of a motorcycle and rolled to the side. It buzzed past him, kicking up clods of golf course. Cormac watched the bike skid and turn a neat 180 degrees. And then it was coming for him again. He scrambled on his hands and knees towards a large bunker and flopped into it. The motorcycle hit the edge of the bunker like a ramp and soared over Cormac's prone body. The front wheel slammed into the sand and the rider was flipped over the handlebars. He landed on the grass with a bone-jarring thump.

Cormac pulled himself out of the bunker, pulling at strands of grass like a Romero zombie digging itself out of a grave. His heart hammered in his chest and his breath hitched. He loosed a short burst of half-insane laughter, marvelling at the fact he was still alive.

The motorcycle's engine had stalled and the heli-copter was now well out of earshot. He was almost suf-focated by the blissful silence. But it was broken by a groan. The man he'd knocked off the back of the bike was coming to. His leather-clad body shook as he came back to his senses. Cormac aimed his Glock and tried to shoot the man but the gun was still jammed. He hol-stered the bastarding thing and reached for his ankle holster.

Empty.

"Fuck."

He'd given it to Donna.

Cormac looked around for an alternative weapon. He spotted a rake at the edge of the bunker. Its shaft was half the length of a standard lawn rake but the head was wider and felt satisfyingly heavy. He gave it a little practice swing and smiled to himself.

Ahead of him, the rider with the smashed visor had retrieved his sawn-off. He used it like a mini walking stick to aid his struggle to stand. It seemed like Cormac had done a real number on the guy. His movements were sluggish but he managed to get himself upright, if a little wobblingly. He raised his sawn-off. Cormac swung the rake and the metal head clattered into the gunman's wrist. The sawn-off flew from his grip before he could squeeze the trigger.

Cormac swung the rake again, this time at the man's head. The ruined helmet gave up the ghost and fell apart. Pieces of it came away like cracked eggshell. Cormac recognised the revealed face instantly. One of the Scullion brothers. Mick. The tough fucker looked damaged and dazed but he remained upright.

"Give it up, Mick," Cormac said. "There's no point, I have you."

"Fuck you, peeler scumbag."

"Be sensible, big lad."

Mick growled and darted forward, his fists swinging. Cormac bobbed and weaved his way out of Mick's path then caught him low in the legs with the rake. Mick toppled over and landed face-first in the grass. Cormac straddled Mick's back and slipped the shaft of the rake under the stubborn bastard's chin. He gripped both ends of the shaft and pulled back to choke him. Mick coughed and spluttered when Cormac eased the pressure again.

"It's over, Mick. Don't make me kill you."

Mick bucked and writhed under Cormac in a bid to escape. Cormac pulled back on the shaft again and reminded the lunatic who was in charge. When he felt the pinned man's body sag he released the pressure again. Mick gargled an indecipherable curse, threat or prayer but was still. Cormac sighed in relief. He got off Mick's back and stood up.

Cormac drew his jammed Glock and took the opportunity to try and fix it. He ejected the clip and jiggled the slide. Something clicked and he was able to rack the pistol. He slipped the clip back in, relieved that he was armed again. Mick had rolled onto his back and was greedily gulping air. Cormac looked to the bunker. The fallen rider hadn't moved. He kicked one of Mick's legs to get his attention.

"Who was on the front of the bike? Your brother?"

"Fuck yourself." Mick's voice was raspy, his throat damaged.

"He's not looking good, whoever it is. Took a very nasty spill. You want me to call an ambulance?"

"Suck my dick."

"God, you're a contrary fucker, aren't you? I'll go find out myself, then. Of course, removing his helmet might cause him even more damage. Shame to take the risk."

"Fuck him too."

"Ah, so it's not your big bro, then."

"Pete's dead."

Cormac bit his tongue. He'd almost told Mick he was sorry for his loss. In reality, the world had lost a psycho. He said nothing, waited to see if Mick would get any chattier.

"This whole move's been cursed from the start. Ambrose lost the run of things. Stupid bastard. And look where it got him. Hope the bastard is dead, and that's no lie. We were doing fine running Belfast. There was no need to get involved with these Brit pricks at all."

"The boss got greedy, eh? Is that aul' Ambrose over there? You must be seriously short-handed if he's in the thick of it, risking life and limb on a motorcycle."

"We were meant to have back-up. Pricks never showed up."

"Why not?"

Mick laughed; a pathetic breathless wheeze. "Wouldn't you like to know?"

Cormac held out his hand. "Come on, get up. We can't stay here all night."

Mick looked Cormac up and down. "Where you planning on taking me?"

"The nearest cop-shop."

"I need to go to hospital. Some English wanker shot me. Same bastard probably done our Pete."

Cormac had missed it at first because of the poor light and the dark leather gear Mick was wearing, but there it was, a gunshot wound in his left flank. And yet he'd still gone after Cormac. Psycho or not, Mick was one tough prick.

Cormac waggled his helping hand. "Come on, get up."

Mick swallowed his pride and reached out. They gripped each other's forearms and Cormac hauled the beaten man upright. Mick took a few steps back and started to unzip his leather jacket.

Cormac raised his Glock. "Hold up there, Mick. What are you up to?"

"Just want to check this wound. Relax."

"I'll relax when you're behind bars." But he lowered the gun.

Rattlesnake-swift, Mick pulled a large hunting knife from inside his jacket and lunged at Cormac. His lips were peeled back in half-crazed savagery. Cormac swivelled on his right heel a quarter-turn. The blade cut through the air he'd occupied seconds before. Cormac snatched Mick's wrist with his left hand. Clamped an iron grip on it to keep the knife at bay. He pushed the muzzle of his Glock into Mick's ear.

"Seriously, mate. Give it up."

Mick reached into his jacket with his free hand.

Used up his last chance.

"You're a fucking idiot, Mick Scullion."

Cormac pulled the trigger.

Lydia felt the helicopter's descent in her stomach before Stephen Black called out from the cockpit.

"We're about to touch down, ladies and gentlemen."

"Have you radioed ahead to the hospital?" Donna asked.

"Our good friend, Captain Giles, has taken care of that."

Donna turned to Lydia and smiled. "Looks like he's going to make it."

Lydia allowed herself a sigh. She looked at John and the icy claw around her heart eased up its grip a little. They were nearly there.

Electric light from the rooftop helipad seeped into the helicopter and tinted everything a pale blue. Lydia couldn't see much from the middle passenger seat except the edges of the hospital roof. The helicopter rocked and swayed like a boat in choppy water before it finally thumped down on its skids. The engine whined to a halt and the whoosh of rotor blades chopping through the air faded. Lydia closed her eyes and drew long, calming breaths into her lungs in preparation for the medical mayhem that would undoubtedly greet them on disembarking the helicopter.

"Let's get a move on, then," Stephen Black said.

He stood in front of her, a grin like a wedge of Edam on his tanned face. He rubbed his hands together with enthusiasm. Lydia unbuckled her safety belt and stood up. She shook some life back into her legs and reached out for Mattie's good hand. Her son made no teenage protests. He interlaced his fingers with Lydia's and treated her to one of his lopsided smiles. His eyes were round with nervous excitement and he looked about three years younger.

Stephen Black slid open the helicopter door. He stepped out onto the roof where the pilot was already waiting. Lydia and Mattie held back while Donna and Rory eased John out of his seat. They guided him to the exit and Stephen Black and the pilot helped him down the steps. Two paramedics in luminous coats wheeled a gurney towards John, careful to stay well clear of the rear rotor even though it had come to a stop. A doctor stood near the doorway leading into the hospital building. He pulled his white coat tight over his flimsy scrubs and thin frame. His expression was less than delighted.

Lydia followed her husband closely, her grip on Mattie's hand tightening. He squeezed back with surprising strength. John was guided onto the gurney with great care and the paramedics snapped the side barriers into place. Donna went to the doctor and after a quick introduction began to fill him in on all the essential information. The doctor's expression was hassled but he listened closely as he checked John's pulse and had a peek under his dressing.

At the doorway leading down into the hospital building, the paramedics wheeled the gurney into a large lift, barely jostling the patient. There was only one button on the control panel; an express trip to casualty. The doors whooshed open after a long drop. Fluorescent lighting glared. Lydia felt woozy. She experienced a lightness of mind that tinged her senses with a dream-like quality. Her surroundings became vague, disconnected; her only tether to reality, Mattie's hand. She would be okay as long as her big brave son kept her grounded.

The doctor spoke to her over his shoulder as the hurried down a grim corridor: "There are some policemen here that want to speak to you."

"How did they find us?"

The doctor's brow wrinkled. "It's the hospital policy for all gunshot wounds."

"Can it wait? I don't want to leave him until I know he's okay."

"He *is* okay. There's a possibility of infection and his blood pressure is low but he'll get that all taken care of here. The wound looks surprisingly good considering the reported stress our man's been put under."

Donna nodded along with the doctor's words. "He's right, Mrs Gallagher. Go talk to the police. It'll pass the time while your husband gets checked over. And they can start looking for the people who did this to your family. Surely that'll put your mind at ease?"

They turned a corner and one of the paramedics punched a button on the wall to open the automatic doors ahead of them. The doctor stopped at a nurse's station and muttered some instructions to a young and fragile-looking girl dressed in a navy-blue tunic. She tugged at her earlobe and nodded along to each order.

"Jenny here will take you to the police. We'll get the patient set up in a bay on this ward. Just return to this station when you're ready." He looked pointedly at Stephen Black and Rory. "Gentlemen, there's a seating area at the bottom of the ward."

Stephen Black looked to Lydia with his eyebrows raised. She nodded to him.

"I'll be fine. Mattie can look after me now."

Before they parted ways a commotion broke out at the doors of the ward. Thuds, shouts and a metallic crash. Lydia felt panic like a nail-bomb in each lung. They were here for her and her boys. Somehow the bastards had found her. She dragged Mattie in behind the nurse's station. Rory and Stephen Black followed her.

"Shit, what about John?" Lydia said.

"The doctor's wheeled him into a bay," Rory said. "He's behind a curtain."

Lydia grabbed Stephen Black's forearm. She felt the little dagger he hid there through the cheap material of his tracksuit jacket.

"Stay with Mattie."

"Where are you going?"

"To find those cops. Obviously the useless bastards haven't heard a thing from whatever room they're holed up in."

"I really think you should stay here, Mrs Gallagher."

"He's right," Rory said. "I'll go."

"No," Lydia said. "You distract them. Make them chase you and draw them away from Mattie."

Rory looked uncertain but nodded. "Fuck it, okay."

The star striker vaulted over the nurses' station counter. His twang, one hundred per cent more Belfast, bounced off the ward walls;

"All right then, ye fuckin' wankers. *C'mon tae fuck!*"

An east London accent matched Rory's volume, "There's the cunt. Have him."

Another man grunted and she heard their hurried footsteps clump past her hiding place. She saw two men dressed in black army surplus fatigues go after Rory. They had guns but didn't fire. The footballer was too valuable to them. But they were determined to catch him. Rory feinted left and right then turned and ran to the bottom of the ward. Towards the seating area the doctor had just pointed out. It could well have been a dead end but Lydia didn't plan to stick about and find out.

Lydia gave Mattie's hand a squeeze then let go.

"I'll be back soon, Mattie."

"You better," Mattie said.

She nodded at him, then scampered on her hands and knees around the counter. On the other side, her head butted into something. She squeaked and looked up: a pair of faded black combat trousers, an army surplus jacket to match, and a cruelly amused face to top it off.

"All right, love?"

"Shit."

The man bent at the waist and grabbed the back

of her neck. He dug his fingers in and rag-dolled her to her feet. The ward spun and he snaked his arm across her throat, hugged her back in tight to his chest. Lydia felt a circle of cold steel kiss her temple. She wanted to puke. A gargled yelp came up instead.

"Let her go."

Stephen Black's voice lacked its usual playfulness. He came into view as Lydia's captor turned to face him. His silenced pistol was drawn and aimed, it seemed, right at Lydia's face.

"Who the fuck are you, mate?"

"Certainly not your *mate*." His lips twisted like he'd bitten into something sour. "Now let her go."

"Seems to me like you're not in any position to tell me what to do. So why don't you fuck off, eh?"

"I'm a very good shot. Do you want a bullet in your eye?"

"Come off it. If you were really that good I'd be dead by now." He began to walk backwards, digging his forearm a little harder into Lydia's throat. "Lads! I've got the bitch. Come on. That Cullen prick will do what he's told now."

Tears rolled down Lydia's face. How could they be back in this position? It wasn't fair. They'd beaten the bastards and were in a safe place. There were cops under this roof for God's sake. Where were the useless bastards, though? She tried to scream but couldn't get her throat to obey her.

And then, "Hey, dickhead."

John?

She felt the pressure on her throat ease as the man changed position. Then she heard a sickening *thwack*. The man let her go. She turned on her heel to see her husband, awake and burning with fury. John held an

IV drip stand over his shoulder like a baseball bat. He swung and the length of stainless steel clattered into the side of the man's head. The man in black fatigues flopped to the floor. John raised the stand over his head and brought it down across the back of the fallen man's neck. Then he righted the stand and used it for support so he could raise a leg and stomp down on the bastard's head.

Lydia backed off a couple of steps, stunned by her husband's sudden violent outburst. She saw Donna approach him, hands raised. The two men who had chased Rory down the ward came up behind them, guns raised. Cold, hard stares.

"Oi, you!"

A flat crack and Donna went down. The man on the left, the one who shot her, cursed. His partner aimed, fired and missed. John charged them, limping at high speed, brandishing his IV drip stand like a Zulu spear. Then both gunmen opened fire on him. Lydia's husband, brave-stupid bastard, fell to his knees and toppled face first onto the cold, hard hospital floor.

"Stop! Police! Put down your guns."

The cops had finally come.

But they were too late.

Lydia went to her husband, sat beside him on the cold, hard floor and wept.

CHAPTER 24

There's not a lot of talk about bungs in the game anymore. Bribing managers and football scouts isn't a dead phenomenon, you know. There are still a lot of fat rich bastards getting fatter and richer off the transfer windows. Everybody knows who's at it. They just don't want to end up in the Thames with stones in their pockets. Loose lips sink Premierships.

Rory Cullen, *Cullen: The Autobiography*

Cormac took a moment to look down at Mick Scullion's corpse. He couldn't say he was sorry the psycho was dead – no doubt he'd saved a few lives by taking his – but there was regret. Regret that the bastard wouldn't be held to account for his actions. That the justice was swift and roughshod and unsatisfying. A bullet in the head was a mercy.

He wouldn't let that happen to Ambrose O'Neill. That fucker would do his penance the hard way.

Cormac stepped over Mick Scullion's body, resisting the urge to spit on him, and made a beeline for the fallen motorcyclist. He could see the rise and fall of the leather-encased chest and an occasional twitch of the limbs. O'Neill was regaining consciousness. Cormac trained his gun on him and proceeded with caution.

When he got within kicking distance, Cormac prodded O'Neill's side with his foot. O'Neill jerked away from the contact and Cormac smiled. He'd jangled some broken ribs by the looks of it. His smile faded when he heard the downed man shout.

"You wanker!"

A London accent.

Cormac dropped to his knees and shoved open the man's visor. A tanned, pock-marked face stared out at him from the helmet. There were two separate eyebrows above this man's angry eyes. It most definitely was not Ambrose O'Neill.

"Who the fuck are you?" Cormac asked.

"Who the fuck are *you*?" the Londoner asked.

"Detective Kelly. PSNI."

"What the fuck's a PSNI—"

Cormac shoved him onto his side.

"Argh! For fuck's sake, mate. I'm in bits here. Go easy."

Cormac ignored him and unzipped a pocket on the back of the Londoner's leather trousers. He shoved his hand in but there was no wallet. A quick frisk turned up no concealed weapons. Cormac pulled him onto his back. He undid the strap on his helmet and tugged it off. The man bared super-whitened teeth.

"I need an ambulance."

"You'll need a hearse if you don't start talking." Cormac backhanded the man's face. "Tell me who you are."

"Jesus, you daft Paddy. Take it easy on the rough stuff, will you? I'll talk. What's the point in keeping schtum now? My prints are on file. Everything's on my record."

"You a tout as well?"

"Tout?"

"A grass."

"Oh." He flashed his pearly whites in a pained, forced smile. "I've been known to help the law with some minor enquiries."

"Honour among thieves, eh?"

"That's a fairy tale."

"All right, then. Start with your name and who you work for. We'll take it from there."

"I'm Brendan Rooney. I do a bit for my cousin, Martin Rooney. I take it even a Mick copper's heard of him."

Cormac maintained a poker face but his guts flip-flopped. Martin Rooney, the fucking Republican-sympathising, London Irish, cocaine kingpin. He nodded once.

"Well, he's been working with some Belfast boys on a big score. Things got a bit messed up and he's called in a bunch of us to try and clean the shit up. Think this whole deal's been cursed from the start, though. Even the clean-up crew's making a mess."

"So, your cousin's hired Ambrose O'Neill and his lot?"

"Yeah. There's a man who doesn't live up to his reputation. He's meant to be a pro. Fucking amateur hour. Totally botched a simple kidnapping."

"Where's O'Neill now?"

"Wanker's meant to be here, backing us up. Things kicked off earlier than we'd hoped but he definitely should have got here with a bunch of Martin's men ages ago. Me and the other Mick – the one who's called Mick! – we were here to scout out the situation and call it in when the helicopter arrived. Then some little fellah started shooting and Mick got all hyped up. Made me go after him."

"Call them now," Cormac said. "Find out where they are."

"Fuck that, mate. There's cooperating and then there's signing your own death certificate."

Cormac couldn't really argue with that, and he knew he was pushing his luck by hanging about. O'Neill could arrive at any moment with a fresh goon squad and a cartload of ammunition. He nodded to Brendan and got to his feet.

"When you see Ambrose O'Neill, tell him Cormac Kelly's looking for him."

"I'll tell him fuck all, mate. Only story he's getting from me is I crashed my bike and was unconscious while a stranger with a gun shot the loopy Mick then took off."

Brendan Rooney obviously had no appreciation for the dramatic. Cormac shook his head and walked towards the shot-up BMW in search of Stephen Black's car. A crowd of gawkers had gathered at the front door of the club. None of them were brave enough to venture off the porch steps. The lack of sirens suggested that none of the useless bastards had thought to call the cops. Cormac flashed his gun at them and shouted across the car park.

"Please go back inside and phone the police. Report this as a fatal shooting. They'll be here soon."

The crowd shuffled back to shelter, nobody feeling up to challenging his authority. Cormac found the big BMW and pushed the button on the key-fob that Stephen Black had given him. Orange lights flashed a few cars down. He headed towards them and clicked the button a few more times. A few seconds later he was at the Vauxhall Vectra. He spotted the bulletproof windows instantly. An ex-police motor. Cormac liked how this little mystery man rolled.

You'll find a small Scottish man in the boot.

Cormac remembered Big Frank Toner. When he'd taken John and Donna away from the hospital, he'd left Frank in the boot of Donna's car. The poor bastard was probably still there.

"Fuck it. I'll tip the PSNI off later."

Cormac decided not to open the Vectra's boot just yet. He'd find somewhere that wouldn't be crawling with police soon. Somewhere nice and quiet where he could have a nice long chat with Mr McGoldrick.

Cormac got into the Vectra, adjusted the driving position and mirrors then gunned the engine. He pumped up the volume on the CD player to drown out the yelled threats from the boot. Black Sabbath's *War Pigs* blasted from the speakers. He nodded along to the high-hat.

"You've got taste, Stephen Black. I'll give you that."

The cops took over. Lydia offered the useless bastards no resistance. She was led to a quiet room and handed some tablets by a sad-faced nurse. Swallowed them without hesitation. The pills made her feel a little numb. A little dumb. She wanted to turn off the harsh artificial light and curl up into a ball. Shut out the world. But that wasn't allowed. Not when you had a son who was just as heartbroken.

Mattie hadn't been offered any pills. Lydia didn't know if she should try and get him some or if he was too young. It seemed unfair that he had to brave the pain with no pharmaceutical filter. She dragged her plastic chair towards his, sat beside him and held her arms open. Mattie snuggled in against her side and cried. Lydia held her son tight, rubbed his back and synchronised her breathing with his.

Time passed, measured only by the tears that soaked into Lydia's cotton top.

Then Mattie lifted his head and rubbed at his eyes with the heel of his good hand. He looked around the room and sighed.

"How long are they going to leave us here for, Mum?"

"The cops? I think they'll wait for us to call them."

"I meant the doctors and nurses." He held up his bandaged hand, his face crimped with teen embarrassment. "My fingers are getting sore again."

"Oh, God, yes. We should get those looked at properly."

"And we should find out about Donna."

"You're right. Jesus. I didn't even ask about her. She could be…"

"Hurt?"

"Yes. Hurt."

"Somebody has to tell Cormac about it."

"Who's… Oh, you mean Detective Kelly. Should I phone him or is it better coming from a policeman?"

Mattie shrugged then rubbed at the back of his neck. "I think Donna used to be his girlfriend. He's going to be pretty upset. Maybe I should do it? We're kind of like friends now, you know?"

Lydia thanked God that she'd been slightly dulled by whatever pills she'd popped. As it was, her heart was just about to burst with pride and love for her little boy. She could see the man he would grow to be in the set of his jaw. The man he would become more quickly now that his father was gone. She nodded.

"Okay, we'll talk to a doctor, find out how Donna is and then you can phone your friend."

They stood together, hugged and breathed deep as one. Lydia kissed Mattie's forehead and patted down a few stray strands of his hair. She probably could do with a major primping herself, but her handbag, which contained her vanity mirror and essential makeup, got left behind in Stephen Black's car. Maybe not knowing how bad she looked was a bit of a mercy.

A uniformed police officer stood outside the room. He smiled at Lydia.

"I'll call the detectives," he said.

"We want to see a doctor, actually."

The officer's smile faded. "I've been ordered to—"

"I'm sure the detectives will be able to track us down, officer. If they can't, then they're pretty shit at their job, aren't they?"

Mattie wheezed, not quite managing to hold back a surprise laugh. The officer widened his eyes for a second then nodded once.

"Fair enough, Mrs Gallagher."

Lydia looked left and right. Tried to remember which way she'd come. Mattie took a baby-step to the left and Lydia followed his subtle lead.

They made their way back to the nurse's station. There were yellow plastic cones set out in front of the counter, providing a warning that the floor was wet. John's blood had been mopped away. The thought of the simple action hit her like a rabbit-punch. A part of John squeezed into a bucket of murky water. Water that would be flushed away into the sewage system. Where the rats live.

"There he is, Mum."

She stepped back from the brink of morbidity. Looked up and caught the gaze of the tall doctor who'd met them on the roof. His shoulders slumped. This was a man who didn't work very hard to conceal his negative emotions. He looked from side to side as if in search of an escape route or a nurse to pass his potential problem on to. Lydia homed in on him.

"Doctor, any word on Doctor, um... Donna?"

"She's in surgery."

"And...?"

"And that's it. The surgeons are working on her. Now if you don't mind, I'm quite busy—"

"Of course you're busy. You're a doctor. Dry your fucking eyes. You want to compare shitty days? My husband just died. You can spare me a few fucking seconds of your time, can't you?"

The doctor puffed up his pigeon chest and jutted his chin. He was set to put her in her place. Lydia crossed her arms and cocked her hips.

Bring it on, dickhead.

He deflated.

"Come this way, Mrs Gallagher."

The doctor led Lydia and Mattie to one of the beds on the ward. He drew the curtain and rested his backside against the side of the raised mattress. Lydia sat in the visitors' chair and Mattie perched beside her on the arm.

"How can I help you?" The doctor's words sounded like an elongated sigh.

"I want to know if you think Donna will live."

"We have a very talented team working on her. There are no guarantees, but she's being given a very good chance."

"And the man my husband... tackled."

"He's dead."

"The other two?"

"Arrested."

"Where are the men who arrived with us? Rory Cullen and Stephen Black."

"They're being interviewed by the police in the canteen. They want to speak to you as well."

"They'll have to wait. First I want you to arrange for an x-ray of my son's hand. And ask a nurse to get him some painkillers."

The doctor glanced at the dressing on Mattie's hand and offered a mouth-shrug.

"I can get the painkillers quickly but there's no radiographer on duty tonight. Soonest he can be seen is tomorrow morning."

"Well, I want you to make sure he's first on the list, then."

"That's not up to me."

"So you get in touch with whoever it *is* up to and persuade them to bump Mattie to the top of the list. He's waited long enough for treatment."

"Fine, I'll do it. But could I ask you for a small favour in return?"

"You can ask."

"Would you be able to get me Rory Cullen's autograph? He told me to fuck off earlier."

Lydia was about to tell him to fuck off but the sound of hurried footsteps on the ward distracted her. The curtain was drawn back by a frowning nurse with glasses too big and fashionable for her middle-aged face. Two men in ill-fitting suits stood behind her. The detectives.

"Mrs Gallagher," the fatter of the two said. "We'd like you to come with us."

Lydia felt Mattie's hand on her forearm.

"Mum, don't forget about Cormac."

She nodded to her son then aimed her best professional smile at the detectives.

"Do you mind if I make a quick personal call?"

The detectives turned to each other and had a quick silent conferral that consisted of raised eyebrow, pursed lips and facial shrugs. Then the fatter one, who Lydia now took to be the senior, cleared his throat.

"I don't see why not, Mrs Gallagher. We'll be at the canteen. Maybe you could meet us there in ten minutes?"

Lydia thanked them and they left her. The doctor looked at his watch and excused himself. He hesitated for a second before pushing through the curtain and Lydia suspected he was working up the nerve to ask for Rory's autograph again.

"I'm sure Rory will be happy to sort you out when things have calmed down a little."

The doctor allowed himself a small smile, nodded and disappeared.

Lydia dug her phone out of her suit jacket. Her heart sped up a little as she scrolled through the screens to get to Detective Kelly's number. She took a deep breath before hitting the green button.

"I'm not looking forward to this," Lydia said.

Mattie held out his good hand. "Let me do it."

"Are you sure?"

"I've already told you, it'll be better coming from me."

Lydia thought it was probably a bad idea, that she shouldn't start down this path of relying on Mattie so soon, but he seemed so grown up all of a sudden.

She handed over the phone.

CHAPTER 25

I can understand why some of the top players need a wee bit of help in the looks department. We're under a lot of pressure to look good for the camera in this day and age. You have no idea how much shit you take for a bad picture in the paper or on the internet. So some of us might need hair plugs or a spot of Botox. It's not a crime, just a bit tragic. After all, you can't really polish a turd, can you?

Rory Cullen, *Cullen: The Autobiography*

Cormac felt the phone buzz in his hip pocket. He pulled the Vectra over to the side of the road and flipped on the hazard lights. The traffic was light and the lanes were wide; little chance that a careless driver would plough into the back of the car and crush his passenger in the boot. Cormac killed the radio and answered the call.

"Cormac, it's Mattie."

"Good to hear from you, kid. They get your da sorted at the hospital?"

"Um… it… fuck. Sorry, Mum." Mattie took a deep breath. "There were men with guns here. They shot Dad…"

"Ah, Jesus, Mattie. Is he…?"

Mattie sniffed. "Yeah."

"Fuck." Cormac gripped the steering wheel with

his free hand as if steeling himself for the next blow. "Did anybody else get hurt?"

"Donna got shot."

His cop instincts had been a step ahead. He'd expected Mattie to say as much. But it still hit him like a wrecking ball in the gut. He rolled down the window to let some air into the car. The old guy in the boot had started kicking and screaming again. Cormac's mouth filled with bitter saliva. He spat it out onto the road. Clenched the wheel tighter. His forearm ached.

"Is she alive?"

"Yeah. But they've got her in surgery. Doctor said she's getting the best treatment."

"Anybody else hurt?"

"No. Dad kind of kept them all busy... he killed one of them before the others shot him." The kid was starting to choke up. "He died like a real hero, you know?"

"You can be proud of him, then."

"The police got the other two."

Cops. Cormac felt like he needed to see Donna but contact with the police could put an end to things. If they checked out his PSNI credentials it would be game over. And with Ambrose O'Neill still at large and another player in the boot of his car, he wasn't ready to call it a day just yet. These bastards had pulled Donna into their shit-storm and they were going to answer for it. He would manufacture their doom.

"Mattie, did these men have Belfast accents?"

"No. They were London hard-man types."

"Okay. Thanks." His mind whirred. "Look, I'm truly sorry for your loss, kid. I promise you, I'm going to get the bastards behind all of this."

"I know you will."

There was a soulful weight to the kid's words that lost none of its impact over the crackly phone connection.

"Can I speak to your ma?"

"Two secs."

The sandpaper rustles of Mattie's hand sliding over the receiver and a murmured exchange preceded the changeover.

"Detective Kelly?"

"Mrs Gallagher. I'm very sorry for your loss."

"Thank you." She paused for a few seconds. "How can I help you?"

"Your security consultant friend gave me the keys to his car so I could meet you all at the hospital. He also told me about his passenger…"

"Oh, Jesus. McGoldrick's still in the car. You need to take him to the police. The bastard set this all up. Oh, and he'll need medical attention. He's been shot in the legs."

"Judging by the racket he's making in the back, there's plenty of life left in him yet."

"Pity."

"He's not a friend, then?"

"As far as I can gather, the old bastard played a big part in this whole mess. My husband is dead because of his greed."

"What do you know about him?"

"He's in with some gangsters and they needed a favour. He handed me and my family to them as a way to get to Rory Cullen. It looks like they want to use him to take some of the risk out of their gambling."

"The men who attacked you at the hospital, they weren't from Belfast?"

"No. Definitely Londoners."

"And they've been arrested."

"Yes."

"I need to find Ambrose O'Neill."

"I'll let you know if he shows up. Are you going to come to the hospital? I think Mattie would like to see you."

"Not yet. I want to question McGoldrick first. See what he knows about O'Neill. But can you call me when Donna comes out of surgery?"

"Of course."

Cormac ended the call and dropped the phone in a cup holder. He turned up the volume on the radio. *Iron Man* smashed through the speakers. In the cocoon of sound, Cormac held his head in his hands. It had happened. He'd dragged Donna into his bullshit and she got hurt. At the time, their breakup had almost been a relief. They'd parted ways before he'd ruined her life. But he'd gone back to her, looking for help, and maybe just a little contact. And now this.

He looked up into the rear-view mirror. Narrowed his bloodshot eyes.

"So, are you just going to sit here and cry about it?"

Fuck beating himself up. Cormac put this on O'Neill and anybody else he could connect to this case. Like the guy in the boot of the car. McGoldrick would pay his dues just the same as the rest of them. But they needed to find a nice private place to spend some time together.

Cormac figured out how to hook his phone up to the Vectra's sound system through Bluetooth and pulled out onto the road again. Headed towards London. He wanted to be closer to Donna even if he couldn't visit her just yet.

It was time to find out just how much trouble he was in. He killed Ozzy's vocals and called Canavan.

"Would you not leave me alone this day, Kelly?"

"Always a pleasure, Canavan. What's the craic?"

"I guess your ears were burning. Just got out of a wee meeting about you."

"So I'm in the shit, then?"

"Officially, you're missing in the line of duty. But it's no great secret that your handler believes you've gone native."

"And did you put them right?"

"Fuck no. I told them the truth. You showed up at my gaff, put my case at risk, shoved a gun in my face, forced me to cooperate with you and robbed my hardware supplies."

"Hey, cheers for having my back."

"I'm not risking my hole for you after the way you came at me."

"I'd no choice."

"Aye, right."

Cormac let the silence swell. He needed more help from Canavan but since he couldn't stick a gun in his face from across the water, he'd have to play on his guilt. Canavan had been right to play it straight with the uppers. They'd have found out eventually, anyway. There was nobody else Cormac could have gone to for help. But now they knew they could rely on Canavan. And Cormac knew that he could too.

"I take it this isn't a social call," Canavan said.

"What did you find out about O'Neill?"

"He's in London. Linking up with Martin Rooney, no doubt."

"Has there been anything back from the Met about Rooney and O'Neill's new relationship?"

"Nothing substantial. Just that they appear to have gotten friendlier; regular meetings with Rooney's underlings and whatnot. He's not been seen in the presence of the big man, though. If they've met in person, they've done it carefully."

"So if O'Neill falls, he falls alone."

"That's how the big boys play."

Time to change the rules.

"Anything else of interest?"

"Oh, yeah. It seems as if Pete Scullion, one of your friends from the kidnapping caper, took a header off a block of flats in London."

Cormac almost told him that Mick Scullion had told him about his brother's death, right before Cormac had shot him in the head. But he decided against it. He didn't have the full story behind Pete's not-so-tragic end. Better to find out what Canavan knew about it. He played dumb.

"Pete's dead? Fuck. Hell of a time to say goodbye to this cruel world."

"Humpty was pushed, mate."

"Figured as much. You got an address for the scene of crime?"

Cormac memorised the address and gruffly thanked Canavan. He reached out to the Vectra's sat nav and fiddled with the touchscreen. The Peckham address came up in the search history. Looked like the so-called security consultant had been to visit the murder scene. Cormac didn't like that this little guy was operating as if the law didn't apply to him. Then it occurred to him that his own recent actions weren't exactly sanctioned.

"But I'm not doing it for profit," he told the rear-view mirror.

There seemed to be little conviction in the reflection of his eyes.

Maybe you should report to the nearest cop shop. Hand over McGoldrick and get in touch with your unit. Give them all your intel and let them take over. Throw yourself at the mercy of an internal investigation. Face the music. Do the right thing.

He gave the idea some thought.

Grunted.

"Aye, right. Fuck that shite."

Cormac set the sat nav to guide him to the block of flats in Peckham and stomped the accelerator.

CHAPTER 26

I don't like to think about what I'll end up doing when football's done with me. Acting could be fun, I suppose. You don't even need that much talent. Just a bad boy reputation would do.

Rory Cullen, *Cullen: The Autobiography*

The detectives had bought her a coffee. Hospital canteen flavour; cheap and weak. Sugar and UHT milk couldn't tart it up. She'd have preferred the can of Coke they'd bought for Mattie. And she'd much rather they'd given Mattie a glass of milk instead of a hefty shot of sugar and caffeine, but she didn't protest when her son cracked it open. There was little chance either of them was going to sleep any time soon, anyway.

The fatter detective, DI Robinson, sipped from a bottle of mineral water. He sighed, set it on the table and scowled at it. His thin moustache rippled when he curled his lip.

"Trying to drink two litres of water a day. My personal trainer recommended it. Is there anything more boring than water?"

DS Scott, the slightly younger and slightly smaller detective shrugged and slurped on a tin of Red Bull. His hair and beard were red and wild like Luke Kelly's, one of John's favourite musicians. Lydia wondered if she could ever listen to the Irish folk singer again now that he'd be forever associated with her late husband.

DI Robinson scanned down his notepad to see where they'd left off. He tapped his pencil on the tabletop and looked at Lydia.

"So, where is this Detective Kelly?"

"I don't know."

"But he definitely hasn't been shot or anything?"

"I told you, I spoke to him on the phone before I came to see you."

"Yes, and told him about…" DI Robinson read from his notes. "Donna Grant. The doctor. And you believe he'll come to see her?"

"He said he'd be here as soon as he could."

"Good, good. I'd like to get his side of the story too."

Lydia omitted the fact that McGoldrick was with him. She'd a feeling that Detective Kelly was going to bend a rule or two to get some answers from the old Scot. Especially since his ex-girlfriend had been caught in the crossfire. It was why Lydia had been eager to let Detective Kelly know about McGoldrick's involvement. John had ranted about the police "back home" on more than one occasion. The thought of McGoldrick experiencing some good old fashioned Northern Irish police brutality gave her something to fantasise about throughout DI Robinson's half-hearted interview.

"I think that's all I need to know for the time being, Mrs Gallagher. Of course, I may need to call upon you again, if that's all right. But I won't torture you. You've been through enough."

"Anything I can do, Detective, don't hesitate to ask. I want all the men responsible for… for *this* brought to justice."

"That's very clear-minded of you. Thank you for your time."

DS Scott spoke for the first time. "What's Rory Cullen like?"

DI Robinson bunched his fists. His subordinate was in for a bit of an earful on the ride back to the station, no doubt.

"I'm sure Mrs Gallagher has more important things on her mind."

Lydia shrugged. "It's okay. I get asked that often. I don't need to think too hard for the answer. He's just like you'd expect. Typical footballer."

"Bit of a prick, then?" DS Scott asked. "Full of himself?"

"Like I said, he's a typical footballer. They all have their flaws. Some more so than others. But yeah, Rory has his moments."

DS Scott sat back in his chair, oblivious to his senior's disapproval, "Knew he was a prick."

"You should know," DI Robinson said. "Right, we're off. Mrs Gallagher, we've organised some police surveillance at your home. Don't be alarmed to find a bit of activity when you get back. It's just a precaution and should only last until we track down..." he consulted his notes again, "Ambrose O'Neill."

When they were out of earshot Mattie tugged on Lydia's sleeve. She looked at him; saw the obvious signs of a sugar rush in his widened eyes and fidgety limbs.

"Are you sure those two were cops?" he asked.

"Why would you doubt them?"

"They're nothing like Cormac. All old and out of shape. He'd kick their flabby asses."

"Some people take their jobs more seriously than others, I guess."

"If those two were more serious, Dad might still be alive."

Mattie slammed his can of Coke down on the table. Light brown suds foamed up and spilled out over the rim. Tears ran down his face and dripped off his clenched jaw. Lydia could tell by the set of his mouth that he was holding back a sob. She cupped the back of his head and drew him into her body. With his face pressed against the flesh below her collarbone, Mattie let some of his anger and grief loose; the sobs and moans muffled. Lydia held on to hers. She couldn't afford the energy.

Rory and Stephen Black entered the canteen. They spotted her immediately but had the good sense to hang back while Lydia comforted her son. She gave them a small wave and pointed to a table in the far corner of the room. Rory returned the wave and Stephen Black nodded once. Lydia knew they all understood that there was more work to be done. She had no faith in the policemen assigned to her. This could only be played out by the likes of Detective Kelly and Stephen Black; those who took their jobs seriously.

Cormac parked the Vectra on the street leading up to the Peckham flats where Pete Scullion had been killed. A pair of police cars sat in the car park and one uniformed officer stood by an area cordoned off with blue and white police tape. Cormac looked up to see another cop on a balcony outside a top-floor flat. The door behind him was criss-crossed by the same police line.

Two marked cop cars should equal four uniformed cops. The other two were most likely going door to door in a fruitless search for witnesses. Cormac figured he was parked far enough away that the uniform on the ground wouldn't hear McGoldrick should he start banging on the inside of the boot lid again. He didn't know if the old guy had given up, passed out or died, but Cormac was in no rush to check on him. They'd need to be parked somewhere very quiet before he opened that can of worms.

Cormac got out of the Vectra and crossed the road. He wished he'd retrieved his PSNI ID from the safe before taking this trip but there hadn't been time. But with any luck, he'd be able to bluff his way through.

The uniform at the police tape looked young and scared. That would work to Cormac's advantage. A trio of black kids in hoodies stood outside one of the ground floor flats. Their chatter stopped dead when they clocked Cormac. They didn't want to miss anything. The uniform noticed him a few seconds later. He held up his hand.

"Do you live in this building, sir?"

"I'm Detective Kelly of the PSNI. I've been working undercover on a case that involves the man who died here. Pete Scullion was part of a kidnap gang I infiltrated."

"Can I see your ID?"

"Like I said, I've been working undercover. It's not a good idea to carry ID on the job."

The uniform's mouth twitched and Cormac could see that he wasn't convinced.

"Do you want to call my handler? I can give you his number."

The young officer relaxed a little. "No, don't worry about it. I've enough on my plate here." He nodded towards the three kids. "What is it you're after, Detective Kelly?"

"I'd like a few minutes up in the flat. See if there's anything in there that'll help me track down the rest of the gang."

The uniform pushed the button on the radio clipped high up on the left side of his vest. "There's a Detective Kelly from the PSNI down here. He wants to go up to have a look at the flat, Malcolm."

The radio crackled. "PSNI...? Right. Send him up, then."

Cormac took the stairs up to the top floor two at a time. He wanted to get in and out fast, before any awkward questions started. The longer he hung about, the greater the risk that they'd find out that he was having an unauthorised poke about.

Malcolm had just stamped out a cigarette judging by the smell of tobacco smoke that hovered around him. He held his hand out for Cormac to shake. Cormac was a little taken aback by his enthusiasm – most cops were ridiculously territorial – but he returned the uniform's firm grip.

"Detective Kelly, all the way from Ireland, eh? My granny was from Belfast."

"You could play for the national football team, then."

Malcolm smirked. "Very good. Here, maybe you could settle an argument between me and young Ronnie down there." He pointed at the uniform in the car park.

"I'm in a bit of a rush."

"Yeah, yeah. Won't keep you a moment."

Cormac turned up his palms. "Go on, then."

"This Pete Scullion. Was he one of those Real IRA boys?"

"No. Ex-Provo turned gangster."

"Good, good. That's what I thought. We've

enough to worry about with the Muslim fundamental-
ists without some mental Micks slinging bombs about."
He held up a placatory hand. "I only say Mick because
I'm part Irish myself. No offence, you understand."

"Aye, none taken. Now if you don't mind...?"
Cormac pointed to the flat's open door.

"Be my guest, mate."

Cormac ducked under the police line. The flat
was a decent enough size. He'd seen much smaller in
Belfast. The décor wasn't up to much, though. It was
every bit the lair of a single man who hadn't done all
his growing up. Big TV, games console, framed posters
of movie scenes and players from the Chelsea squad.
Cormac looked at a stack of junk mail piled on a small
table by the door. The credit card and loan offers were
addressed to Brendan Rooney. Nothing too surprising there. At best, Cormac could conclude that they'd
gotten sloppy in their haste, allowing the Belfast boys
to come here despite Brendan's obvious connections to
the big cheese, Martin Rooney.

The kitchen area showed a few small signs of a
struggle; a broken plate on the linoleum, the kitchen
drawer open, its contents jumbled like a hand had swept
through it frantically for a weapon.

Back in the living area, Cormac noticed a laptop
charger plugged into the wall but no laptop nearby.
He looked into the bathroom. Nothing in there but
the threat of E. coli and hepatitis. He closed the door
quickly.

There were two bedrooms, one used as sleeping
quarters, the other a storage/dump room. He checked
out the spare room first. Found little of interest. Judging
by the thick layer of dust, the junk in there hadn't been
disturbed in some time.

In the bedroom, Cormac found a poster of Rory Cullen in his old Chelsea gear. Somebody had added a crudely drawn penis to his face and a speech bubble pointed to his mouth with the witty statement, "I'm a knob face traitor", scrawled within. The handwriting was child-like. There was nothing in the dresser drawers other than clothes, and the wardrobe was just as fruitless.

Cormac went to the bedside cabinet and pulled out the top drawer. Amid a tangle of headphones, gold chains and knick-knacks rested a plastic wallet with the Chelsea logo printed on it. Cormac flipped it open and found a current Stamford Bridge season ticket. He checked in behind it and found a different coloured ticket. It was an executive box ticket for a match the weekend after next. Chelsea vs. Manchester City. The first game Rory Cullen would play against his former squad.

A foot soldier like Brendan Rooney was lucky to afford a season ticket, but to land a spot in an executive box for a match as hyped as this one? He'd either come into a bit of money and blown it on this or been gifted the ticket by somebody in a high place. Somebody like Martin Rooney. Perhaps as an award for pulling together a caper that'd give them more control over the outcome of the game. It seemed like Lydia Gallagher's theory wasn't all that far-fetched.

Cormac pocketed the tickets and left the flat.

"Find anything useful in there?" Malcolm asked.

"Not really."

"Neither did our boys. Good luck rounding up the rest of them."

Cormac considered giving Malcolm his mobile number in case he found out anything about O'Neill's whereabouts. It seemed unlikely that the information would trickle down to him though, and it was probably a bad idea to leave anything that might allow his superiors to track him down. He skipped down the stairs, breezed past young Ronnie the uniform and got back in the car.

It was time to chat to McGoldrick. He just needed to find a nice private spot.

"It makes more sense to stay at my place," Rory said. "There's the security system and Stevie here has agreed to a sleepover as well."

Lydia considered Rory's proposal. It seemed sensible. And the longer she put off spending her first night in her own bed without John the better. But she had to consider Mattie. Maybe it would be better for him to get back to normal as soon as possible.

"What do you think, Mattie?"

"Can Cormac stay too?"

Lydia was getting uncomfortable with Mattie's apparent fascination with this cop. She would have to take the time to talk to Mattie and find out exactly what he'd been through, what he'd seen and what Detective Kelly had done over the past few days. The gaps in her knowledge unnerved her.

"I'm sure he would appreciate the offer," Stephen Black said. "But I believe Detective Kelly is out looking for the last of the scoundrels who kidnapped you, young Mattie."

Mattie looked Stephen Black up and down then turned to Lydia. "Can you text Cormac with Rory's address, Mum? Just in case he does need a place to crash tonight?"

"You should be asking Rory. It's his house."

Rory tapped the tabletop, one finger at a time. "Another guy with a gun in the house? Seems like a good idea to me. Even if he is a peeler. Just don't tell any of my mates back home, all right, kid?"

"Thanks!"

Lydia tapped out the text. Mattie watched the phone's screen over her shoulder to make sure she didn't do something wrong. He didn't relax until she hit send.

"So what now?" Lydia asked.

"We'll need to call a taxi," Stephen Black said. "Good ol' Nathan will have made himself scarce in his whirlybird by now, no doubt."

"You think so?" Rory asked.

"Wouldn't you, dear boy? I mean, it had to have been him who told the thugs we were on our way to this hospital."

Lydia thought about it for a moment. "He'd have had plenty of time, I guess."

Stephen Black nodded. "It would have taken just one quick text or a coded message over the radio."

Rory slapped the table. "Sneaky fucker."

"He was just doing his job, I suppose," Stephen Black said. "Probably didn't fully understand what he'd done."

"I'm tired," Lydia said. "Let's just get going."

"Do you think you should tell those English cops that you're not going home? They might want to reroute their surveillance boys."

"No, I don't want to talk to anybody else tonight. And sure, they should be there anyway in case anybody comes looking for me. Until I hear that somebody somewhere has arrested that Ambrose O'Neill bastard, I don't want anybody thinking they can relax."

Chapter 27

You need to surround yourself with the right people or this game will eat you alive.

Rory Cullen, *Cullen: The Autobiography*

Cormac disabled the CCTV cameras on the top floor of the multi-storey car park before he opened the Vectra's boot. The place was closed for the night and the bays were mostly empty. Just a few cars on each floor remained, their drivers maybe having decided to hit the pub and take a taxi home that night. He'd been able to raise the barrier with a good shove and hadn't set off any audible alarms. He figured there wasn't much to safeguard after hours in a place like this.

The only light in the building came from the Vectra. It was enough. Cormac reached into the boot and pulled the little man out and dumped him onto the concrete floor. McGoldrick rolled onto his back, took a deep breath but didn't scream. Maybe he was too scared, perhaps he wanted to save energy; either way, Cormac wasn't overly concerned. So long as McGoldrick was willing to talk when he urged him to, they'd get along just fine.

"Can you walk?" Cormac asked.

"I don't know." In just those three words his Scottish accent rang through.

"Have a go."

He watched as McGoldrick rolled onto his belly and ever-so-slowly went from all fours to a kneeling position. Then the old Scot used the Vectra's rear bumper as a handhold and climbed to his feet. Cormac considered slamming the lid of the boot shut on his hand when he used the rim to steady himself, but he didn't want to send the old bastard into shock. He waited until McGoldrick was upright and looked confident that he wouldn't keel over.

"Do you think you lost much blood?"

"I'm still conscious, aren't I?"

Cormac noticed that McGoldrick had managed to tear lengths of cloth from his polo shirt and fashioned some tourniquets for his upper thighs. He pointed at them.

"Very inventive."

"Who are you? What the fuck do you want?"

"Let's concentrate on you."

McGoldrick puffed his chest and squared up to Cormac. He was a game wee bastard, he had to give him that.

"All right, pal, how about this. Do you know who *I* am? Do you know what I could have done to you?"

"Ah, the old rich man favourites. Yes, I'm starting to get a handle on who you are, Mr McGoldrick. You're a millionaire who didn't make his money without breaking a few rules. One thing led to another and you got in bed with a very bad man called Martin Rooney. Now you can arrange to have people kidnapped. So, yeah, I know exactly who you are and what you can do. The question is, do you know how much shite you're in right now? Here's a hint. You can't throw money at this problem."

"What the fuck do you want from me, then?"

"I haven't decided yet. This caper of yours has cost me a lot. I've burnt a lot of bridges, ruined my career and somebody very close to me has been badly hurt. I could blame you for that and act accordingly."

Cormac drew his Glock and levelled it at McGoldrick's head. The old Scot stared back defiantly, but Cormac didn't miss the slight quiver in his hands before he folded his arms across his chest.

"I have to tell you, McGoldrick... that option is in the lead right now. A double-tap in your face won't repair my life. It'd make it worse in the long run, really. But it'd be very fucking satisfying."

"You said you haven't decided yet," McGoldrick's voice was strong and steady. A negotiator to the end. "What else are you considering?"

"I'm thinking about how much more useful you could be to me if I left you alive."

McGoldrick's shoulders dropped slightly as tension eased from his frame. He was relaxing into the situation, ready to barter for his life.

"Okay. How much is this going to cost me, then?"

"I've already told you, you can't throw money at this problem."

"What do you want, then?"

"Martin Rooney."

McGoldrick ran his still shaking hands through his hair. It flopped back into place and the old Scot whistled a descending note.

"How am I supposed to deliver something like that?"

"Give yourself up and implicate Rooney as a co-conspirator in this kidnapping case as well as the other illegal activities he's helped you out with over the years."

"Nothing's going to stick to him. He's been distancing himself from the illegal shit for years now. Everything is done through middlemen. Rooney keeps his hands clean."

"He'll have fucked up somewhere. They all do. You confess your sins, roll over on Rooney and let the investigation take care of the rest."

"So I can lose everything, go to jail and get killed by one of his lackeys? I'd be better off getting shot in the head here and now."

"If that's the way you think it's going to play out, you need to fire that high-powered legal team you undoubtedly have on your payroll, mate."

McGoldrick sat on the rim of the boot. "Sorry, I'm not fit to stand. My legs are killing me."

"That's okay. Saves me picking you up off the floor after I kill you."

"You're so brave, picking on an unarmed and injured man."

"Don't forget old and grey." Cormac smirked. "I've seen first hand what you're capable of, even if you do pay others to do the dirty work for you. Forgive me if I can't dredge up much sympathy. Must feel a bit strange, though. To be on your own, I mean. All that money useless to you."

McGoldrick sagged. Cormac could have continued the torment. It was easy to belittle someone then kick them when they were down. But he wasn't in the market for that sort of perverse satisfaction. He just wanted results. And if he could hand the Met a case that would take down Rooney, maybe it'd stand in his favour when he had to face the music back home.

"I can't do it," McGoldrick said.

Cormac sighed and tucked his Glock away. The old Scot looked up at him, confused but hopeful; like maybe he'd called a very convincing bluff. Cormac rolled his shoulders and then rushed McGoldrick. He grabbed the old Scot's polo shirt and yanked him back onto his feet. Stitches popped but the seams held on. McGoldrick loosed a surprise hiss of breath. He started to struggle and Cormac head butted him. A cut opened along McGoldrick's left eyebrow. Cormac had done him a kindness, delivering a little tap to the forehead instead of crushing the old Scot's nose. He just wanted to keep him under control. And it worked. McGoldrick softened like wet cardboard.

Cormac led McGoldrick to the edge of the car park. There was a four-foot concrete wall and no guard rail. Wind whipped McGoldrick's hair into his face. Cormac pushed him against the low wall. He looked over the edge. It was a long drop to the ground.

"How about we stop pretending you have a choice in this matter, McGoldrick?"

"You're a fucking psycho!"

"No I'm not. I promise you, I will regret throwing you over the side. Your screams will haunt me for a long time to come. But that's not going to stop me. This deal is non-negotiable. Either you agree to take down Rooney, or you're dead."

McGoldrick's mouth opened and closed but he couldn't engage his voice. Cormac hunkered down and wrapped his arms around the old Scot's shot-up thighs. The pain would keep everything in sharp focus. Cormac lifted McGoldrick off his feet and plonked his arse on the wall. Then he regained his grip on the polo shirt and gave him a little jolt. McGoldrick's arms pinwheeled and he wailed like a siren. Cormac eased him further over the edge; let him feel gravity's greedy pull. The polo shirt started to stretch.

"Okay, okay! Fuck you. I'll do it. I'll do it! I'll do whatever you want. Just let me go."

Cormac refrained from pointing out the reality of letting him go in this position. He helped McGoldrick down from his wobbly perch and led him to the car. The terrified old man stumbled over his own feet but managed to stay upright with Cormac's support. It had been a bit of an extreme move – and it had probably shaved a few years off McGoldrick's life expectancy – but you couldn't argue with the results.

"All right then, Mr McGoldrick." Cormac put a little upbeat singsong into his voice. "We'll see about taking you to a nice police station now. No point delaying the inevitable, eh?"

"Fuck yourself."

"Ach, don't be like that. I'll tell you what. You can ride in the front with me instead of that aul' boot. Sure it'll be a bit of a treat, won't it?"

McGoldrick said nothing. Cormac suspected it would be a quiet, uncomfortable drive.

Lydia kissed Mattie goodnight and left him in Rory's spare bedroom. They both knew there was little chance of him sleeping but they had to go through the motions at least. Try and cling to some semblance of reality. Rory had lent him an iPod with some good "chill-out" tracks and a bunch of simple games for a mindless distraction. Mattie had accepted it with automatic politeness but no real feeling. The boy was numb.

Rory and Stephen Black waited for her in the kitchen. They sat at opposite sides of the table, a pot of tea in the centre. Lydia took a seat at the head of the table.

"Want a cuppa?" Rory asked.

"You must have something stronger than tea, Rory?"

"You know I do, but, sure, have this first. I'll make you a sandwich to go with it."

"I'll not be able to eat."

"Wouldn't blame you, but I'll make it anyway. Take it or leave it."

Rory got up and clattered about the kitchen. Lydia looked at Stephen Black. He frowned at his phone, unaware that she'd switched her attention to him.

"You're unusually quiet," she said.

"Sorry," he said, but didn't look up from the small screen. "Just a little preoccupied. I tried to get a trace on the phone Ambrose O'Neill was using earlier but he must have pulled the battery. My contacts have come back empty-handed."

"So we don't know where he is but he'll not have to try too hard to find us."

"Yes, I suppose you're right. If you're not at your own house then I'm sure this will be the second place he looks. Luckily, Mr Cullen has this place very well kitted out."

"And you're here."

"Indeed."

"So we just sit and wait and see if he shows up?"

"I'm afraid I don't have a more satisfactory alternative."

"And that's why Rory opted for tea? In case anything happened?"

"Rather sensible of him, don't you think?"

Rory worked away in the kitchen, pretending that he wasn't listening to their conversation. It wasn't that long ago he'd chased her through this house, furious that she'd betrayed him by letting two thugs in through the front door to ransack the place. She wondered if it was wise to come back here. It was good that Stephen Black was about to supervise, but still, who knew what sort of ill will lingered?

She made a conscious effort not to dwell on it.

"I think we should call Detective Kelly," Lydia said. "He didn't reply to the text I sent and we don't know what he's done with the little bastard, McGoldrick."

"What do you want him to do with McGoldrick?"

"Kill him." It was out before she could filter it.

"Understandable," Stephen Black said.

"It is?"

"Of course. You must be thinking that he's responsible for the death of your husband. That his plan set the course of events and all that."

"And you think I'm wrong?"

Stephen Black finally looked up from his phone. He regarded Lydia with sympathetic eyes and a slight grin. "On the contrary, I agree with you."

Lydia waited for him to start laughing. He didn't. She noticed Rory had finished making the sandwich but wasn't ready to return to the table yet. His gaze was fixed on the kitchen worktop, shoulders hunched.

"And Mr Cullen suspected you'd feel this way too. He's already negotiated a fair disposal rate with me."

"As in…" Lydia searched for an unambiguous phrase, "a contract killing?"

"Well I tend to avoid paperwork, but yes, that's the essence of what we're talking about."

"But won't the police put me and Rory in the frame for something like this if it happens so soon after I've accused him of setting the kidnapping up?"

"Yes, they will. Which is why it won't be happening any time soon, you understand? You'll need to bury this down for a while. And if at any point this course of action no longer sits right with you before then, we'll call it off."

"Are you all right with this, Rory?"

Rory turned to face her. He leaned back against the worktop and folded his arms. "I can't believe how I reacted earlier, after those bastards came in here and... well, you know what happened. I wasn't just out of order. I threw an off-the-chart psycho. I need to do something to make that right with you. If this is what you need, so be it. I can't say I'll be sorry to see the wee shite go."

"So what now?" Lydia asked.

"We wait. Detective Kelly seems like an honest chap. I'm sure it won't be long until he delivers Mr McGoldrick to the police," Stephen Black said.

"But if he goes to jail, how are you going to get at him?"

"To be honest, I'll be surprised if he serves time. The evidence will be circumstantial, no doubt. He's not a stupid man. He'll have covered his back somehow."

If that were the case, Lydia doubted she'd have a change of heart. She shook her head. "May as well have him dropped off at his house, then."

"No, no. I rather like the idea of him at least spending a couple of nights in a cell, don't you?"

Rory came to the table and placed the sandwich in front of Lydia. He gave her a big goofy grin. "With any luck, he'll have a big strapping cellmate to help him pass the time."

Lydia forced a smile. The tablets she'd taken at the hospital were beginning to wear off and she could feel reality seeping in through the wall of fuzz that had insulated her from her grief. It wouldn't be long until the full impact of John's death worked her over like a loan shark's collector. She wanted to be alone when the time came.

"I'm sorry to ask, Rory, but could I have your bed tonight? I don't want to disturb Mattie."

"Of course, yeah. I should have offered it sooner. I'm probably going to stay up and keep aul' Stevie company anyway."

"Thanks, Rory."

Lydia stood up and put a hand on his shoulder.

"Just so you know, I'm not going to hold what happened earlier against you. Clean slate, okay?"

"If you can offer me that, I'm not going to turn it down. Thank you. You're brilliant."

"Don't worry about it, Rory. I need all the friends I can get right now. Bygones."

Rory looked like he might cry. Lydia excused herself and went to Rory's bed. She collapsed onto the mattress, pulled a pillow tight against her chest and squeezed it.

John was never going to hug her in the night again.

She buried her face in the surrogate bed companion and prayed that her son couldn't hear her muffled wails.

Cormac had been able to find a police station easily with the aid of the sat nav. He followed the directions mindlessly and got halfway there before he had a change of heart. There was no way he'd get out of a cop shop without identifying himself. Once they verified his information with his unit who knew what would happen. His handler might order the Met boys to detain him until they could arrange to have him shipped back directly to a PSNI station. He couldn't let that happen. Not when Ambrose O'Neill was still out there.

But the uniforms at the flat in Peckham had already accepted him as an undercover cop. A quick adjustment to the sat nav, and it wasn't long before he rolled into the car park, relieved to see Ronnie and Malcolm still manning the same positions.

Cormac turned to McGoldrick. The old Scot had fumed silently for the whole trip. Cormac could almost feel the heat from his fury. Again, he adopted his upbeat singsong voice, just to piss him off a little more.

"Okay, big lad. This is your stop."

McGoldrick clenched his jaw. Little muscles in his face pulsed. Cormac got out of the car and rounded it to open the passenger door. He reached over the old Scot and unclipped his seatbelt.

"You going to get out on your own or am I going to have to drag you by the scruff?"

McGoldrick stared dead ahead but he reached up for the Jesus handle and heaved himself out of the seat. He hissed and cursed under his breath. His wounded thighs must have been giving him gip. But he was upright and Cormac wasn't feeling much pity for him. He clamped his hand around McGoldrick's upper arm. His fingers sank into doughy flesh. Take away his money, all the bluster and bravado, and McGoldrick was just a weak old man.

Cormac led McGoldrick towards Ronnie. The young uniform gave them a guarded look.

"Hello there, Detective..."

"Kelly." Cormac shoved McGoldrick a couple of

steps forward. "Could you take this guy off my hands?"

"Who is he?"

"He's connected to the murder here and a shitload of other badness. If you could cuff him and stash him in the back of your car you'd be doing me a major favour."

"Could you not just bring him to a station?"

"I need to keep moving, mate. Don't want to get lumbered with a bunch of paperwork and questions from some jobsworth. You know what those desk jockeys can be like."

"I don't know... Let me check with Malcolm, yeah?"

Cormac made a show of glancing at his watch but maintained a friendly demeanour. "Aye, mate. Whatever you need to do."

Ronnie relayed the situation to Malcolm. He got radio silence for a few seconds before Malcolm responded.

"I think this might be above our pay grade, mate. Best to leave decisions like that to the big boys. They've got Robinson and Scott on this one."

"Yeah? Fucking Bert and Ernie? Muppets."

"They're on their way to check on our... Oi, oi. Here they come now. Look smart, Ronnie. Or give it a go, at least."

Ronnie's frame stiffened when he caught sight of the Ford Mondeo rolling through the car park entrance. He adjusted his hat and rubbed one of his shoes on the back of his trousers, his earlier irreverence now completely gone. Whether or not these superiors were muppets, they would be shown respect.

Cormac could feel the situation get more complicated by the second. He wanted to walk away and let the Met boys figure out what to do with McGoldrick themselves. But he couldn't. He needed to make sure they understood that the old Scot was at the eye of this shit-tornado.

The Mondeo pulled up alongside the Vectra and its engine cut out. Cormac couldn't see through the tinted windscreen; moonlight casting a milky glare. The driver opened his door and stepped out. He had a mop of wild curls and a bushy beard. His brow was knotted with suspicion.

"What's happening here, Ronnie?"

"This is Detective Kelly from the PSNI. He reckons this other fellah has something to do with the boy who flew off the balcony."

"PSNI? What the fuck are you doing over here?"

"He says he's undercover," Ronnie said.

"What are you, his interpreter?"

"Sorry, sir."

"Well, Detective... what's your story?"

The passenger door opened and a fat guy with a receding hairline and a Freddie Mercury moustache got out, placed his hands on the small of his back and stretched. He sighed loudly then rested his elbows on the roof of the Mondeo and looked Cormac up and down.

"Who's this?"

"Detective Kelly, apparently," the curly haired one said. "He's PSNI."

"What's he doing here, then?"

"Just been wondering that myself."

McGoldrick cleared his throat. "This man kidnapped me, beat me and shot my legs to force me into making a false confession. I want him arrested."

Cormac almost laughed. But then he saw the looks on the two new arrivals' faces. They looked at the blood on McGoldrick's chinos and then at Cormac.

"Are you carrying a gun, Detective Kelly?" the cop with the Freddie Mercury moustache asked.

"I didn't shoot him."

"That's not what I asked."

"This aul' fucker's just chancing his arm. Take him in."

"I'd like to see your ID, Detective Kelly."

"I don't have it on me. I'm working undercover."

"Convenient," the red-haired cop said.

"Perhaps you'd be so kind as to accompany us to the station, Detective Kelly? You could fill us in on the whole story."

"I don't have time. I'm tracking another suspect."

"Let me make this a little plainer," the redhead said. He strutted up to Cormac and pointed a thick finger in his face. "You're fucking coming with us. Get in the car."

"Ah, fuck this," Cormac said. He grabbed the redhead's wrist and pulled him off balance and straight into a tight uppercut. The punch connected with the tip of the redhead's chin, his beard almost cushioning Cormac's knuckles. His head snapped back and his legs wobbled. He folded forward onto the tarmac.

Cormac drew his Glock as Ronnie laid a hand on his shoulder. He turned and pushed the uniform backwards. Aimed the gun at his chest.

"Stay back, kiddo."

"You fucking nutcase," Ronnie said, "you can't do that."

"Just did. And now I'm going to tootle along, just like I planned. Before I do, cuff this old bastard and bundle him into your squad car. If I find out that you didn't take him into custody, I'll find him and shoot him."

Cormac sensed movement to his left. He turned slightly but kept his pistol trained on Ronnie. The fat Freddie Mercury had a telescopic baton in his hand.

"I wouldn't recommend it, mate. Hit me with that and this gun's probably going to go off. Do you want to explain that fuck-up to wee Ronnie's ma?"

"Put the gun away."

"Will do, as soon as I'm a safe distance from here. And I'll leave as soon as I see Mr McGoldrick cuffed and bundled."

Ronnie's radio crackled. Malcolm had noticed the ruckus and wanted to know what was going on. Ronnie ignored him and went about following Cormac's request.

"You're making a big mistake," McGoldrick said.

Cormac nodded. "It wouldn't be the first one, mate."

Chapter 28

Every second counts in pursuit of that final score. You can't let up or drop your guard.

Rory Cullen, *Cullen: The Autobiography*

Light penetrated the blinds. Lydia rolled onto her side. She was half-aware. Stranded between dreams and reality. As she came to she went through her mental checklist. What day is it? Am I working today? Where the fuck am I?

Info trickled through holes in the wall of fatigue. Then the dam burst. She was flooded by the events of the previous days. Their force punched her to full consciousness with the highlight of tragedy – the brass knuckles – being her husband's death.

Lydia sat up. It was Sunday but there was much to do. She needed to check on Mattie for a start. And then find out about collecting John's body. There would be a wake and a funeral. She needed to get in touch with John's family back home. Get in touch with her own family. Pick a funeral home, a coffin, flowers. Decide on a venue for the mad Irish attendees to get blitzed at after the service. She'd been to a few of their funerals.

John needed to be seen off properly.

And what about Rory? Stephen Black? They were both downstairs. What were they doing? What were they going to do? Rory had a match to prepare for. Stephen Black would probably be called in for surveillance duty while he trained. But where did that leave Lydia and Mattie?

Ambrose O'Neill was still out there. Unless Detective Kelly...

Lydia reached out to the bedside cabinet for her phone. She noticed that there was a missed call first. Then she saw the time.

11:37.

She'd slept for hours. Proper sleep. The pills and exhaustion had overcome her need to grieve. She would have to make the most of her energy. Who knew when she'd be able to switch off like that again.

Lydia got out of the bed and stretched. Her clothes were damp with sleep-sweat and her mouth felt grimy. She craved a shower and a toothbrush. But she would have to ask Rory first. After everything that had happened, she still wasn't really free.

She went to the window and parted the blinds. It had rained. The street looked cleaner. A car shushed past, orange sunlight reflecting from its windshield. She let the blind fall back into place and called Detective Kelly.

"Hello? Lydia?"

"I've a missed call from you."

"Yeah, sorry I called so late. Only let it ring a couple of times on the off chance that you'd be awake."

"It's okay. You didn't reply to my text."

"Yeah, had just seen it when I called. It was a busy night."

"I'm sure."

"McGoldrick should be in custody by now... I think he might squirm out of this, though."

"It is what it is. Have you seen Donna yet?"

"Not sure if I should. Things got complicated and I might be in a bit of trouble. Maybe you could check on her for me?"

Lydia felt like telling him to fuck off. She had enough on her plate as it was. But he'd brought her back her son. And he'd kept John alive long enough for her to see him one last time. It wasn't as if he was asking much.

"I'm sure I'll be at the hospital later. I'll call you if I can get in to see Donna."

"Thank you."

"What will you do now?"

"I... I really don't know. Like I said, things are complicated. I want to track down O'Neill but I can't... Look, you don't need to hear all this. But I should meet you somewhere later. I need to return Stephen Black's car and, you know, I'd like to see Mattie if it's all right with you."

"I'll call you in a bit."

Lydia didn't know if it was all right for this cop to see Mattie. She didn't like how so many things about him were "complicated". But she felt bad for ending the call without throwing him a bone. It was just too much to think about. Her first priority had to be her son.

The landing floorboards creaked as she treaded towards Mattie's door. She peeked in and saw the jumble of a disturbed duvet and sheets but no Mattie. Her heartbeat ratcheted but she fought the urge to panic with deep breaths and common sense. The boy had woken up and gone downstairs to look for food.

Nobody had snatched him away in the night. All the same, she took the stairs a little too quick and noisy.

Mattie, Rory and Stephen Black were in the kitchen concentrating on her laptop, a newspaper and a disassembled pistol respectively. The smell of men and breakfast was in the air. Rory looked up at her and wordlessly went to the cappuccino machine. It hissed and spat coffee into a little white cup. He added milk without asking if she wanted it and sat it in front of the seat beside Mattie.

"Thanks," Lydia said.

"Morning, Mum." Mattie broke away from the screen for a few seconds to look at her apologetically. "Hope you don't mind. Just passing the time, you know?"

"Course not."

Lydia took her seat and blew on the coffee's surface. The first sip sent a fizzle of calm across her skin. She started to believe that she could actually cope with the challenges of the day. Just so long as she got through the whole cup of bliss. She closed her eyes and breathed in the steam from the cup. Opened them and found her gaze drawn to Stephen Black's pistol.

"Could you put that away, please? I've seen enough of them to last me a lifetime."

Stephen Black folded away the oil-stained cloth he'd been cleaning a piece of the gun with.

"Sorry about that. Just two ticks."

His nimble fingers went to work. In seconds the silenced pistol was back in one piece and tucked away under his tracksuit jacket. The gesture didn't do much to settle Lydia. She was tempted to ask Stephen Black to leave – remove all traces of violence from her proximity – but she knew that they were safer with him around for the time being. But she looked forward to a time when she never had to deal with the likes of Stephen Black or Detective Kelly again.

The sooner they took care of McGoldrick, the better.

Cormac stood at the reception desk and waited for the disinterested hospital employee to grace him with her attention. He considered disguising his accent – his Scottish lilt was passable – but figured the effort would be wasted. Even if somebody had circulated his description, the lady in question was unlikely to have paid much attention to the memo. She yawned then looked at him with watery eyes.

"Help you?"

"I'm looking for Donna Grant's ward."

"She a patient here?"

Cormac took a breath before answering. "Yes, she is."

The receptionist tapped on her keyboard with her index fingers. She sighed and interlaced her overworked digits. Cracked her knuckles and stretched her arms in front of her.

"No record of a Donna Brand here."

"I said Grant."

"Oh. Must be your accent. Hold on. I'll try again."

Tap, tap, tap.

"Okay, Donna Grant. Ward 13C."

"And I'll find that...?"

"On the twelfth floor."

"Lifts?"

She pointed one of her typing fingers to the wall to her right. "Follow the signs for 'Lift Core 5'. Take the lift to the—"

"Twelfth floor. Right, got it."

He wanted to leave her with a snarky reply or simply turn around and storm off but that would have left a lasting impression. Instead, he smiled like a harmless idiot and made his way along the corridors to Lift Core 5. Inside the lift he faced away from the CCTV bubble camera above. He wiped a thin sheen of sweat from his brow. A good cop would smell the unease off him. He was yet to meet one since he'd arrived in London, though.

The lift doors eventually pinged open on the twelfth floor and he stepped out. Cormac had checked ahead and knew it was half an hour into visiting time. He'd used the hours before then replacing his battle-worn clothes. His newly bought Primark duds were comfortable enough but he knew they weren't so chic. He hoped Donna would be awake and in the mood to take the piss out of them.

A sour-faced nurse pointed Cormac towards Donna's bay. The curtains were drawn around the bed but the nurse didn't forbid him from seeing her. He looked around for signs of increased security. Nothing. Not even the standard bored uniform on a stool. Jesus Christ. The hospital had been a shooting gallery the night before by all accounts and Donna had been involved. They couldn't spare one officer to keep watch over her?

Cormac took a few seconds to breathe the hospital aromas deep and allow the irritated scowl on his face to fade away. His gurney gob was the last thing Donna needed to see. He concentrated on the positives. The appalling lack of security made his life a lot easier. He crossed the ward, the soles of his cheap canvas shoes squeaking on the hard floor, and drew back Donna's curtain.

Ambrose O'Neill looked up from the visitor's chair and winked.

"The security here's shite, isn't it?"

Cormac's hand went for the shoulder holster underneath his black fleece. O'Neill raised a snub nose .38 from its resting place on his lap. He shook his head.

"Let's keep it civil for now, Kelly, eh? Draw that curtain and keep your voice low."

Cormac did as he was told then looked to Donna for signs of harm. Apart from the obvious dressed gunshot wounds, he saw nothing. She was unconscious; oblivious to their presence.

"I haven't done anything to her, Kelly. Not yet."

Cormac thought about diving for him, but he'd have to vault Donna's raised hospital bed first. There was no way he'd make those few feet without getting himself, and possibly Donna, shot.

"What do you want?"

"What the fuck do you think I want? My crew's been wiped out, because of you. And I'm in the shit up to my oxters with a drug-dealing, scumbag cockney, because of you. My life's basically fucked, because of you... do you see a pattern forming?"

Cormac shrugged. "So, what now?"

Donna gasped like she'd just come up from under water. The sudden noise distracted O'Neill long enough for Cormac to snatch the Glock from his shoulder holster. O'Neill returned his attention back to Cormac, saw the gun in his hand, and his mono-brow dipped down in the middle.

"Put it away, Kelly."

"What's happening, Cormac?" Donna looked from side to side. Her voice was sleep-slurred. "Am I in a hospital bed?"

"It's okay, Donna," Cormac said.

"It fucking isn't, Cormac. Why am I in hospital? Did you let me get hurt?"

O'Neill sneered.

"I wasn't there, Donna. I couldn't…"

"Whatever, Cormac. Just get this caveman out of here and stay out of my life, okay?"

"Bit of a ladies' man, are you, Kelly?"

It was easy to ignore O'Neill's shitty comment. Donna had already done more damage than the bullish prick ever could.

"…*stay out of my life*…"

"Let's go, O'Neill."

"Why should I?"

"I've got a gun in your face."

"Snap." O'Neill thumbed the hammer. "Stale-mate, mate."

Cormac looked at Donna. She turned away from him. He lowered his gun.

"All right, O'Neill. You win."

"There's a sensible lad. No point in you getting this pretty girl all shot-up again."

A single tiny sob escaped Donna. It was a shotgun blast in Cormac's chest. He wanted to reach out and touch her. Knew that he couldn't.

O'Neill stood up and held out his free hand. "Give me your gun."

Cormac flipped the Glock around and handed it to O'Neill, handle first. The gangster snatched it from his grip. He grunted with satisfaction.

"C'mon then, dickhead." Ambrose said. "Head for the lifts."

Cormac hoped that Donna would spare him a glance before he walked away from her, but she remained on her side. Her chest hitched every few seconds and Cormac blanched at the thought of the pain each one caused her wounds. He stored his anger, ready to release it on a hair-trigger.

Cormac drew back the curtain and moved across the ward. None of the nurses so much as spared him a glance, each one focussed on whatever task they had at hand. Most of the conscious patients were occupied with visitors and had no interest in anything beyond them. He looked back at O'Neill. The gangster had a jacket draped across his forearm, concealing his pistol. He eyeballed Cormac.

"Watch where you're going, Kelly."

Cormac faced front and stopped just before colliding with a small Indian nurse. He apologised and she gave him that calm and serene Indian smile and stepped around him. At the lifts, Cormac hit the call button. The machinery clunked and chunked behind the sliding doors. They waited for an eternity for the lift to climb the levels. All the while, Cormac prayed that it would be empty.

Finally, the doors slid back and revealed that Cormac's prayers had been answered. Nobody there. He stalled for a second, knowing that O'Neill wouldn't be able to resist. Then he felt the pressure of a snub nose .38 muzzle pushed into his lower back. It was his final chance. He grasped it.

Cormac turned sharply on the ball of his right foot. His right arm moved in an upward arc and connected with O'Neill's gun hand. The snub nose spat lead into the empty lift. Cormac grabbed the back of O'Neill's neck with his left hand and charged into the lift. He rammed O'Neill's head into the siding and the capsule shook violently. Then he threw a couple of sharp right hooks to the gangster's greasy head. O'Neill roared, threw himself backwards and bowled into Cormac. The doors had slid shut and they bounced off them, contained.

O'Neill tried to catch Cormac with an elbow as he turned to face him. Instinctively, Cormac shoved him away and the elbow sailed past his nose. It was a stupid move. O'Neill gained enough space to raise his revolver. Cormac kicked out before the gangster had time to aim. The shot went wild; the bullet pulverised the button panel. Cormac almost lost his balance as the lift shuddered to a stop.

Through the ringing in his ears, Cormac could vaguely make out the squeal of an alarm. O'Neill bent forward to retrieve the snub nose. Cormac smashed a cheap canvas shoe into his thick-featured face and the gangster fell back onto his arse. He went in for the kill, connecting a knee to O'Neill's forehead then attempting a head-stomp. The gangster jerked to the side and Cormac's foot slammed down on the lift floor. He turned to soccer kick the bastard into oblivion but felt an iron grip shackle his ankle.

"Ah, fuck."

O'Neill jerked Cormac's weight-bearing leg out from under him. His head bounced off the side of the lift and he landed on his backside, his shoulders propped against the doors. He saw O'Neill's fist come at him too late. White light flashed and he went blind for a second. But he managed to raise his arms to fend off the next haymaker. He countered with a jab at his blurry target.

His fist met flesh and he felt something give way. He blinked until his vision sharpened and saw the mess he'd made of O'Neill's nose. It was kinked to one side and belching blood. Cormac threw a right cross from a sitting position. O'Neill's head jolted backwards but he didn't go down. Tough bastard still had a boxer's punch resistance.

"Give it up, O'Neill."

"Fuck yourself, kid."

O'Neill tugged the confiscated Glock from the waistband of his trousers. He tried to level it at Cormac but his aim wavered; blood and tears mixed in his eyes. His hesitation was a gift from God. Cormac flopped onto his side. Ambrose squeezed and the pistol barked; blew a hole in the lift doors. The ringing in Cormac's ears kicked it up a notch. He twisted and got his feet against the lift door. Pushed himself forward and grabbed at O'Neill's wrists. O'Neill took advantage of his position and rolled on top of Cormac. The gun got trapped between their chests.

"You're dead now, Kelly."

Cormac couldn't hear the words but he could read O'Neill's lips just fine. He felt O'Neill's fingers scrabble. Cormac bucked hard, twisted his hips and pushed O'Neill sideways. The Glock fired as he tried to wrestle it away.

"Oh, shit," Cormac said.

He ran his hands up and down his chest in search of a wound. Nothing. He checked his face and head. Sore but not shot. Then he looked at O'Neill.

Ambrose O'Neill lay in a spreading puddle of blood. His body jerked. He clasped at his throat. Blood bubbled over his thick fingers.

Cormac retrieved the guns from the lift floor. He

tucked the Glock back in its holster and tucked O'Neill's snub nose into his waistband. His hearing was returning. He could make out a high-pitched whine. O'Neill, caught in a dying panic, welcoming death a hell of a lot quicker.

Cormac stood over Ambrose O'Neill, careful not to step in his mess. He watched him writhe and spurt gobs of blood. The lift doors were cranked open. Chaos snatched at him. Cops, cops and cops. Where had those fuckers been when O'Neill was paying Donna a visit?

Cormac interlaced his fingers behind his head and waited. They took O'Neill out of the lift first. Even this close to medical care it didn't look good for him. Then the cops threatened, cuffed and manhandled Cormac out of the lift. He didn't resist. Just went with the flow. Thoughts of a rest in whatever cell they took him to made him want to smile. But that wasn't the done thing when you were pulled from a grisly, blood-splattered scene. He didn't want these uniforms thinking he was some sort of psycho.

EPILOGUE

On the pitch, I'm sublime. Beyond human. I'll give you your fairy tale ending.

Rory Cullen, *Cullen: The Autobiography*

Rory Cullen saw the goal happen in his head before his foot made contact with the ball. It played out exactly how he imagined it. Times like this, he always had a vague feeling that there was something more to him than quick reactions, stamina and gifted skill. He was practically supernatural on the pitch. The ball was his. He commanded it. Goals were easy.

Three defenders and a keeper, not one got near that volley. The net strained to contain his power. The keeper yelled at his defenders. The defenders scratched their heads.

Rory ran towards his teammates, his arms spread wide like wings. He crashed into them and they raised him up off his feet. Into the air. Rory Cullen flew. The players from his old team looked at him as if they wanted to spit in his face. He mouthed a clear "fuck you" for the benefit of his old skipper. *Never liked that philandering fuck-nut, anyway.*

And the crowd. The clamour. They bayed in the stands. Sang their tribal chants; brimming with passion but indecipherable until they unified in a chorus of *Blue Moon*. Rory pointed to the City fans, their roars swelled. He lapped up the glory until the boys lowered him to the ground. The ref called for them to return to the centre of the pitch. They had more work to do and Rory was not going to shy from it. His heart pounded in a way that no drug could ever simulate – and he'd tried most of them so he knew that to be fact.

The madness of last week couldn't have been further away. Gangsters had tried to clip his wings but nobody held that sway over him. Even if McGoldrick and Rooney's plan had worked out, he'd never have been able to take orders from them. He couldn't throw games by missing easy goals or getting sent off at a crucial point in the match. There was no containing—

At the centre spot, the ref held the ball under his arm a little too long. He had a hand to his earpiece and wore an expression of confusion. He tilted his head from one side to the other as if trying to dislodge water from his ears. His ruddy cheeks were fading to grey.

"What's wrong?" Rory asked.

"We have to get off the pitch."

"The fuck we do. We're in the middle of a game, ref."

"Somebody's just been murdered. Up in one of the boxes. The cops are locking the place down."

Rory forced a shocked reaction to the news. But inside he felt a mix of panic and anger. The bastard wasn't meant to die until the final whistle blew. They'd fucked his debut game for City at his old stomping ground. It was bad enough that the plan would have detracted from his performance that day, but to interrupt it, make it not worth a damn... He'd have to have words with Stephen Black.

###

Lydia sat on the edge of the couch and stared at the tick-ertape newsfeed at the bottom of the screen. Somebody had been murdered at Stamford Bridge. No name had been released but Lydia knew who it had to be. She'd been there when the idea had first been explored and thought that she'd managed to talk Rory out of it since then. But he'd gone ahead with it. Rory had paid Stephen Black to kill Martin Rooney.

She decided there and then that she'd have to drop him from her client list. Yes, he was her cash cow. He was also dangerously close to becoming a friend after all they'd been through. But she was done with violence now, and she was determined to cut all sources of it from her life.

Which was why McGoldrick was going to live a few more years yet.

Rory had offered to pay for that hit too. It took a few days for her to begin to think straight, but she'd realised that she couldn't be responsible for anybody's death. Not even the death of a man who was arguably responsible for her husband's murder. She would destroy the one thing that brought joy to McGoldrick's life, though.

His career.

She called McGoldrick's mobile.

"What do *you* want?"

"Now, now. I just wanted to check you were holding up all right. I believe a very close friend of yours has just died."

"I have no idea—"

"Martin Rooney is dead. He was shot at Stamford

Bridge today. The gunman walked right into the executive box, shot him and disappeared."

Silence.

"I realise this must be quite a shock. Not even a crime boss like Rooney is safe. What hope would you have if somebody decided to come at you?"

"Don't you dare threaten me."

"Oh, that wasn't a threat. I don't want you dead. I want much more than that."

"You trying to blackmail me, hen? Here's the thing, whatever you think you have on me, it's bullshit. There's no evidence that'll support your conspiracy theory shit. And you need to stop calling me. If anything, I could have *you* done for harassment."

"Well, you say that, Mr McGoldrick, but it's just not true. You should check your emails before your PA goes through them in the morning. Turns out, my late husband had been gathering a bit of evidence about you. Kept it in a safety deposit box I didn't know about until his solicitor gave me a call during the week. I've scanned a couple of compromising photos for you to check out."

"Photos? They'll not hold up. I'm not so old that I haven't heard of Photoshop."

"These were taken with a Polaroid camera. Old school. You'll appreciate that. And they're just the tip of the iceberg. My hubby really did his homework. I'm starting to suspect he was going to blackmail you to cover his gambling debts but he couldn't go through with it. Even in his darkest hour he was ten times the man you are."

"And yet you're happy to blackmail me."

"But I'm not doing it for money. I'm doing it for control. For revenge. And my first demand will be for you to sign over your top three earners to my agency. I'll expect the paperwork by lunchtime tomorrow."

"You're out of your mind, woman. I'll do no such thing."

"Check out the selection of photos I've sent your way first, then get back to me, McGoldrick. It's been nice doing business with you."

Lydia ended the call then slumped on the couch. The breaking news from Stamford Bridge played on a loop. She let it wash over her and pondered the guilty thought that maybe Rory had been right to do what he did. Maybe it was the only way to protect himself against that psycho. But was it worth the risk? Time would tell.

The doorbell sounded and Lydia sighed. She'd have to smile and be sociable. Before she got up, she switched channels to connect with the CCTV camera at her front door. Detective Kelly's stern face filled the screen, as she'd expected, but she was going to check every caller from now on. Rory had paid for the same security system he had at his own house and arranged to have it installed before letting her spend a night at her own home.

Lydia stopped at the bottom of the stairs before she opened the front door.

"Mattie! You have a visitor!"

She heard the double thump of her son's feet hitting the floor. He didn't move that fast when she called him to do her a favour. But she could understand his excitement. This was the first time he would see Detective Kelly since the night they flew in the helicopter. And most likely the last.

Lydia went to the door to let an agent of death into her home.

Cormac smiled at Lydia Gallagher when she answered the door. She looked thinner, paler, older, but pretty nonetheless. Prettier still when she returned his forced smile for a few seconds. She stepped aside to let him in.

"Go on through to the kitchen," she said. "I'll put the kettle on."

The carpet was spongy under his feet and the hallway was roomy and bright. The house had that "expecting company" smell that could only be achieved with plug-in air fresheners. Cormac followed Lydia to the large kitchen and sat on a high stool at the granite-topped island she indicated with a sweeping hand gesture. For a woman living with her dead husband's gambling debts, she seemed to have a very nice house.

"Hiya, Cormac."

Mattie stood at the door, an uncertain look on his face. His arms were folded in a way that made it look like he was trying to hug himself. He'd grown an inch in a week. Cormac stood up and met him halfway between the island and the door. There was an awkward moment where they clasped clumsily at each other's extended hands, getting the handshake wrong. Then Mattie surprised him by stepping in and throwing his arms around him. His chest hitched once but when he broke away from the hug there was no sign on his face that he might cry.

Cormac went back to his stool and Mattie sat next to him. There was enough room between them that it didn't feel too uncomfortable. They smiled, raised eyebrows and rolled eyes at each other for a few seconds before Lydia asked Mattie if he wanted anything to eat.

"I'll just have some juice, Mum."

"You know where the fridge is. Coffee, Detective?"

"Please, call me Cormac. And, yeah, coffee would be brilliant. Black, just."

Lydia nodded and poured him a cup from a percolator. "I'll leave you boys alone for a bit."

She left the kitchen but Cormac assumed she would be within earshot. As she should be.

"How's it going, big man?" Cormac asked.

Mattie scratched at the back of his head. "Pretty shit, to be honest. I miss Dad."

Cormac noticed the nice clean dressing on Mattie's damaged hand. The bruises on his face had mostly faded. The fingers would heal too. But the emotional scarring; that would last forever.

"I'm sure you do." Cormac couldn't think of anything else to say. He let the silence stretch.

"What about Donna?" Mattie asked eventually. "Have you seen her?"

Cormac shook his head. "She wants nothing to do with me. I found out through her doctor that she's recovering well, though. She was transported back to Belfast a few days ago. I might leave it a few weeks before I try calling her again."

"I'll have to see if she's on Facebook," Mattie said. "I never got to say bye to her. She did a lot for me, like."

"I'm sure she'd be delighted to hear from you."

"When are you going home?"

"Today. Heading to the airport from here. Not really looking forward to it, to be honest. My boss is collecting me. That'll be a fun drive."

"Think you'll get fired, then?"

"If not that, I'll definitely be demoted and transferred somewhere shite. Not sure I could stay if they put me back in a uniform. I hate traffic cops."

"Maybe you could work for the police here?"

"Nah, your boys don't get guns. I'm way too much of a cowboy for that aul' craic. Who knows what I'll do? Probably drive a taxi like everybody else who loses their job in Belfast."

"What about becoming a private investigator or something?"

"God, no. That'd be worse than traffic duty. Spying on rich people having affairs with other rich people? No thanks."

"Well, Stephen Black told me he's going away soon. Maybe you could work for Rory Cullen? He was allowed a gun."

"Yeah, I'm not sure who allowed him to have the gun... and I don't think Rory would have me."

"Why? You a United fan?"

"Nah. I don't watch football at all. Boxing's my game. That's a real sport."

"Dad always said boxing's been 'shite' since Lewis retired." Mattie lowered his voice when he cursed. He knew himself that his mum would be eavesdropping.

"He's right. But I live in hope."

"He *was* right."

Cormac wasn't comfortable. He'd wanted to say goodbye to Mattie and leave things on a positive note. It seemed like all he'd managed to do was bring the kid down. He had to turn things around.

"I got you something," Cormac said.

The kid sat a little straighter on his stool, his interest piqued.

Cormac dug into the inside pocket of his pea coat and pulled out a small box wrapped in brown paper.

Mattie stripped away the paper and popped open the little velvet box. His face lit up when he saw the contents.

"It's a Claddagh ring," Cormac said. "I know you probably don't think much of Ireland right now, so I understand if you don't want to wear this, but I wanted to give you something meaningful."

"Why? What does it mean?"

"It's a token of friendship and loyalty."

"It's cool."

"Ah good. I was worried you'd think it was a bit gay."

This time Cormac lowered his voice. They shared a conspiratorial smile.

The kid took the ring from the box and tried it on his middle finger. It was a couple of sizes too big. He looked a little crestfallen.

"You'll grow into it. Maybe you could wear it on a chain until you do?"

"Yeah, I guess so."

"And sure, you wouldn't want one you'd grow out of, would you?"

"That's true."

Cormac felt good. He'd pulled their goodbye out of its nosedive. They'd part ways on a high. He gulped down the last of his coffee and stood up.

"I think I'll hit the road, mate."

"So soon?"

"Can't risk missing this plane."

"Will you visit again?"

"Certainly. Might even check out that Facebook thingy and add you as a follower or whatever."

"That'd be cool."

They got off their stools and hugged again, this time less awkwardly.

"I better say bye to your ma as well."

"It'd be rude not to, Detective Kelly."

Lydia stood in the kitchen doorway, the ghost of a smirk on her face. Cormac ruffled Mattie's hair until the kid slapped him away. He went to Lydia and offered her his hand. Her grip was firm and businesslike.

"Please, call me Cormac."

"Sorry, yes. Cormac. Cormac Kelly." She drew a card from the back pocket of her jeans. "Stephen Black asked me to give you this."

There was a mobile phone number printed on one side. No name. On the other side somebody had written a short note in fastidiously neat cursive. Cormac squinted at the small letters.

Thank you for the football ticket, Detective. I plan to put it to good use. If things don't work out well with the PSNI call the overleaf number and we'll explore some employment opportunities. Your work ethic and skill-set impressed me.

Regards

Stephen Black

"You going to take him up on the offer?" Lydia asked.

"I doubt it," Cormac said, but he slipped the card into his back pocket.

Lydia nodded. "I'm not sure how legal his 'security' business is."

"I have my own doubts about that as well." *But you weren't exactly Johnny Law last week.* "Probably better off out of it." And yet the card remained in his pocket.

Lydia and Mattie saw Cormac to the door. He walked the short distance to his rental car, parked in their roomy driveway, and turned for a final wave goodbye. They smiled at him from the porch. There was a gap between Lydia and the doorframe where Cormac imagined John would have stood.

He revved the rental car's engine. The boxy little Toyota felt like a toy compared to Stephen Black's kitted-out Vectra. He put a lid on an emerging swashbuckling fantasy inspired by the little security consultant's note. There were other things he needed to concentrate on in the immediate future. Saving his job and getting back into Donna's good graces were his top priorities.

But if it all went wrong, at least he had a plan B.

35669821R00189